GET THE DWARF OUT

GET THE DWARF OUT
DWARF BOUNTY HUNTER™ BOOK TEN

MARTHA CARR

MICHAEL ANDERLE

THE GET THE DWARF OUT TEAM

Thanks to our JIT Team:

Dave Hicks
Diane L. Smith
Jackey Hankard-Brodie
Peter Manis
Deb Mader
Dorothy Lloyd
Kelly O'Donnell

If We've missed anyone, please let us know!

Editor
SkyHunter Editing Team

"If they're gonna charge people this much for drinks, the least they can do is get a bigger bathroom. Come on." Hux stumbled down the alley outside the bar in Yuba City, drunker than a skunk, and fumbled to open his fly without flashing his unmentionables to the world. He wouldn't have made it if he'd had to wait inside any longer.

Not that he'd make it much longer out there, either.

The yellow lamplight from across the street fell across his back as the transformed shifter turned halfway toward the wall and tried to hide his business.

Galfrey and Jake would lose it on me right now if they knew what I was doing. Serves them right for choosing this crappy bar in the first place.

He gave himself another moment to be sure his bladder wouldn't turn on him again, then zipped his fly with extra care and staggered against the wall.

We shouldn't have started talking to that stupid dwarf in the first place. He can gel up that mohawk all he wants and stride around like a biker, but we all know what he is—a transformed.

"Exactly like us," he slurred and stabilized himself against the rough-plastered bricks. "And we're all screwed."

The roar of two heavy engines approached the front of the bar, and he turned toward the parking lot to stumble to the front door. Multiple car doors opened and slammed shut again, but the engines didn't turn off. He didn't think anything of it until he saw the massive figure step out of the first SUV's driver's door.

When his somewhat bleary-eyed gaze settled the tiny crimson-haired witch in her black trench coat who accompanied the giant, he froze.

"Shit. Galfrey! Jake!" He staggered toward the entrance even though a part of him shrieked that he should simply sneak around to the back where his friends were waiting for him on the patio. Unfortunately, he seemed unable to make his drunken body follow his sloshed brain's directions. "We're in deep—"

"That's him!" a young shifter bellowed. "That's one of them."

"Quiet," the giant shifter responded harshly.

Veron. That's his damn name.

Hux couldn't run in a straight line to save his life—even though his life probably depended on it. The witch in the trench coat strode toward him followed by a horde of other shifters in dark clothes. He managed to yell a final, "Help!" before two hounds on the bar's back patio began to bark wildly.

Before Hux could register what he heard in the hounds' frantic barks and howls, Veron's witch reached him and blasted a brilliant, bright red light into the side of his head. He dropped onto the sidewalk in a heap and wished the world would stop spinning before he blacked out entirely.

"Johnny!" Rex howled and jumped frantically in the grass while Luther raced around the bar's back patio at record speed. "Johnny, something's wrong."

"Tons of shifters, Johnny," Luther added. He stopped abruptly, sniffed the air, and uttered a bloodcurdling bay. "The angry kind."

Where they were seated at the corner patio table with Galfrey and Jake, Johnny and Lisa exchanged a concerned glance. The bounty hunter raised an eyebrow at the terrified transformed shifters who'd been on the verge of sharing their story. "Are y'all expectin' company?"

"Are you kidding?" Galfrey's eyes were wide. "Who would we—"

"Help!" The desperate cry rose from the parking lot, followed immediately by a bright red flash and a thump.

"Hux," Jake whispered and his already pale face blanched even more.

"What's that idiot doing outside?" his friend demanded in a harsh undertone.

"Last time I checked," the dwarf muttered as he stood from his chair, "even transformed can't do magic like that."

"We'll go check it out," Lisa added and pushed quickly to her feet as well.

"Hey!" Charlie shouted from the other side of the patio. "What's going on?"

Johnny waved his cousin off as the two of them headed toward the alley on the other side of the patio wall. "Y'all hang back."

"We smell 'em too." One of Charlie's transformed shifter biker buddies sniffed the air. "It doesn't look good."

Charlie slammed his drink onto the table in front of him and sniffed. "Then let's go check it—"

"They're all in on it!" a man shouted in the front parking lot and his voice broke at the end. "We have to find the bastards who—"

"Where do you think you're going?" another shifter roared. "Do you want to blow this entire thing—"

"I don't care!"

"Get in the car or you'll ride in the back with him—unconscious like he is too."

A muffled shout was followed by multiple car doors opening and slamming shut again quickly.

Johnny and Lisa raced down the alley and Charlie's shifter friends created an uproar on the patio as they pushed their chairs back and rushed after them.

As the bounty hunter rounded the corner and stumbled into the parking lot, he caught a glimpse of red sneakers being shoved into the trunk of a black SUV as a second vehicle accelerated out of the lot and down the road with a squeal of tires and a burst of white smoke.

The SUV's back hatch closed behind the unmoving red sneakers and the tiny witch with crimson hair he'd seen once before darted around the side of the vehicle. Her black trench coat fluttered behind her before she slid into the front passenger seat. The car hurtled away from the bar before she'd even closed the door.

"Stop!" Lisa sprinted into the parking lot but by the time she'd taken two more steps, the last SUV to leave was already making a sharp turn halfway off the curb to enter the street.

Charlie and his shifter friends spilled into the open space with snarls and growls, ready for drunken action. The mohawked dwarf clenched and unclenched his fists and looked around the space that was now filled with cars and his buddies' bikes but no attacking shifters. "Where's the action, huh?"

The bounty hunter stared after the unmarked vehicle with a grim expression. He thought he caught a glimpse of the crimson-haired witch looking at him through the passenger window before the vehicle disappeared down a side street.

Rex and Luther continued to bark madly from the grassed yard behind the bar. "Johnny! Johnny, something happened."

"Yeah, what's going on there? Do you want us to come rip 'em apart?"

"That's what I wanna know," Charlie added as he stalked across the parking lot. "And who's been throwing spells here without sticking around to answer for it?"

Johnny stared at the dark road ahead where the vehicles had vanished. "Did you see who climbed into that getaway car, darlin'?"

"Yeah." Breathing heavily, Lisa turned to him with wide eyes. "The same witch we saw at Kaiser's farm. She's a little hard to not recognize."

"Uh-huh." He sniffed, rubbed his mouth vigorously, and spun to stride down the alley.

"Where you goin', 'coz?" Charlie shouted.

"To get some damn answers."

"All the answers drove off into the night." The mohawked dwarf scowled and stormed toward his bright orange Harley parked beside the row of his friends' bikes. "Well, someone had better get after those assholes—"

"Whoa, Charlie." The bald and completely tattooed biker shifter lunged after him and held him away from his motorcycle. "This is not a good time to go out for a ride."

"Are you kidding me? Come on, Romeo. Do you think a few drinks are gonna put me out?"

His buddy chuckled and hauled him toward the mouth of the alley. "You bet I do, brother. They'll take you off the road and right through it."

"Aw, piss off." Despite his grimace, he begrudgingly let his friend lead him to the back yard and the patio.

After she'd scanned the parking lot with little hope that she'd see anything of value, Lisa shook her head and turned to follow the group of transformed shifters who seemed to love the open road as much as Johnny's cousin. *Leave it to a Walker not to know how many drinks he's had or when enough is enough.*

When she reached their table, the bounty hunter had already rejoined Galfrey and Jake. The hounds had settled from their frenzy and they pranced toward her and bounded around her feet as she crossed to her partner and the two transformed shifters they'd been interviewing.

"Lisa. Hey, Lisa. What happened?"

"Yeah, did you guys get the guys?"

Rex snorted and looked sharply at his brother. "What?"

"You know. The shifter guys. And the shouting guy. And the —" Luther sniffed the air. "There was a witch here, right?"

"There was," she muttered. She stopped in front of the table and grimaced when the shifters they'd met barely fifteen minutes earlier looked at her with matching expressions of horror. "Are you sure that was your friend out there?"

"No." Galfrey swallowed thickly. "We're not sure but it sounded like him."

"It wasn't him," Jake protested and shook his head violently. "No way. He went to the john. I'll prove it."

He stood abruptly but Johnny stepped in front of him to block his path. "Did he have red sneakers?"

The man froze. "What?"

"Was your boy Hux wearin' red sneakers?"

The shifters glanced at each other and Jake sat slowly.

"Yeah," the second man said. "How did you—"

"They took him." The dwarf pulled his chair out with a loud scrape of metal across the patio paving and sat.

"Who?" Galfrey leaned forward and looked desperately from Johnny to Lisa. "Who took him? Who are you talking about?"

"The only one I saw was that witch with the red hair. The tiny one."

"Oh, no…" Jake groaned.

"And if I had to guess, I'm sure we'd have seen old Tall-Hulkin'-And-Ugly in one of those SUVs too."

"Who?" Galfrey's eyes practically bulged from their sockets.

"Veron," Lisa clarified impatiently. "Kaiser's right-hand shifter. But you two already know that, don't you?"

"Oh, Jesus, man!" Jake dragged his hands down both sides of his face. "They took him. They found us—how did they find us?"

"They only found Hux," his friend muttered and stared in disbelief at the bounty hunter and his partner.

"Yeah, but they know we were together. They must know." He turned toward his companion and grasped him by the lapel of his leather jacket to give him a little shake. "They'll snatch us next, man, and take us to wherever they're taking Hux to dump our bodies on top of his. We gotta get outta here. We gotta—"

Johnny pounded the side of his fist into the metal patio table and the harsh clang echoed somewhat. "Y'all need to sit and shut up."

Jake immediately released his friend and spun in his chair like a grade-school troublemaker being threatened with a trip to the principal's office. Galfrey closed his eyes and exhaled a long, shaky sigh.

"Now's the time to spill it," the bounty hunter added in a tone that brooked no argument. "'Cause y'all are holdin' onto somethin' heavy and y'all's poker faces are shit."

"We can't talk about it." Jake pressed his lips together and shook his head. "We can't. Not now that they have Hux. We'll never get him back and they won't stop until they find us too."

"Well, it's a good thing y'all are sittin' down with about the only two magicals who give a damn about what happens next." He felt Lisa's stare as she sat slowly beside him again and he darted a sidelong glance at her before he cleared his throat. "And who ain't more worried about savin' their own skins first."

Jake rocked miserably in his chair, still shaking his head, and groaned in terror.

"Hey." Lisa leaned forward and fixed Galfrey with her gaze because the other transformed shifter wouldn't open his eyes. "We've already been looking into this whole situation of the faction skirmishes and how Kaiser's involved. But we can't do anything if you guys don't help us."

Jake stopped shaking his head, at least, but he still wouldn't look at them.

"Once you do, we can make it a priority to find Hux before anything happens to him."

The dwarf snorted and looked sharply at her. "We will?"

"Yeah, Johnny, because this isn't Kaiser's MO, is it? Snatching one transformed shifter at a time and taking them away without talking to anyone." She raised an eyebrow at Galfrey and nodded. "Right?"

"How the hell am I supposed to know how that asshole operates?"

"Watch your mouth, pal." Johnny pointed warningly at him. "I ain't sayin' she can't take care of herself but you don't wanna find out the hard way."

Lisa pressed her lips together and tried to hold back a smirk.

"Sorry." The man shook his head. "But I can't believe…we've been laying low for months and they find us here, of all places."

"Someone ratted us out, man," Jake whined.

"So y'all are hidin' somethin'."

"Not like that." Galfrey shot his friend a warning look but the other shifter was too lost in his paranoia to notice. "We didn't even do anything wrong, okay? It was self-defense but it went…it went sideways faster than any of us expected."

"Yeah." Jake shrieked a laugh. "All because of you and your screwed-up mission to protect everyone when we can't even protect ourselves. And now Hux is as good as dead."

"Hey, no one was supposed to die that night, okay? That was the whole point."

"And it went so well." His friend rolled his eyes. "Screw this, man. Screw the war, screw Kaiser and his fucking crusade, and screw you." He lurched out of his chair again. "You can stay and tell stories around the goddamn campfire. I'm getting outta here before they—"

Johnny whistled shrilly and both hounds left their grass-sniffing to bound dutifully to their master's side. Their claws scrabbled across the patio cement as they skittered to a stop and blocked the shifter's escape.

"Do you want us to tear him up, Johnny?"

"Ooh, hey. That'll be easy. He smells like a rabbit right before I crush its neck in my teeth." Rex snapped his jaws but stayed where he was with his tail pointed straight out behind him.

Luther chuffed. "Bro, he's one of those weird new shifters, not a rabbit."

The larger hound bared his teeth and uttered a low snarl. "Fear, dude. Same fear, same smell."

"Oh. Yeah. That makes sense. He stinks."

Jake blinked at the hounds, then looked at Johnny. "You know what I am, right?"

"Uh-huh."

The shifter swallowed. "Then you should know you can't scare me with a couple of dogs."

Johnny folded his arms and leaned back in his chair. "Wanna bet?"

Luther jumped forward with a snarl and Jake immediately raised both hands in concession. "All right. Jesus. Okay."

Galfrey stared at his friend, who sat slowly. "This has gone on way too long, man. We gotta tell them."

"Whatever. Lemme get another drink first."

"Do you think Hux would have had that many beers if he knew he'd be attacked and shoved in one of Kaiser's cars? Come on, Jake. Get a grip."

The other shifter gritted his teeth. "I can't do this."

"It looks like all you gotta do is sit there quietly and let your buddy say what's on his mind," Johnny interjected. "And maybe answer a few questions if we have 'em. Then your next round's on me."

His gaze fixed on the hounds, the terrified shifter shook his head. "Whatever, man."

"So go ahead," Lisa prompted. "Let's hear your side of the story."

"Yeah, okay." Galfrey removed his newsboy cap, ruffled his short dark hair, and tossed the hat onto the table. "A couple of months ago—"

"For crying out loud," Charlie shouted from where he sat with his biker friends and pounded the table with a fist. "What's a dwarf gotta do to get some goddamn habanero nachos in this joint?"

The bikers exploded into raucous laughter and jostled him before one of them went inside to place an order.

Galfrey nodded toward the mohawked dwarf and frowned. "What's his deal?"

Johnny grunted. "We ain't got that kinda time tonight. Trust me."

"He knows he's not only a dwarf, right?"

"That moron can't decide what he is and ain't when he's sober. Ignore him and start talkin'."

CHAPTER TWO

Galfrey shrugged and ran his fingers across the metal mesh of the tabletop. "A couple of months ago, we got a…an invitation from Veron to meet him and the rest of Kaiser's posse. It was one of those deals he's made with transformed shifters all over the country."

"We know what Kaiser's doing." Lisa nodded. "Who's we?"

"Our crew, I guess." He shrugged. "I can't honestly call it a pack at this point. It's more a group of transformed shifters trying to live as peacefully and quietly as we can. But the more we heard about what Kaiser was trying to do—at least in the beginning—the more we realized we had to stick together and show a united front—"

Jake scoffed. "Look how well that worked out. A united front that gets half shot to pieces while the other half scatters into the wind."

"Do you wanna tell the damn story, dude? Or you gonna shut up and let me finish?"

"Whatever."

Galfrey glowered furiously at his friend and drummed his fingers on the metal table. "We honestly believed taking a stand would work. That maybe if Veron had to go back to Kaiser and tell his scumbag of a boss that we had stood up to him, banded together, and refused to be bullied into working with the guy so they wouldn't pick us off one by one, things might change."

"Did Veron give you any details about what this kinda deal entails?" Johnny asked.

"No. As far as we know, the only thing he tells anyone is we can join Kaiser's ranks for a greater shifter world or be put down in the street where we belong."

"Those are his exact words?" Lisa asked.

Galfrey looked bitterly at her. "It's heavily implied."

"So you got the invitation," the bounty hunter prompted. "Did that happen the night Addison Taylor was killed?"

Jake groaned again but didn't say a word.

The other shifter winced. "No. Veron contacted one of our other guys first—Paxton—and told him to spread the word to anyone who might be interested to meet him on the docks a week later. We could face him in person and give him our answer to take to Kaiser."

"And your answer was no." Lisa didn't state it as a question.

"It was always no. Look, most of us aren't like that crazy-ass dwarf over there." Galfrey nodded toward Charlie again, who'd launched into another drinking song but this time, gave his performance from the relative safety of a patio chair. "We merely want to live our lives the way we've lived them until now. Most of us were human first. You know…before. We don't want to be involved in all this other shifter crap and didn't ask for any of this."

"No one's sayin' you did." Johnny frowned as he considered what he'd heard and tugged his beard a few times. "So you went to the docks that night to tell Veron that he and Kaiser could stick their offer where the sun don't shine."

"Basically, yeah." The man sighed heavily. "Veron chose the location. We merely arrived to give our answer in the best way we knew how that wouldn't make us look like a group of terrified little kids."

Jake shook his head. "They never should have been there."

Lisa shifted in her chair. "Who?"

"That Taylor girl," Galfrey muttered. "That wasn't us and we had no idea who she was until after."

"They hardly covered it on the news," his friend whispered. "No one wants to get caught in this mess, especially us. But despite the lack of news reports, we seemed to hear about it everywhere we went. Bronson Harford, San Francisco's millionaire-shifter darling, lost his freaking girlfriend in a tragic accident. And if you'd let her go—"

"How the hell was I supposed to know they were together, huh?" Galfrey all but snarled in what sounded like a mixture of guilt and frustration. "It's not like I give a damn about natural-born shifter politics or kids who have eaten from a silver spoon all their life."

"Wait, what do you mean by let her go?" Lisa glanced at Johnny in confusion but he fixed his gaze firmly on the shifters across the table and studied their reactions.

These fellas ain't as badass as they tried to seem three months ago. They got a helluva surprise for tryin' to be brave.

Galfrey slumped in his chair, tilted his head back, and groaned. "I didn't know, man. I swear if I had, I wouldn't have stepped in."

"You're gonna have to explain more than that," the bounty hunter grumbled.

"I know. I know, but…" The shifter squeezed his eyes shut and ruffled his dark hair again before he turned his attention to fiddling with his newsboy cap on the table. "Look, when this Kaiser asshole started his whole campaign, it was in secret, right? More than it is now, at least. We heard stories here and there of Veron coming to visit transformed in their homes. Before everyone knew his name, he was the shifter you did not want to see walking up your front steps. Those were quiet meetings—one-on-one and sometimes with a whole family if someone had their kids with them. It didn't matter if it was only one transformed who tried to keep their secret. This guy made sneaking around his calling card."

Jake sighed and sounded like he was about to break down in tears. "Not anymore."

"We arrived at the docks when we were supposed to," Galfrey continued. "Or maybe a little early, as I recall. There was little more than a dozen of us and we were gonna make a stand. But this other transformed chick was already there and simply stood on one of the piers and looked terrified. Then this natural runs out of the warehouse and yells about how they have to get outta there. He tells her to come with him and that they didn't want anything to do with our mess. Hell, I thought it was some kinda return to Veron's old tactics—lure a single transformed out into the open for a private chat. I thought maybe the guy had tricked her into being there."

Johnny tilted his head and regarded him with a scowl. "Fixin' to do what?"

"I don't know, man. Give her the same kinda choice Kaiser's given the rest of us. Maybe hold her against her will and make her watch the way he eliminates anyone who stands against him. We all knew it was gonna get ugly and that chick kept asking what was going on and looked so confused. Honestly, she looked as scared as we were."

"And you didn't think maybe she looked so damn scared 'cause y'all's posse was rollin' in for the kinda fight that has happened repeatedly over the last year?"

The shifter glared at him. "It's a little hard to think straight when you're standing up for yourself and don't expect to get out of there alive."

"It sounds like maybe you got a little rougher than you meant to."

"No. It wasn't like that—"

"It kinda was," his friend muttered.

"Dude."

"That Harford kid and his friends tried to clear it all up." Jake shrugged. "We didn't have time to find out what was going on before Veron and his black-magic witch on a leash arrived with almost as many shifters as we had."

Galfrey swallowed and his face grew paler by the second. "I swear I had no idea who she was and I didn't know the Harford kid either. We all thought they were in on Kaiser's campaign—him and his friends. All I wanted was to get her somewhere safe and out of the way so she could make her choice without being manipulated into what sounds a hell of a lot like serving a heart-less dictator."

"Then what happened?" Lisa asked.

The bounty hunter narrowed his eyes. "Did you kill her?"

"Johnny—"

"What?" Both shifters stared at their interrogators in dumb shock before Galfrey shook his head. "No. No way. Hey, I didn't do a thing to that Taylor girl, okay? Yeah, I tried to drag her away from the docks but that's 'cause I was trying to protect her and everyone else."

"It's hard to protect anyone when the other guys have auto-matic weapons and that redheaded witch," Jake snarled.

Lisa drew a sharp breath. "They brought firearms with them?"

"Yeah. Every single one of them had a gun from what I remember."

Jake hugged his waist and stared at the tabletop. "I can't believe we made it out of there—only the three of us."

"You two and Hux."

"Uh-huh." The other man shifted forward in his chair and stared at the two investigators with a desperate plea in his eyes. "We knew we'd have to fight our way out. Although we didn't expect the guns, we were ready to fight back in one way or another. The Taylor girl being there was an accident, okay? She tried to get away but it's not like Veron gave two shits one way or the other who was part of our group that night and who wasn't. All he saw was another transformed shifter with the rest of us, and she—"

"Man," Jake muttered. "That kid's screams when she went down…I never heard anything like it."

"You saw Addison Taylor get shot on that pier?" Lisa asked.

Galfrey nodded and pointed at the right side of his chest. "Here. She fell back into the water and her boyfriend completely lost it."

Johnny raised an eyebrow. "You can't blame him for it."

"I don't. I blame myself." With a bitter grimace, he drew a deep breath through his nose and his eyes shimmered with unshed tears. "No, I didn't pull the trigger but I had the wrong idea about everything."

"It sounds like you were trying to help." Lisa shrugged. "Granted, you had the wrong information but you were forced into a seriously tough decision to begin with."

"If you're trying to lighten the load on my conscience, lady, that's not gonna do it. I should have minded my own damn business."

"Naw, I reckon folks doin' nothin' more than mindin' their own damn business is part of what got this whole mess twisted up in the first place." The bounty hunter pointed at him. "You did all right tryin' to stand up for your friends. Hell, if I made all the right calls half the time, I coulda saved myself a helluva lotta headaches. I know that much. A couple of mistakes don't make a fella right or wrong for makin' 'em."

His partner turned in her chair to study him in surprise but he didn't react to her gaze.

Yeah, I said it, darlin'. Somethin' is wrong with me if I can't admit I ain't always right.

She shook her head and turned slowly toward the transformed shifters with a frown. "Did you see Addison Taylor at all after she fell into the water?"

"With her sprayed clean through with bullets?" Galfrey hissed a sigh. "No way. She went down and that was it. That poor girl died in the bay."

"What about Bronson Harford and his friends?"

"They hightailed it out of there like any sane person would." He shrugged. "It probably would have been a hell of a lot worse for us if he'd stayed and been killed in the slaughter too. High profile and all that, right?"

"Not lately." The dwarf tugged his beard thoughtfully. "How many friends did he have with him?"

"I don't know. Two?"

"No, man. Three." Jake nodded. "I know it was three 'cause I remember it took all of them to hold him back so he wasn't killed exactly like the girl was. The guy was as strong as an ox, man."

"Rage and grief will do that to a fella, sure." Johnny scratched the side of his face through his wiry red beard and jerked his chin at the shifters. "Y'all said you think you're the reason this whole thing went from bad to worse over the last three months—since that night."

"Yeah." The two shifters exchanged a worried glance. "Yeah, we think—"

"Don't put words in my mouth, man." Jake folded his arms. "I don't know what the hell to think. I'm simply trying to stay alive."

"Fine. You guys have heard about this Tyro asshole too, right? The one running around killing transformed 'cause of what we are without trying to hide behind the shitty offers Kaiser's been making?"

"We've heard of him, sure." Johnny nodded.

"I think… Shit. I think it's 'cause of us. Of me. Or at least that's what I thought until they snatched Hux."

His friend groaned again.

"Someone must have heard the story of what happened,"

Galfrey continued. "That I tried to take the Taylor girl with us so we're the reason she couldn't get away and was killed for being in the wrong place at the wrong time. Whoever this Tyro guy is, I think he's punishing whatever transformed shifters he can find in an attempt to reach me. All because I couldn't pull my head out of my ass long enough to realize—"

The shifter buried his face in his hands with a strangled sob.

Jake stared at his friend with a mournful grimace. "Now, we're dead."

"No, you ain't. Not yet. And y'all are gonna stay kickin' while we work the rest of this out." Johnny stood from the table and turned to head to the bar's back door.

"Where are you going?" Lisa asked.

"I promised these fellas a round after our little chat, darlin'." He stopped short when Charlie leapt out of his chair on the other side of the patio and thrust both hands in the air.

"Johnny! Hey, remember that time at the swimming hole on Grampy's farm? The time you got those leeches all up in your—"

"Say another word and I'll make damn sure you ain't gettin' back on that eyesore on wheels."

"It's all good, 'coz. See?" Charlie held his huge glass of water up, which was almost empty. "I'm on number three here and sobering up."

"Sure, and I can destroy that bike up in ten seconds flat whether you're sober or you ain't."

The mohawked dwarf's smile faded as he sat slowly in his chair. "Aw, come on. You don't mean that."

Half his biker friends chuckled good-naturedly. The other half scowled at Johnny and shook their heads.

The bounty hunter turned to face Lisa, Galfrey, and Jake and thrust a finger in the air. "One drink. Then we're gettin' the hell outta here."

CHAPTER THREE

When Johnny said one round, he'd meant it. By the time they'd finished their drinks, the transformed shifters had fallen into a morose silence but they didn't try to argue when he told them what came next.

"I think the best thing now is for y'all to lay low."

"That's what we've been doing."

"Sure. But now y'all have a little extra protection." When the shifters gave him blank looks, he scoffed and spread his arms to gesture to himself and his partner. "Personal protection—me and Lisa and the hounds, too."

Jake's eyes widened. "Why are you sticking your necks out for us like this?"

"Because someone's gotta. Y'all didn't have a clue what y'all were doin' the night Addison Taylor was killed. This Tyro asshole, though? He knows exactly what's goin' on, what he wants, and all the lines he's willin' to cross to get it. It doesn't have to make sense to anyone else as long as it makes sense to him. But knowin' a thing's wrong and doin' it anyway makes him a hell of a lot trickier to deal with."

"You'll merely get caught in the storm," Galfrey muttered.

"Naw. I'm fixin' to make the storm come to us. Until then, y'all need a safer place to stay than this dump with all those yahoos fallin' all over themselves." Johnny stuck a thumb over his shoulder to indicate Charlie's table, where the mohawked dwarf and his biker buddies erupted in another wild round of laughter. They pounded the table and scattered nacho crumbs all over their laps and the patio.

"Johnny." Lisa swallowed the last her gin and tonic and turned to him with a confused frown. "We're not going back to Florida."

"'Course we ain't, darlin'. The least we can do is keep these fellas from leavin' a paper trail. What's the worst place you can think of to stay? The kinda place you wouldn't suggest to your worst enemy?"

The two shifters frowned at each other. "I don't know. Any place out on 99."

"Great. Then that's where we'll stay."

"Are you for real, man?"

"As real as they get." He whistled for the hounds, who immediately dropped the stick and plastic water bottle they'd been playing with to join their master as he strode off the patio and down the alley. "The worst place you'd never go is the last place anyone will think to look for ya. Charlie!"

"What's up?"

"We're headin' out. Come make yourself useful, huh?"

"Yeah, sure. Text me wherever you're going, and I'll—"

The bounty hunter spun and glared at his cousin. "New deal. You come with us right now or you'll spend the next week pickin' up the parts of your ride from the highway. Your call."

"Damn." The dwarf shifter stood from his chair and clapped one of his friends on the shoulder. "When Johnny means business, he means business. Let me know where you guys are heading tomorrow. I'll catch up—"

"The hell you will!" Johnny called from the alley.

Lisa hurried to join him and left Galfrey and Jake to bring up the rear. "Are you sure it's a good idea to threaten motorcycle dismemberment?"

"It ain't a threat, darlin'. He knows I could do it before he has enough sense in him to stop me."

"No, I know that. But we could also simply let him know what hotel we're staying at once we get there."

He snorted. "If we give him the option, he'll jet outta here without a word—again. And I aim to put my cousin to work since he's fixin' so hard to be all involved."

"Put him to work doing what?"

The dwarf opened the back hatch of their rental and nodded for the hounds to get in. "Babysittin'."

"Whoa, whoa, whoa, Johnny." Luther spun on the SUV's carpeted floor and cocked his head. "We don't need that."

"Yeah." Rex sat at his master's feet and looked at him with wide, glistening eyes. "Babysitters are for babies."

"Not y'all."

"Oh, whew." Rex bounded up after his brother, then shouted, "Hey, why are we in the way-way back?"

The hatch shut with a click and Johnny opened the back door for Galfrey and Jake. "Y'all are comin' with us."

"Nah, man. That's all right." Galfrey pointed at a beat-up black Subaru Outback parked across the lot. "We got our own ride."

"Sure." The bounty hunter wrinkled his nose at the vehicle. "Ridin' around in something like that is bound to get you noticed. If you don't wanna get picked up like Hux, I suggest leavin' your ride exactly where it is."

"Dude, is he serious?"

Galfrey bit the inside of his bottom lip and settled his gaze on the SUV's open back door. "He's got a point."

"Fine. It's a pile of junk anyway." Jake stormed toward the rental and climbed in.

"Oh…" Luther sniffed the back of the skinny shifter's head. "I get it. Hey, Johnny. How come you're not putting the shifters in the back?"

"Yeah, the back seat's ours." Rex panted and stared at Galfrey as the shifter slid in beside his friend and shut the door.

He turned to glance at each of the hounds and muttered, "Does he make you wear a seatbelt?"

"Oh-ho! No way."

"Johnny never straps us in. Are you kidding?"

"Then that's why you're in the back and we're not." Facing forward again, he accentuated his point by buckling up nice and tight.

Johnny pretended to ignore the entire exchange and slid behind the wheel as Lisa scrambled into the passenger seat. He cranked the engine, strapped himself in, and turned to hold his hand out toward the shifters in the back seat. "Wallets and cell phones, fellas."

"No way can he be serious about that," Jake muttered.

"Do I look like I'm yankin' y'all around?" The dwarf wiggled his fingers. "Let's go."

"We're not, uh…in the habit of handing our personal possessions to a stranger." Galfrey adjusted his newsboy cap on his head and shrugged. "Maybe this was merely an elaborate plan to rob us."

"If I was fixin' to steal y'all's valuables, I woulda done it an hour ago. And y'all wouldn't have noticed until tomorrow. Hand 'em over."

Jake wrinkled his nose and shook his head. "Yeah, I'm good."

Johnny turned in his seat and cocked his head. "Did you hear that, darlin'?"

"Hear what?" Lisa raised an eyebrow.

"The sound of a couple of fellas who still don't know what's good for 'em. Lemme ask you somethin'. If you were runnin' for your life from a mysterious bastard no one knows who's huntin' your kind indiscriminately for a type of revenge no one else has pinned down but you, how tempted would you be to make a few phone calls or swipe your credit card a couple of times to get from one place to the next?"

"Hey, we get it, man," Jake cut in. "We won't call anyone or use—"

"And if you were that mysterious bastard, how easy would it be to find the fellas you're after merely by hackin' into phone records or lookin' up bank statements?"

"Fairly easy," Lisa replied, her voice flat and expressionless.

"Wait, what?" Galfrey leaned forward. "You think that's how they found us?"

"If that witch on Kaiser's payroll has been huntin' transformed the way I heard she does, I reckon that's got somethin' to do with it. And I ain't fixin' to wash y'all down if it's only the smell of you and nothin' else."

"Yeah, okay. Here." Jake fumbled in his back pockets before he produced both wallet and cell phone. The latter toppled out of his hand onto the floor before he could hand it over, but Lisa waited patiently for him to retrieve it before she took his personal belongings.

Johnny looked into the rearview mirror and widened his eyes at Galfrey. "This ain't gonna work if you're only goin' in halfway."

"Jesus. Fine." The second shifter handed his valuables to her and stared at them as she shoved everything in the glove box. "We get all that back, though, right?"

"Sure. As soon as we find where they're keepin' your buddy Hux and after we crack down on Tyro and discover what the hell's been goin' on in Shifterland."

Luther sniggered. "Shifterland. What does that even mean?"

As Charlie rounded the corner out of the alley, Johnny rolled his window down and whistled at his cousin. "You're followin', understand?"

"Oh, come on." The mohawked dwarf spread his arms in a gesture of frustration as he walked backward toward his orange motorcycle. "Are you trying to bleed all the fun out of everything for me or what?"

"It ain't supposed to be fun, Charlie. And I'm only gonna tell you this once." The dwarf pointed at his cousin. "You screw around with this, you'll wish you'd kept runnin' your mouth about those damn leeches instead."

"Yeah, yeah. I got it. Where are we going?"

"I ain't tellin' you—"

"The Gold Motel off 99," Jake muttered.

The biker dwarf grinned. "Yeah, I know the place. That's a real dump, Johnny. Are you sure that's where you wanna—"

"Damnit, Charlie. Get on the damn bike and stay behind me." The bounty hunter rolled the window up with a growl of aggravation and shoved the gear shift into drive. "From now on, no one talks to that dwarf unless I give the go-ahead."

"Sorry." The shifter shrank into himself and gazed out his window. "I was only trying to remind you and didn't think he could hear me."

"Dude, he's a shifter dwarf," Galfrey muttered. "That was the first thing he told us."

"Well, I'm sorry I can't remember everyone's life story, man. I'm a little preoccupied with making sure mine doesn't end tomorrow, okay?"

After he'd checked the side mirror to make sure his cousin had mounted the damn bike, the bounty hunter drove out of the parking lot and nodded at Lisa. "Do you have the right place down?"

She tapped her GPS. "Yep."

"Hey, whatever your phone says," Galfrey added, "there are at least three faster routes if you take—"

"We ain't takin' back roads." He pressed the accelerator. "And I need a quiet ride so everyone sit tight and zip it."

Lisa smirked and cleared her throat.

The bounty hunter divided his attention between the road,

her directions, and continual glances in the rearview mirror to confirm that his pain-in-the-ass cousin on the bright orange Harley was still behind him.

If he tries anythin', I swear I'll make up for our boyhood days in a single move.

For the first fifteen minutes of the drive out of Yuba City, Charlie followed the SUV exactly as he'd agreed to do. By the time they'd reached 99 under the warm night air with only a handful of other cars on the road, however, the roar of the Harley's engine kicking up blared from behind the rental.

In the next moment, the biker dwarf streaked past them in a blur of orange and black. The tips of his heavily gelled mohawk fluttered in the wind as he vanished into the darkness ahead of them between the highway lights.

"Dammit, Charlie." Johnny gritted his teeth and glanced at Lisa's phone. "How much farther?"

"About ten miles."

"If he ain't waitin' there for us, no one's gettin' any shuteye tonight."

"I'm sure he'll be there."

He frowned at her and snorted. "No, you ain't. The only thing anyone can be sure of with that bonehead is that he ain't good for a single word outta his damn mouth."

Lisa leaned her head against the headrest and sighed. "And what if he proves you wrong, huh?"

"It won't be provin' me wrong, darlin'. It'll be him tryin' to prove he can do whatever he wants and get away with it in the end."

"Oh, yeah? Should we hold everyone to those same standards?"

He did a double-take at her raised eyebrows and rolled his eyes. "You're talkin' about me, ain'tcha?"

"I merely said everyone else."

"Yeah, well, everyone else ain't Charlie Walker. And there's already one too many of those. I tell you what, darlin'. If you wanna compare him to me, you gotta take a look at the whole picture."

"Which you still haven't told me."

He looked into the rearview mirror and caught both Galfrey and Jake staring at his reflection before they both looked away quickly. Rex and Luther, however, gazed dutifully into their master's squinty eyes and panted with their tongues lolling out of their mouths.

"What's up, Johnny?"

"Yeah, fancy seeing you here."

"Shouldn't you be watching the road or something?"

The dwarf grunted and returned his full attention to driving. "It's a story for another time, darlin'."

"Uh-huh." Lisa folded her arms. "And when exactly will we have the time now that we're providing a makeshift WITSEC courtesy of Johnny Walker Investigations?"

"I'll work that part out when we get to it."

And if this Gold Motel doesn't have two empty connectin' rooms, we ain't stoppin' until we find one that does. I'm done sharin' accommodations with all the strays I can't seem to avoid takin' in. No way in hell will I share a room with Charlie, neither.

CHAPTER FOUR

The bounty hunter wasn't particularly surprised to find that neither Charlie nor his orange Harley was waiting for them in the motel parking lot. Still, it left him in a sour mood that didn't improve even when he learned that the Gold Motel had one set of adjoining rooms on the second floor.

He paid for both before he signaled for the crew waiting in the SUV to come up and get settled in. As Galfrey and Jake reached the top of the stairs, the roar of Charlie's beefed-up motorcycle shattered the relative silence and the mohawked dwarf turned into the parking lot with a skid of rubber on asphalt. The growling rumble of his engine sputtered to a stop.

"Take these. Get 'em settled in." Johnny held the keys for both rooms out for Lisa, who took them carefully.

"Johnny, he's here. That's what matters, right?"

"Not even a little." Without taking his eyes off his cousin, the bounty hunter stalked down the stairs and his knuckles popped when he clenched his fist.

"Whew!" Charlie swung a leg over his bike and laughed. "What a night, huh? Man, I saw that straight open highway and couldn't help—"

Johnny's fist met the other dwarf's jaw in a fierce right hook and the biker staggered back, his eyes wide in dumbfounded shock.

He raised a hand slowly to his face and scowled at his cousin. "Shit. What the hell was that for?"

"You know damn well what it was for." He pointed at him. "I told you to follow but you go hurtlin' off down the road anyhow and you ain't even here before us."

"Aw, come on, 'coz. Don't tell me you'd be able to hold yourself back from…well, from whatever it is you love. If a traveling salesman opened a popup store for all his crazy-cool weapons, wouldn't you ignore the rest of the world simply to have a good look at the merchandise?"

"That's—" Johnny shook his head. "All right. First, there ain't no popup weapon shops."

"It's hypothetical, man."

"Well, this ain't!" He stepped close enough to his cousin that their faces were mere inches apart but forced his hands to his sides again when all they wanted to do was batter the mohawked dwarf. "I already saved your ass more times than I care to admit and I ain't fixin' to add another one to the list. Understand?"

Charlie glanced at the second floor of the motel, where Lisa stood with one foot in the open door of the shifters' room as she debated whether or not she wanted to see any of this. Finally, he looked at the bounty hunter and gave him a weak smile. "Johnny, don't you think it's been long enough that you can let all that go now?"

"You tell me, 'coz."

"Look, I'm good, okay? No problems. Straight as a whistle, I promise."

Johnny folded his arms and raked his gaze over his cousin despite the short distance between them. "You ain't given me one good reason to believe it."

"Hey, I'm here, aren't I?"

"Uh-huh. You're always around when you want somethin', Charlie. But how about after you get it, huh? Trust me, I have no problem cuttin' you outta this whole mess if you can't pull your shit together—"

"It's together, Johnny."

"Not until you prove it."

"Come on. Why would I lie to you?"

He leaned closer until their noses almost touched and his bristling mustache was a breath away from scraping against his cousin's face as he searched Charlie's eyes and muttered, "I think we can both think of at least two reasons, yeah?"

His teeth gritted, he slapped a hand against the shoulder of the biker's leather riding jacket and shoved him away. The mohawked dwarf chuckled bitterly but didn't say a word.

"Don't give me another one." Johnny turned and marched toward the motel stairs again. "Are you comin' or what?"

"Well, make up your mind, huh? You want me here. You don't want me here. And hey, don't think I didn't hear you talking about a babysitter. I swear, Johnny, if you think I'm gonna sit around and let some friend of yours tell me what to do because you don't trust me—"

"I don't. But right now, you're all we have."

Charlie paused at the foot of the stairs and frowned at the bounty hunter's retreating back. "Huh?"

"You ain't gettin' a babysitter. You are the babysitter."

"Oh." Scratching his head, he hurried up the stairs. "Wait, for the shifters?"

Johnny stormed into the open room where Galfrey and Jake both sat on the edge of one twin-sized bed.

Lisa leaned against the side of the dresser with her arms folded and watched the dwarf with undisguised curiosity. "Is everything okay?"

"As much as it's gonna be. It depends on how far he's willin' to go to set things straight." He jerked his thumb over his shoulder as the other dwarf entered the doorway.

Jake looked sharply at the newcomer. "Why? What did he do?"

Charlie snorted. "Answering that kinda question's gonna take us a few weeks we don't have. So these are the digs, huh?" A cockroach skittered out from under the old-school radiator and disappeared under Galfrey's bed. "Cozy."

"Where are the hounds?"

"In here, Johnny!" Luther barked from the adjoining room.

"Yeah, guess how thin the walls are." Rex uttered a warbling howl to make his point. "It sounds like I'm right in your face, huh?"

Johnny snapped his fingers. "That's enough, boys."

The hounds sniggered and padded around the other room.

"So how long are we supposed to stay here?" Jake asked. "I'm only asking for peace of mind."

"Y'all let us worry about that."

"It kinda feels like a hostage situation when you don't tell us, though."

The bounty hunter glared at the shifter and swept his arm behind him to gesture toward the open door. "You ain't a prisoner. If you're feelin' lucky enough to take your chances out there on your own, go ahead. I estimate that you'll last maybe twenty-four hours before you find one of those posse cars hot on your heels and a giant shifter with his tiny witch hoppin' out to say hello. And you won't even be able to pretend that I didn't tell you so, but there ain't no use in warnin' you against it."

Charlie folded his arms and smirked. "I think that means you'll be kidnapped or dead before—"

"I know what it means!" Jake hunched his shoulders and stared at the stained carpet. "I get it."

"Do you honestly think they're gonna put that much energy into finding us again?" Galfrey asked.

The bounty hunter shrugged. "Y'all said they were lookin' for you in the first place. Are you takin' it back now?"

"I don't…think so."

"Well then, we should all keep movin' forward and assume your gut was right." He fixed them both with a look that effectively quelled any further questions. "And I'm turnin' in."

"Good idea." Charlie pulled the door shut and hurried after his cousin. "Where's my room?"

"You're standin' in it."

"Ha. No, seriously."

Johnny turned in front of the door connecting the adjoining rooms and stared unrelentingly at his cousin. "Seriously. There should be a cot or somethin' in the closet. Don't get too cozy."

Before the other dwarf could respond, he pulled the door open and disappeared into the other room.

Lisa cleared her throat and took her wallet from her purse slung over her shoulder. From that, she removed a twenty-dollar bill and slapped it on the dresser. "The office should have change. You know, if you need snacks or something."

"Huh." Galfrey stared at the money as the Light Elf crossed the room. "I think my appetite's been kicked into next week but thanks."

"Hey, if you don't want it—"

"Charlie." She spun around halfway through the adjoining doorway and pointed at him. "That's not for you."

The dwarf gave her a crooked smile. "I don't get to enjoy the amenities too?"

"Sure. If you think your life's in danger for pissing off the wrong magical, feel free to hand your wallet and your phone over. Oh, and your keys."

He responded with a bitter laugh and waved her off before he moved to the closet to pull the cot out.

"If you guys need anything," she added and nodded at the other two transformed shifters, "well…you know where we are."

"Yeah. Thanks." Galfrey hadn't moved his gaze from the twenty on the dresser. Jake heaved a sigh and flopped onto the bed.

"Okay. Goodnight." Lisa closed the door and turned to find Johnny pacing along the narrow strip of walkway between their motel room's exterior door on one side and the bathroom on the other. "I guess that couldn't have gone any—" Her gaze settled on Rex and Luther who had curled on the second twin-sized mattress. They stared at her and panted through their houndish smiles. "Are you two supposed to be there?"

"Oh, come on." Luther uttered a low whine. "One time isn't gonna kill you. Or us."

"Yeah, Lisa." Rex lifted a hind leg and demonstrated the feat of canine flexibility required to nip the inside of his thigh while still lying mostly curled on the mattress. "And it's not like you two-legs aren't gonna share the other bed. This one can be ours."

"We gonna snuggle too, bro?"

"Maybe."

Rolling her eyes, Lisa moved to the bed not conquered by the coonhounds and sat on the edge. She watched Johnny pace for a moment longer before she cleared her throat. "If it bothers you this much to have him in the next room, maybe we should find someone else to do the job."

"Huh?"

"Charlie."

"Naw, he'll stay." Johnny waved dismissively. "It's possible he's finally ready to prove he can do something right. And he wanted to be involved in this case anyhow."

"Okay…" She kicked her sneakers off and scooted backward on the mattress before she pulled her legs up under her. "So why are you prowling across the room like an angry animal?"

"I'm thinkin'."

She glanced at the hounds and raised an eyebrow.

"Always a good idea, Johnny," Rex said and continued to nibble his hind leg.

"Yeah. Thinking's good." Luther settled his head on his forepaws and stared at her. "We should do more of that."

His brother snorted. "Says the hound who doesn't ever think at all."

"Yeah, but I'm—hey."

Lisa shook her head, rested her hands in her lap, and returned her attention to her partner's contemplative pacing. "I'll wait."

"For what, darlin'?"

"For you to tell me what's going through your head so I can give you a fresh perspective on it. Then you'll have an epiphany and act like it was your idea in the first place, which is fine because we'll go out to find whoever we need to find and close the case however we need to close it." She shrugged. "But if you need a little more time to get the ball rolling on this one, that's fine. I'll wait."

He stopped pacing and scowled at her. "Is that how you think this works?"

Despite her better judgment, she couldn't help but flash him a brilliant grin. "How do you think it works, Johnny?"

"All right. Fine." The bounty hunter snorted and approached the bed to sit on the edge and stare blankly at the floor. "I can't put my finger on it yet but somethin' doesn't sit right about Kaiser's little gang showin' up at that bar tonight."

"Why? Because it took them three months to find the transformed who refused his offer and managed to escape?"

"Sure. But that ain't the main part." He turned abruptly to look at her. "If Veron and his gang were huntin' our new friends deliberately, why did they stop at one?"

"You mean with Hux."

"Yep."

"Hmm." Lisa narrowed her eyes and tapped two fingers against her lips. "My guess is they probably weren't."

"Uh-huh. That's what I think too. Which means they were there for someone else." Johnny's gaze drifted slowly across the adjoining wall and settled on the door between the two rooms.

The sound of the TV clicked on, followed by Charlie's cheerful chatter. "Do you guys like watching those crime shows? No? Yeah, they are probably a little much given the circumstances. Hey, how about the Discovery Channel? When in Rome, right?"

Lisa snorted and fought back a laugh before she whispered, "That's all an act, right?"

"What?"

"Saying things that make absolutely no sense."

The bounty hunter scowled at the connecting door. "Maybe he's aimin' for comedic relief. He's been tryin' to gloss over everythin' that way his entire life but it simply makes him sound a whole nail shy of a damn safety holder."

She laughed in confusion. "I don't follow."

"It means he's a smartass dwarf who sounds like an idiot. And it makes him more trouble than he's worth." He sniffed and looked away. "How many of his biker buddies do you think were in that bar?"

"Six, maybe seven." Lisa's eyes widened and she turned to look at the door before she lowered her voice. "You think that's why Veron and his guys arrived? For Charlie and his friends?"

"It ain't outta the question, darlin'. You heard that shoutin' match the two of 'em got into once we picked up on somethin' goin' down, yeah?"

"I did." She took a flat, lumpy pillow from the pile behind her and folded it in her lap to prop her arms up. "'They're all in on it.' That's what I heard."

"Uh-huh." He ran a hand through his hair and scanned the motel room as he tried to recall what he'd heard during the attack neither of them had seen. "They drove into the parkin' lot, found Hux out there answerin' the call of nature, and popped him on the spot, magically speakin'.'"

"Well, Galfrey certainly thinks they're after him and Jake. Maybe Veron decided he'd found one and that was enough."

"Naw. I'd be willin' to bet it was Veron we heard shoutin' at the other guy and threatenin' to shove him in the trunk with a passed-out Hux." He tugged on his beard. "He said somethin' about blowin' the operation and the other guy wasn't gettin' the picture."

"So you think the witch tracked a group of transformed shifters to the bar." Lisa nodded as she worked through each step. "And found Hux instead."

"You bet. If they'd been trailin' our desperate friends on the other side of that door, Veron would have drawn 'em out and snatched all three of 'em. Or if Kaiser wanted 'em dead, they would be dead already. I think what we heard out there was contention in the boss man's ranks. Someone ain't playin' the game the way he was told to play it."

"And that's why they left." She frowned. "To avoid something they couldn't clean up without giving themselves away."

"That's exactly what I think, darlin'. I wish I'd had a look at whoever was shoutin' to 'find the bastards.' The bastards who did what, huh? Escaped Veron's death sentence three months ago? Or those who someone workin' for Kaiser wants to pin the blame on for Addison Taylor's death?"

"Or who wants an excuse to wage a secret war against all transformed shifters no matter who they are or if they're willing to join Kaiser in the first place."

"Someone like this Tyro guy."

Lisa shook her head. "That doesn't make sense, though. Everyone we've talked to about these shifter supremacists says the two are completely unrelated."

"Except for killin' transformed." Johnny stared at the stained bedspread for a long time before he looked sharply at her. "Did you see anyone else's face?"

"Nope. Only the back of that witch's trench coat before they disappeared. You?"

"I had a damn good look at her face. I think she had one of mine too."

"Are you sure?"

"No. But it wouldn't surprise me." He kicked his shoes off and tossed them onto the floor. "Well, I suppose we'll find out when we go back to Kaiser's pot farm on Friday."

"What? Johnny, if that dark witch saw you and recognized you, we'll completely blow our cover with Kaiser and his entire operation. We can't go there."

"We can, darlin', and that's exactly what I'm fixin' to do. Nothin' has changed."

"He'll know we were at the same bar as the shifters Veron intended to 'talk' to and the shifters they've been looking for. Those who got away." Lisa nodded toward the connecting door. "If he didn't already think there was something fishy about the two of us wanting to buy fifty pounds of—" She grimaced and lowered her voice. "Of marijuana, Johnny, he'll certainly be suspicious when we arrive after witnessing a kidnapping carried out on his orders."

"We don't know who decided to bag Hux like that. It felt like a last-minute decision to me."

"Either way, it's a bad idea."

"But it might be exactly the kinda bad idea we need." Johnny slid toward the head of the bed and pulled the covers back on her side. He gestured for her to get under the turned-down comforter.

She fixed him with a deadpan expression. "You can't say something like that and simply expect me to go along with it and call it a night."

He got into bed, patted the mattress beside him, and cleared his throat.

With a heavy sigh, she shrugged out of her light jacket, tossed it over the arm of the one armchair beside the bed, and crawled under the covers. "You'd better tell me what you're planning or you can sleep with the hounds."

"Hey, now. That ain't a way to—" He stopped when he rolled over to see Rex and Luther passed out on the other bed. "Damnit. Who told them they could upgrade from the floor?"

"You were busy thinking."

"All right. Fine. Listen, darlin'. My gut's tellin' me Kaiser's playin' a long game of hardball. One slip from one of his guys one night ain't enough to make him fly the coop so we'll go there on Friday, make the deal for our outstandin' business, and see how he reacts. If he mentions us bein' at Veron's little showdown gone wrong tonight, we'll know he ain't worried about it. If he clams up...well then, we have to assume that we have more on our plate with Mr. Join My Shifter Army than we thought. Either way, it's more information than we have now. We might be able to learn where they took Hux too."

Lisa closed her eyes, pulled the comforter up to her chin, and snuggled into it. "Then I guess Friday will be one hell of an enlightening day."

"You bet." Johnny clicked the bedside lamp off and tried to get comfortable on the lumpy mattress with the unyielding pillows and itchy sheets. After another minute, he growled and shifted again. "Chargin' folks to sleep in a place like this oughtta be illegal."

"It's the worst motel I've ever stepped foot in," Lisa muttered.

"Yeah. At least those shifters ain't yankin' our chains."

CHAPTER FIVE

At The Resort's off-the-radar property in the North San Juan valley, Carp paced furiously across the office on the fourth floor.

Kaiser sat behind his desk and watched the young shifter burn through his aggravation and rage.

If he doesn't pull himself together soon, we'll have more than an uncooperative prisoner on our hands. We'll have complete chaos.

After another five minutes of alternating his attention between the administrative work on the computer in front of him and the young shifter who seemed set to wear through the floor of his office, he took a deep breath and removed his reading glasses. "I brought you up here for a chance to cool down in private, not to work yourself up all over again. It's time to drop it, Carp."

The young man finally stopped pacing and spun toward him with wide eyes. "We need to kill him."

"That was already attempted once before, don't you remember?"

The young shifter snarled, lurched toward the desk, and slapped both hands on the surface. "And now we need to finish the job. How many other transformed have gotten away from you, huh?"

"None. Because you know I don't go out to conduct those meetings."

"Away from Veron, then. Everyone else who's turned down the offer to join you for a better shifter world was taken care of the minute they said no except for those assholes who escaped that night on the docks."

"Well, we have one of them."

"It's not enough." Carp pounded the desk with a fist but stepped back immediately when Kaiser rose quickly from his chair in one fluid motion.

"It sounds to me like you think you're the one giving orders around here." The older man raised an eyebrow. "That's premature."

"I'm just saying." The kid gritted his teeth and whirled to pace across the office again. "What kind of message are we sending if we don't kill that pathetic excuse for a shifter right now? Or if we don't track the other two and make them pay?"

"This isn't about my reputation, Carp. It's about your pain. Don't give credit for your rage where it isn't due."

"Then let me kill him."

"No."

"Why?"

Kaiser drew a deep breath, smoothed his hair away from his face, and gave the young shifter a tight, bitter smile. "Because the one transformed you and Veron captured last night is not our only target. You know that."

"Please. Like you and I have the same goals."

"Don't we?" He crossed the room to lay a hand on Carp's shoulder. "Look at me." The young shifter slowly did as he was told but his jaw muscles worked furiously beneath his scowl. "You have an agenda with these particular transformed. I'm happy to help you meet those needs where I can, but we can't lose sight of the bigger picture, son. The ultimate goal."

"You've been working toward this ultimate goal for how many years now?" The young man scoffed. "If helping me with my goals takes as much time as you've needed for yours, I'm better off doing this on my own."

"That's one way to look at it." Kaiser removed his hand and spread his arms in a non-committal gesture. "But from what I've heard, not even the infamous Tyro can pinpoint his own targets. He has help. And you would never have found that transformed in our custody if you hadn't gone out with Veron last night. But hey, if you think you no longer need me, then sure. Let's part ways. Right here and now."

Carp rolled his eyes and couldn't look at him again. "You don't mean that."

"Of course I do. I won't hold you against your will, son." He tilted his head and studied the young shifter's face to gauge his reactions.

If he thinks he's a prisoner here, we're doing this all wrong.

"You always have a choice," he added. "I welcomed you with open arms when you came to me looking for community and support. You wanted the chance to be a part of something bigger than yourself but if you haven't found what you're looking for with me, then by all means look somewhere else. I promise I won't hold it against you."

Carp scoffed and darted his boss a sidelong glare. "Do you know who you sound like right now?"

The older shifter chuckled. "In this regard, at least, I wouldn't count it as a bad thing. Anyone who runs a large organization with so many moving parts knows the importance of making sure each and every individual within that organization is satisfied with their station and the part they play."

"That's the problem," the boy retorted. "I'm not satisfied."

"I can see that." Kaiser clasped his hands behind his back and raised his eyebrows as he waited for him to continue. Fortunately, Carp decided not to push the issue. "Is that your decision, then? To leave, call off our arrangement, and search for what you want somewhere else? Without my help?"

"No." The young shifter swallowed and shook his head as he lowered his gaze to the floor. "That's not what I want."

"Good." He turned swiftly, marched to his desk, and stopped behind it to rest his fingertips on the smooth, polished surface. "The only thing I'll ask you for now is your patience. I know you feel like you missed an opportunity last night—"

"I did. The others are still out there."

"May I finish?"

Carp lowered his head.

"It all feels so very close—right there at your fingertips." Kaiser lifted one upturned hand and clenched it into a fist. "But you know what happens if you grasp something too tightly before it's time, don't you? It ends up slipping through your fingers."

"I won't let that happen."

"I know you won't. Because you'll stand down and carry on like nothing's changed until it's time to finally seize what you want. And I'll help you get there, son. Believe me. For now, you should focus on your other responsibilities."

The young shifter scoffed. "I don't need to focus on anything else."

"You have a duty, plain and simple. And if you can't fulfill any of your other roles, I'll make the decision for you. You'll be on your own without my resources or my help. Got it?"

Carp glared at him like he'd been unforgivably insulted. "Yeah. I get it."

"Great. Don't bring this up again until we've both put our other pressing responsibilities behind us. I'll tell you when it's time." Kaiser sat in his chair, slipped his reading glasses on again calmly, and returned his attention to the work on his computer.

"I'm going home," the kid muttered.

"As you should."

"And I don't know when I'll be back."

The older shifter looked over the rims of his glasses. "That's fine. I don't expect you to need a babysitter. When you're finished with your personal business, you know where to find me."

Carp glared across the room for a moment longer, then spun and stormed toward the office door to fling it open. It cracked against the wall and he barreled into the hall before he grunted in surprise and muttered, "Jesus. Do you have to lurk like that all the time?"

Whoever he spoke to didn't give any reply, but Kaiser smirked as the younger man under his care—at least when he was on The Resort—marched down the hall toward the staircase at the end.

His office and the hallway beyond fell silent again, but it seemed this wasn't the time for him to return to the forms and paperwork he'd intended to finish since he'd first sat at his desk two hours earlier. The light, brief knock on his open office door made him look up.

"Agnes." His lips quirked in mock sternness. "Have you been lurking?"

"It's not my fault if these young pups of yours can't pay attention long enough to notice who's standing around the corner."

He chuckled. "They're more than pups."

"Where it counts. Mostly." The crimson-haired witch inclined her head and stared with a blank expression at the head of the organization. "Do you have a minute?"

"For you?" He removed his reading glasses again, sighed, and kicked his chair away from his desk to get a better view of her without the computer monitor getting in his way. "I have all the time in the world for you."

Agnes stepped quickly into the office, turned and shut the door behind her, then walked purposefully to the center of the room and stopped. Her black trench coat flapped around her ankles as she moved and her black combat boots clicked when she brought them together at attention.

Kaiser smirked and settled both arms on the armrests of his executive desk chair as he leaned back. "What's on your mind?"

"The transformed from last night—at the bar."

"Don't tell me you're already having trouble with the drunk."

"No. And he's sober now. He probably has a hell of a hangover but that's not my problem."

"Is he cooperating?"

"Not yet but I'll get him to talk." She slipped her hands into her jacket pockets and shrugged. "But I'm talking about the other ones. The transformed shifters I found."

"The ones you never got to talk to because Carp had a moment of all-consuming vengeance."

She stared at him in silence, then raised an eyebrow. "Yeah. The bikers were there. And the dwarf."

"Oh? Veron told me you never had a chance to approach them."

Agnes shook her head. "I mean the other one. The new investor. Him and his Light Elf partner."

"Johnny Walker?"

She nodded.

"Well, he's sticking around at least until Friday. As far as I know, his plans haven't changed. And they weren't the only ones in that bar."

"Do you honestly think it was a coincidence?"

Kaiser raised his eyebrows and shrugged. "Yuba City isn't exactly LA."

"But seeing him at that same bar with the sob story we bagged last night and the transformed we were supposed to meet? One of them also being a dwarf and a biker?"

"Not all dwarves work together for a common goal," he replied with a crooked smile and gestured around his office with a sweeping hand. "Not all shifters either. Or all magicals, for that matter, if we look at the whole picture."

"Sure. It could be a coincidence. But seriously, Kaiser, what are the chances?"

"Of the two of us, you're the one who knows the numbers. You tell me."

Agnes glanced briefly at the back of the computer monitor on his desk and frowned in thought. "Low. Way too low given everything else that's going on."

"Okay. So to you, this means…"

"Nothing. But it could mean much more if he brings it up on Friday. Walker saw me."

He widened his eyes. "Are you sure?"

The witch nodded. "He knows we have that transformed shifter in our hands now."

"No, he knows you and Veron have the hostage—captive, prisoner, whatever we're calling him. Did Veron see him?"

"No. Only me. I haven't even brought it up until now."

With a heavy sigh, Kaiser looked at the kitchenette at the far side of his office and nodded. "I know I don't have to tell you how competent you are, Agnes. I appreciate the update."

"Do you want me to find him?"

"Walker? No. If that dwarf has anything to do with the bikers or our newest guest, I assume he'll bring it up on Friday and we'll get to the bottom of it then. Keep doing what you're doing for now."

After a brisk nod, she whirled on her heels, took long strides across the office, and paused long enough in the hall to pull the door closed gently behind her. Her exit was much more silent than Carp's had been.

For throwing her chips in with a pack of shifters, you'd think a witch would be the loudest one among us. She's certainly not the most naïve, either.

He lowered his head to pinch the bridge of his nose.

It could have been a coincidence, of course. For all intents and purposes, Johnny Walker and Lisa Breyer could merely have happened to choose that particular bar in a comical twist of fate. They weren't hunting transformed shifters, after all.

But if the bounty hunter had seen Kaiser's greatest asset spiriting away a transformed who'd refused the offer to join him and had somehow avoided meeting his end because of it... Well, that would put a whole new spin on things.

Agnes didn't lie and she didn't jump to conclusions.

Johnny Walker will tell me everything I need to know on Friday, whether he realizes it or not.

"Dude, this is awful," Bronson muttered in the passenger seat of Corey's car.

He laughed and did an exaggerated double-take before he adjusted his grip on the steering wheel. "Are you kidding? It's Crimson Spray."

"And they suck."

"Whoa, whoa, whoa." Jeff leaned forward in the back and grasped the side of Bronson's seat to pull himself closer to the front. "Are you saying you can't get behind the epic classic that is Crimson Spray?"

"It's not even music. Honestly, it's noise."

"Well, if you were driving, I'd let you choose whatever music you want." Corey pointed at his friend. "But you're not so it's Crimson Spray or nothing—"

Bronson lurched forward to punch the radio's power button, then slumped in his seat. "Then nothing."

The car fell silent.

In the back seat, Jeff and Adam exchanged a nervous glance.

Corey cleared his throat. "Okay, then. So how about—"

"Just drive, man, okay?" Bronson shook his head and stared

directly ahead at the road in front of them that wound out of the mountains. "Silently."

"Come on, Bronson," Adam muttered. "The whole point of a vacation was to make you feel better before you go back to the daily grind. That's what this was supposed to be, man. To get your head out of the funk-space it's been in."

"Yeah, well, it didn't help."

"Dude, everything's gonna work itself out," Jeff added. "You'll see. You gotta give it time—"

Bronson lurched in his seat to glare at his friends in the back. "That's what I've been doing. Do you think there's some kind of magic timer when someone's supposed to move on with their life and forget about the shit they can't get out of their head?"

"That's not what I meant, man."

"Then say what you mean." Gritting his teeth, he faced forward again and thumped his elbow on the armrest of the passenger door. "I shouldn't have to deal with this shit from you guys too."

"No one's trying to make you do anything." Corey pulled the driver's sun visor down and raised his chin to make the shadow fall over his eyes. "Except for maybe lighten up."

"Oh, yeah? Can you tell me when I'll be able to let this go?"

"You gotta get rid of the anger first, man."

"Get rid of the anger?"

"Yeah," Jeff added. "You know, like, release it. Forgive the douchebags you don't wanna forgive."

Adam snorted. "It sounds like a load of touchy-feely crap when he says it like that but it works, Bronson. You remember the shit I had going on with my dad a couple of years ago. It took a while but I forgave him for what he tried to pull after Stanford. It blew my mind how easy it was to get over the bastard's issues after that."

Jeff barked a bitter laugh. "You don't even talk to your old man anymore."

"So? Just because you forgive someone doesn't mean you have to be their best friend." Adam folded his arms. "Or suffocate yourself trying to be the trophy son they always wanted. For real, Bronson. You should give it a try."

"I'm good."

Corey shrugged. "Usually, he's full of shit, man, but in this one case, I kinda agree with him. Maybe if you—"

"Yeah, maybe if I had Adam's dad, my life would be a hell of a lot easier," Bronson snapped.

"Dude," Adam said and shook his head, "there isn't any comparison here—"

"Yeah, no shit. It's easy for you to toss forgiveness around like it's your new fucking religion, but your dad didn't murder your girlfriend and dump her body in the bay."

The car fell into a tense silence again.

Adam leaned back in his seat and stared out the window.

Jeff studied him for a moment, then turned his gaze to the back of Bronson's head. "No one's saying it's okay, man—what they did. No one's saying you have to get over it. We're only trying to help."

"You wanna help?" Bronson's voice cracked and he swallowed thickly before he turned away and gazed out his window to hide his face from everyone. "Tell me how to stop dreaming about her every night. That's a good start."

"Damn, dude," Jeff whispered. "Hey, have you thought about seeing someone to help with that?"

"Yeah, I'm seeing someone." Bronson sniffed and forced himself under control. "And he's helping me decide exactly how to make it right."

After the next ten minutes passed in complete silence, Corey pointed at the radio but couldn't bring himself to look at his friend. "You can put whatever you want on. Music, I mean."

Bronson lunged forward again, punched the radio's power button, and sank back against his chair without a word.

He wasn't listening to the music anyway.

I can't even get away for a week without this whole thing following me around like a damn curse. And now I gotta go home and be the Bronson Harford everyone thinks I am. After the gala, I'm out. Then I can focus on what needs to get done, even if I have to do it myself.

CHAPTER SIX

The next morning, Johnny woke with a crick in his neck and a mood that couldn't even be described as bad. He was livid.

"Dammit, I paid damn near six hundred dollars for these rooms. They can't even put a coffeemaker in here that does anythin' but drip sludge into a flimsy cup." He pounded on the top of the tiny single-cup coffeemaker, which sputtered and emitted a burst of steam beneath his hand.

Lisa frowned wearily as she crawled out from beneath the covers. "I'm very sure most people who come to stay in a place like this aren't all that concerned about the quality of the coffee."

"What's that supposed to mean?" He tapped the appliance again and studied it from all angles before he shoved it across the narrow ledge beside the bathroom that served as a counter. Hot water sloshed everywhere but he didn't bother to clean it.

"Take a look around, Johnny." She gestured at their surroundings. "The worst hotel we've ever stayed in is guaranteed to look even worse during the day."

Luther's yawn finished with a sleepy canine squeak. "Could've been worse."

"Oh, yeah?" Johnny grunted. "How's that, huh?"

"You could've had mice crawling across your bed all night."

"Oh, jeez." Lisa leapt out of the bed and stumbled sideways before she stopped and stared at the rumpled sheets with a grimace of disgust. "Please tell me that was a worst-case speculation."

"Nope. Only the truth."

Rex stretched his front legs and hind legs out as far as they would go and chuffed. "Except for the fact that you slept on the floor."

"Yeah. It was my bed. And you missed out on all the midnight snacks, bro. So there."

"Oh, come on." Lisa rolled her eyes and ran a hand through her hair. "Luther, do you seriously have no idea how the way you say something affects what everyone else thinks you mean?"

"Huh?"

"Never mind."

The hound licked his muzzle and rose slowly to all fours. "Hey, Johnny. I know you said we could go in the shower and everything, but I checked it out earlier. A hound can't do his business with all that staring back at him."

"Ew." Lisa scrunched her face and headed toward her jacket and purse that rested on the armchair.

"I don't even wanna know." Johnny snapped his fingers and moved toward the motel room door. "Keep that one to yourself. There's enough space for y'all outside."

"What about the grass, though?" Rex leapt off the bed and trotted after the bounty hunter with Luther beside him.

"I wouldn't count on it, boys. I doubt this place has seen better days since it was first built. Or worse days, either."

"As long as the parking lot doesn't smell like that shower." Luther sneezed, snorted, and shook his head. "Whew."

"I'll be out in a minute," Lisa called after them.

"Yep." Johnny led the hounds down the exterior walkway along the row of second-story rooms and down the outdoor staircase to the ground level. The door to their connecting motel room opened and closed again and Charlie's hurried footsteps raced after him.

"Johnny. Hey. Where are you going?"

"I'm lettin' the hounds out." He looked over his shoulder to catch a glimpse of his wide-eyed, grinning, fully alert, and awake cousin. "And if you can't turn off all the chipper, you can go back upstairs."

"Chipper?" Charlie snorted and hurried after him and the hounds toward the back of the motel. "It's only regular old Charlie, although I realize you probably don't want even that around you."

"Nope." They stepped through the alley exit and into the back lot of the motel, which was littered with soda cans, damaged trash bags, and piles of chipped asphalt that had somehow been dug out although the reason why wasn't clear. Now, the holes left were overgrown with green-brown weeds.

The bounty hunter folded his arms and squared his stance while the hounds sniffed in an attempt to find the best place for their morning business. "Whatever it is, it can wait."

"Hey, I'm only trying to make conversation here."

"Uh-huh."

Charlie stopped beside his cousin, drew a deep breath of the crisp morning air, and sighed happily. "So what's the plan?"

"You mean besides comin' out here alone for a little early morning peace and quiet?"

"Funny. No, I mean about Hux. You know, the shifter who was kidnapped last night by the same guys who have been picking us off in groups over the last three months. We'll go out to look for him today, right?"

"Nope." Johnny shook his head without looking at his companion.

Charlie's crooked smile disappeared. "Seriously, though. What's your first lead?"

"I ain't got a lead, Charlie." He wrinkled his nose and stared blankly across the horribly neglected space. Even the hounds no longer held his attention.

I'm tryin' to not lose it with Mr. Chatty here. I oughtta hang a sign on my face.

He shook his head, sure that something as simple as *don't even try it until I've had my coffee* would make no difference.

"Wait, but you saw who took the guy, right?" The shifter dwarf stepped forward and turned to look his cousin in the eye. Johnny glared at him. "You heard the other guys last night. Hux is gonna end up in a body bag if we don't find him soon—or whatever we can find of his body."

"Does Kaiser usually chop up the transformed who flip him and his offer the bird?"

"No. They are gunned down and left in the street for anyone to find. That's all." Charlie scoffed. "And you don't even look like you care."

"Just 'cause I ain't pullin' my hair out doesn't mean I don't care." He grunted disapproval and studied the junk pile at the far end of the lot. "Kaiser ain't gonna kill him."

"Oh, yeah? Did you have a private talk with the guy after midnight?"

"Hux is fine for now. It might be Kaiser had a different plan for these transformed who got away, but that was before last night."

The biker dwarf kicked a crushed soda can and it skittered across the asphalt. "Sure. I get it. 'Cause you two came to an understanding when you went out to his property and met face to face and you can read his mind now. Is that it?"

"Don't get smart with me."

"Hey, try this out." Charlie pointed at the back of the motel. "How about you get your head out of your ass and go help the guys who are locked in that second crappy motel room thinking their friend's already cut into a million pieces and that they're next. And…you know…let me come with you."

Johnny closed his eyes and drew a deep breath through his nose. "You ain't listenin'. Kaiser ain't gonna touch a hair on that shifter's head 'cause by now, he knows I know who took Hux. And if he doesn't, his problems are a helluva lot bigger than I thought."

"What?" Charlie sniffed the air and flared his nostrils as Luther bounded over the top of the junk heap. Broken plastic, stripped tire rubber, and loose paper trash scattered around him before he reached the asphalt. "How does he know?"

"Witchy redhead caught a good look at me before they high-tailed it outta there. They ain't gotten this far with what they're doin' by lettin' a group of idiots tag along on their little missions. I'm sure the witch who tracks transformed shifters has at least enough smarts to tell her boss what she saw."

"You mean you."

"I mean me."

"Shit." Charlie shook his head. "That's not good news."

"It ain't bad."

"Well then, what are we gonna do about it? 'Cause it sounds bad to me."

Johnny finally turned to look at his cousin. "We ain't gonna do a thing. Lisa and I have some business to handle with the guy tomorrow, and I aim to put everythin' together today before we head out."

"Business." The biker shifter frowned and extended his hand absently when Rex trotted toward him. The hound shoved his head under the mohawked dwarf's hand and panted happily.

"Oh, yeah. Yeah, right there. That's—"

His master snapped his fingers and while the hound didn't pull away from the scratch-fest, he at least stopped talking. "Business you ain't a part of." He pointed at his cousin. "You have a job to do here anyhow."

Luther raced across the lot and his ears flapped and tongue protruded from the side of his mouth as he passed his master and scrambled down the narrow alley between the motel's front office and the rows of vacant rooms. "Time to go for a ride. Yes! We're getting outta here."

Rex nudged Charlie's hand but the dwarf no longer paid him any attention. "Fine. Be that way."

The hound trotted after his brother and caught up to Johnny, who was already stepping beneath the shade of the overhanging walkway.

"Johnny." Charlie scanned the back wall of the motel, then hissed his frustration and jogged after his cousin. "Hey! Hold on a minute. I'm not staying here."

"Damn straight you are."

"No. No, no. You told me to keep an eye on Galfrey and Jake. I did that. Now, I'm coming with you."

"Dammit, Charlie. Keep an eye on 'em don't mean lie on a cot for one night and call it good 'cause they didn't happen to drop dead in their sleep."

"But I'm… I mean…" The mohawked dwarf gazed longingly at his orange Harley that glinted under the morning sunlight. "Come on, 'coz. I'm not built to stay in one place."

He snorted. "Tell that to the dwarves still livin' underground instead of in the cities."

"You know what I mean. What am I supposed to do here all day, huh?"

The bounty hunter pointed at the door to the shifters' room. "Keep an eye on 'em. Do you think you can do that? 'Cause it sure as hell seems to me like the easiest thing in the world, even for you."

"Aw, come on. Can't I at least—"

"No." He opened the back door of the SUV for the hounds, who leapt dutifully onto the seat and seemed to have decided that the argument between the Walker cousins didn't warrant adding their two cents.

"Johnny—"

He shut the door and pointed at Charlie again. "Here's how it's gonna be. You stay here with those two shifters until I say so. And if I get one whiff of you sneakin' around while I'm gone, thinkin' I'll never know the difference, you're out. No more poppin' by, no more talks, and no more info about what Lisa and I find out while we're doing our jobs. Understand?"

Lisa stepped outside and leaned over the balcony. "Are we leaving now?"

Johnny nodded at her, folded his arms, and glared at his cousin. "Sorry. I didn't hear your answer. Do you get what I'm sayin'?"

The shifter dwarf scrunched his face up and scratched the shaved side of his head. "This is bullshit."

"Well, maybe next time, you'll think a little harder about breakin' into my house askin' for help and not takin' no for answer when I say we ain't got room for extra hands on a case."

Lisa reached the bottom of the stairs and moved toward them but her smile faded when she picked up the tension between the dwarves. "Is everything okay?"

"You bet, darlin'." Johnny nodded at the other dwarf. "Charlie's gonna stay here and keep an eye on things for us. You and me are gonna go pull us out a rainy-day fund."

Charlie looked quickly from one to the other. "For what?"

"A deposit on Kaiser's merchandise." The bounty hunter stormed around the hood of the rental and slid behind the wheel without another word.

"Wait, what?" The other dwarf's disappointment morphed instantly into wide-eyed excitement, and his grin returned with full force. "Johnny. Are you serious? You're gonna buy from Kaiser?"

The only response he received was the SUVs engine turning over before it revved as if in a warning.

Lisa stopped beside the passenger door and cocked her head. "Charlie."

"Yeah?" A childlike laugh of excitement escaped him.

"The next time you give us a wrinkled map and terrible directions, make sure it includes the kind of business we're stepping into."

"Ha!" He clapped a hand to his head. "You didn't know?"

"The guy uses a fake name on a property that doesn't even exist on a current map." She raised her eyebrows. "How were we supposed to know Kaiser runs a marijuana farm in the middle of nowhere?"

"Well, it…I don't know. That's basically all anyone does out here."

She shook her head, opened the door, and slid in. As soon as she closed it again, Charlie's palms smacked against the passenger window and he fixed them both with another crazed grin.

"Hey." Johnny pointed at him. "Hands off the car."

"One thing. One more thing, guys." He gestured for the window to be rolled down, and Lisa obliged him with an exasperated sigh.

"What?"

"What are you gonna do with all that weed, huh?" He bounced on his toes and grinned like a lunatic. "You're not gonna…you know, keep it all for yourselves, right?"

"It's none of your business." Johnny pressed the button to roll the window up again.

"Wait, wait, wait! Hold on." Charlie stretched his neck higher in an attempt to keep his mouth level with the elevating glass. "I can help you with that. Let me know, okay, and I'll—"

"You're stayin' out of it." Once the window was completely closed, the bounty hunter jerked the gear shift into reverse and lurched away from the sidewalk. When he turned the SUV fully and faced the road again, he caught a glimpse of his cousin through the rearview mirror.

Charlie stood where they had left him with one hand on his hip while the other rubbed the shaved side of his head. The idiotic grin remained plastered on his face as he bounced with excitement.

"I shouldn't have told him about the deal."

Lisa turned to look at the mohawked dwarf again before Johnny pulled them onto the main road. "It doesn't matter, though, because we're not buying anything from Kaiser."

"Nothin' but information and a foot in the door, darlin'. But my idiot of a cousin ain't gonna take no for an answer. He never does."

CHAPTER SEVEN

Two hours later, Johnny stormed out of the fourth bank they'd visited with his fiercest scowl of the day firmly in place.

"Uh-oh." Luther shrank into himself in the back seat. "He doesn't look happier this time."

"No, he looks madder," Rex muttered.

The bounty hunter threw the driver's door open and slumped behind the wheel.

Lisa pressed her lips together and studied him warily. "I take it you didn't find what you were looking for at this one either."

He grunted. "There's somethin' wrong with the banks here if they ain't even got enough money inside 'em when a fella wants a withdrawal."

"Well, you are trying to draw almost sixty-five thousand dollars, Johnny. In a state you don't live in, I might add."

"It's my money, darlin'. I should be able to get however much of it I want wherever I want at any time I feel like it."

She chuckled. "Did this teller ask you what the withdrawal was for too?"

"Exactly like everyone else."

"Did you give them an answer this time?"

He shifted in his seat to face her. "Why the hell should that matter, huh?"

"Oh, I don't know. It might have something to do with the IRS and the FDIC. Not to mention that this part of California is a hotbed for exactly what we're not buying from Kaiser with over sixty thousand dollars."

Johnny sniffed and backed out of the bank parking lot. "Everyone is tryin' to sniff around in business that ain't their own. How the hell am I supposed to get the guy his money if I can't even get mine?"

"Well, do you want to try it your way again with another bank or would you like to listen to my suggestion now?"

He shook his head as he turned down the side street and headed across town again. "Do you have someone around here who owes you what we need in cash?"

"No, Johnny. But a cashier's check wouldn't raise nearly as much suspicion."

"Oh, sure. I'll have 'em make it out to Kaiser Bossman. That'll do fine."

Lisa glanced at him in exasperation and sighed. "Make it out to me. Then we'll go somewhere else and I'll cash it."

"You'll what?"

"I'll cash it and we'll say it's for our business. I have an excellent track record with my bank."

"And you think I don't?"

She chuckled. "Maybe not after you went into four different branches asking to withdraw an amount like that without giving any answers."

"Fine." They lurched through the traffic light and Johnny jerked the SUV sharply to the right to pull into the parking lot of a coffee shop with an illegible marquee sign hanging crookedly off the awning. "After we get more coffee."

"That giant cup first thing wasn't enough?"

"I'm loadin' up, darlin'. I paid for a week at that piss-poor excuse for a motel and if I ain't gettin' my joe in the room, I gotta get it somewhere else."

"Hey, Johnny." Rex scooted forward on the back seat, leaned closer, and licked his muzzle. "How about a snack, huh?"

"Yeah, they don't have those in the motel either," Luther added.

Their master glanced at them in the rearview mirror. "Catchin' mice ain't enough to keep you full?"

"Hey, that was all Luther."

"Yeah, and they weren't very big." Luther belched. "But I think they gave me heartburn."

Lisa waved a hand in front of her face before she opened the door to get out. "I'll go put an order in. Then we'll get the money for the most ridiculous transaction of my life."

Johnny snorted. "How do all these folks out here manage their business when the banks won't give 'em their damn money?"

"Probably by not putting their money in the bank in the first place." She closed the door and hurried into the shop to purchase two large coffees and snacks for two private investigators and their hungry coonhounds.

And now we're joining the ranks of under-the-table drug dealers. This is ridiculous.

After a stop to buy a plain duffel bag from the Yuba City Goodwill, her plan to cash Johnny's cashier's check made out in her name worked perfectly—excluding the strange looks the bank teller had given a sweetly smiling Lisa Breyer.

With the bag stuffed full of cash and hidden on the floor of the SUV, the duo stopped at the Raley's grocery store to stock up on as many non-perishable food items as they could find to feed Charlie and their new shifter friends who would remain under Johnny Walker protection for the next few days.

They returned to the motel and the bounty hunter almost exploded in fury when he didn't immediately see the orange Harley in the parking lot. The hounds sniffed it out right away though. A new guest of the motel had parked their truck with an attached trailer directly behind the motorcycle.

Johnny muttered an obscenity and scowled at the Harley while Lisa lugged their groceries and the duffel bag full of cash up the stairs. "Who parks like this, huh? Pinnin' a guy in like that?"

"It's a motorcycle, Johnny. He can get out if he needs to."

"Well, I suppose he ain't goin' anywhere." After looking over his shoulder quickly to see her at the top of the stairs, he squatted beside his cousin's bike and checked under the engine to make sure the tracking device was still exactly where he'd left it. It was and he felt some of his tension dissipate.

With a grunt, he stood again and turned to where both hounds sat behind him, stared at their master with wide eyes, and panted heavily. "What are y'all doin'?"

"Watching you, Johnny."

"Yeah. What are you doing to his thing on wheels?"

"Not a damn thing." He wagged his finger from one to the other. "And y'all ain't gonna say another word about it, understand?"

"Oh, right." Luther sniggered. "'Cause he can totally hear us."

"Super-weird, Johnny." The hounds trotted after their master as the bounty hunter turned and strode toward the stairs. "Two dwarves who can hear us at the same time."

"Yeah, I never thought that would happen."

Rex stopped to sniff an old stain on the sidewalk and snorted. "Hey, Johnny. Did you have no idea your cousin had some shifter all mixed up inside him?"

"We're droppin' the topic." He pulled the room key from his pocket and slipped into the room.

Lisa had already opened the adjoining door between rooms and was halfway finished setting up the closest thing they'd have to a buffet table.

Jake stared at the spread of crackers and Cheese Whiz, beef

jerky, apples, bananas, bottled water, and cans of baked beans. His frown deepened when he picked up one of the cans. "Do people still eat baked beans out of a can?"

"They do when they're not allowed to leave the motel room," she muttered as she emptied the last bag of its paper bowls and plastic utensils. "There are no mini-fridges here, but at least your room has a microwave."

"And a coffeemaker," Charlie added as he rubbed his hands together vigorously and focused on the makeshift feast.

Johnny glared at him. "Does it work?"

His cousin shrugged. "It heats the water. That's about it."

"Well, it's a good thing I thought ahead." The last items Lisa pulled from the final bag drew everyone else's attention as she slammed them onto the small table in the shifters' room.

"Oh…" Charlie wrinkled his nose. "You expect us to drink instant coffee?"

"With powdered creamer and sugar if you want it." She snatched an apple, took a bite out of it, and turned to enter her room, where she could enjoy her fruit in relative solitude.

"What, uh…" Galfrey ran his fingers through his hair and stared at the food on the table. "What happened to the steaks and mashed potatoes?"

"Yeah, and green beans," Jake added as he set the can down. "Not baked beans."

"I ain't said a thing about all that."

"Well, not to us. But Charlie said you'd bring real food."

"That is real food." Johnny squinted at his cousin, who spread his arms with a sheepish smile.

"I might have said a thing or two about dinner."

"Uh-huh. So you decided you'd make these fellas a promise that wasn't yours to make in the first place. Or keep, for that matter."

"Hey, I merely recalled what I know about you and what you like to eat. I didn't think you'd stock up on camping food."

"Well, we're campin' here." The bounty hunter pointed at the food. "So y'all have to make do with what you have now."

"Yeah." Galfrey selected a bag of beef jerky and ripped it open. "Thanks for bringing us something."

"Hold on a sec." The shifter dwarf shrugged. "These guys had their hearts set on a decent meal, 'coz. If you don't feel like going out to get it for them, I'm happy to go and pick something up—"

"Nice try but it ain't happenin'. You're stayin' right here with the rest of us." Johnny studied the can of Cheese Whiz and grimaced. "Make yourself a cracker sandwich or somethin'."

"Johnny, I can at least go pick up something to go."

The bounty hunter set the can down again and folded his arms. "A steak dinner for everyone on your dime?"

"Well, no. But…" His cousin leaned sideways to peer past him and into the adjoining room. "You have enough for dinner in that bag, right?"

As she took another bite of her apple, Lisa hooked her heel around the side of the duffel bag and slid it across the floor until it was under the bed.

"You ain't heard a thing we said about what's goin' down tomorrow." Johnny shook his head. "The answer's no."

"Wait, what's happening tomorrow?" Jake asked as he opened the lid of the Cheese Whiz and dolloped a huge glob onto a cracker.

"Serious, Charlie? You told these fellas they'd be gettin' a fancy supper tonight but you forgot to tell 'em about the one thing that is relevant?"

"Yeah, I forgot."

Johnny rolled his eyes and picked two bottles of water up. "We're payin' Kaiser another visit."

His cousin grinned. "And they're buying weed."

Galfrey choked on his beef jerky and the strip he'd meant to put back in the bag fell onto the floor instead to be quickly gobbled by Rex.

"Yes! Hey, guy. Feel free to drop more anytime you want."

Luther sniffed the stained carpet. "Hey, no fair. I've been standing here the whole time."

"You gotta be quick, bro."

"Hold on." Ignoring the hounds, the shifter cleared his throat. "You're going to see Kaiser tomorrow? To buy—"

"What does that have to do with anything?" Jake asked. "You guys said you'd find Hux. That's the whole point of this. You can't storm in there and make a drug deal with the guy. Are you crazy?"

"We ain't." Johnny shrugged. "Lisa and I made this appointment with him before we knew the three of y'all were in town. But it's a way for us to get in there and investigate. If they have your friend somewhere on the property, we'll find him."

"And blow this whole thing wide open." Galfrey shook his head. "That's your plan? Kaiser won't think twice before he puts a bullet through both of you."

"He won't." He stepped through the door into the room he shared with Lisa. "As far as he's concerned, we're a couple of PIs tryin' to expand our business operations and we ain't bringin' any transformed with us. So if he thinks we're onto him and he tries somethin', he'll be riskin' a huge chunk of change and blowin' his cover."

"How's that, exactly?" Jake looked like he might be sick.

"The guy ain't mixin' his campaign against the transformed with his other business on that farm." He shrugged. "He has a couple of dozen young shifters there who think all they're doin' is growin' the plants and getting' ready for harvest. My guess is that most of 'em ain't heard a thing about these other faction skirmishes, and I bet that's how Kaiser wants to keep it."

"But what if he—"

"Y'all worry about eatin' and stayin' in this motel. Let us worry about the rest." Johnny snapped his fingers and both hounds scurried out from under the small table to race into the adjoining room. He shut the door and locked it with a harsh click.

Lisa's apple core pinged into the trashcan. "How long do you think they'll stay here quietly before they decide our way of doing things isn't the way they want to go about this?"

He tossed her a bottle of water and sat on the other bed with a sigh. "I assume they'll play along until we come back from this meetin' tomorrow. Dependin' on what we find, it could go either way."

"And what if we do find Hux there?"

"Then we get him out and bring him back to his buddies."

She opened the water bottle and took a large sip before she added, "That still doesn't resolve the Tyro problem."

"Nope. But snatchin' a prisoner out from under him is gonna put a serious dent in whatever else he's up to. And if we wound the head of this whole messed-up crusade, I imagine the pain's gonna trickle down the line to Tyro anyhow."

"So you think they're working together."

"Darlin', anyone targetin' the same group of magicals and killin' 'em for no reason is workin' together, whether they know it or not."

CHAPTER EIGHT

The next morning, Johnny, Lisa, and the hounds packed a few leftover snacks and the duffel bag of cash into the rental with them to return to Kaiser's property for the meeting. Charlie, Galfrey, and Jake had very clear instructions to not leave the motel for anything.

"But if you get a call," the bounty hunter added, "make sure you answer the damn phone this time."

"What, so I can cruise onto the base of the guy who tried to have me killed two nights ago to rescue you from the worst idea you've ever had?" Charlie quipped.

With a grunt, Johnny closed his door and accelerated out of the parking lot.

The drive to Kaiser's farm went more smoothly than the first time. They managed to avoid backtracking along the main road to find the turnoff—still marked by the giant boulder—as well as any head-on collisions with trees.

Kaiser was expecting them, which also simplified things.

When they exited the car and walked across the valley toward the front of the main house, a group of young shifters came to greet them exactly like they had on their first visit. They didn't question them this time and instead, the guy leading the group smirked at the duffel bag slung over Johnny's shoulder and nodded.

"You're right on time. He's waiting for you."

"Uh-huh."

"Up in his office. Do you need someone to show you up again?"

"What's your name again?"

The young shifter folded his arms. "Bull."

"Yeah, that's right. Y'all have all kindsa crazy names out here, don'tcha?"

The others behind Bull sniggered but didn't join the conversation.

"I tell you what, Bull." Johnny pointed at the main house. "If your boss is comfortable lettin' us walk through on our own, we'll do fine without an escort."

"Suit yourself." The young shifter turned and stepped aside to let them pass. The others didn't move at all but watched them stroll across the dry grass.

"Y'all don't mind a couple of hounds runnin' around either, do ya? They've been cooped up in a bad motel room for a while."

"As long as they stay out of the warehouses."

"Wait, Johnny," Luther called as he trotted after his master. "Aren't we supposed to stay with you? You said we needed to—"

"Go on, now," he said without turning, snapped his fingers, and pointed in the general direction of the gigantic open space in the bottom of the valley. "Y'all run it out. Git."

"But Johnny—"

Rex snarled and leapt at his brother.

Luther yelped when he found himself pinned to the grass. "Hey! What gives, bro?"

"Quit talking, dummy." Rex snapped at his face in warning. "Let's go run around while Johnny does his thing with the guy."

"Oh. Oh, right." The smaller hound scrambled to his feet again and uttered a sharp bark before he raced across the field. "I bet I can catch a bird before you even see one!"

With a snort, the other coonhound turned and looked at his master.

The bounty hunter nodded in Luther's direction and Rex raced away to coral his brother into not doing or saying anything stupid that would give them away.

Those hounds had better keep their mouths shut out here. The last thing we need is a whole pack of shifters hearin' every little detail of what they're lookin' for while we're handin' cash to the boss.

Some of the shifters who'd come to greet them chuckled as they followed the hounds around the side of the main house. Fortunately, none of them seemed to have noticed that Luther had almost blown their already thin cover.

When the two investigators stopped at the front door, Lisa looked over her shoulder to where Bull stood exactly where they'd left him, his arms folded and an amused smirk playing on his lips.

"How likely do you think it is that everyone here knows why we came back?" she muttered.

Johnny opened the door and gestured for her to step inside first. "It's a pot farm, darlin'. I suppose anyone who spends time here on the regular knows exactly why folks visit."

His partner looked at him with a raised eyebrow before she entered the sparsely furnished house.

She ain't talkin' about the money changin' hands and we ain't got a chance in hell of havin' a private conversation with shifters listenin' to every damn word.

He followed her inside, closed the door, and cleared his throat. "But I'm willin' to bet the chat we have with Kaiser stays between the three of us."

She nodded. "Sure. You're probably right."

Johnny knew she'd picked up on the aggravatingly subtle hint —that Kaiser's young shifters barely out of adolescence most likely believed their surface reason for being there, as evidenced by the duffel bag full of cash. But if anyone had suspected that they had come to either scan the property for the kidnapped Hux or to question Kaiser about his involvement in said kidnapping, they probably wouldn't have been given free rein to show themselves to the boss' office.

It's wishful thinkin', sure. The guy headin' this operation is as wily as they come. I assume we'll find out exactly how much he knows while we're pretendin' to talk about everythin' else under the sun.

They found the back staircase at the side of the building easily enough. The cables and electrical wiring tacked to the wall of the stairwell looked exactly as Johnny remembered them, although the low electric hum of who knew how many generators was louder in the stairwell than last time.

They either amped the power up to this place for those warehouses or they're plannin' somethin' else that needs extra juice. Like a holdin' cell for a transformed shifter they ain't decided what to do with yet.

No one else passed them on the first floor, in the stairwell, or on the top floor where Kaiser's office was located. The main house was considerably emptier today than it had been on their last visit, but he took it as a good sign. The boss didn't want to be disturbed while he sat down for a little chat and an under-the-table transaction with a planet-renowned bounty hunter and his ex-fed partner.

When they reached the closed office door, he knocked briskly.

"It's open."

The dwarf opened the door slowly and cleared his throat.

Kaiser sat behind his desk at the back of the room and looked up with a growing smile. "Johnny. Lisa. You made it."

"You told us to come on Friday at ten." He spread his arms expansively. "And here we are."

"Here you are." The shifter studied his guests for a moment

longer, then gestured toward the center of the office. "Please. Come on in."

They complied and Johnny paused inside the door. "Do you want this closed?"

"Go right ahead. My guys are busy out back today so we shouldn't be interrupted. But I appreciate a private conversation behind closed doors just the same."

It shut with a soft click and Kaiser stood to retrieve three folding chairs stacked against the wall before he opened them one by one and positioned them in a spacious triangle in the center of his office. "Right now, hard metal's about all we have for guests. Can I get you anything to drink? I know it's not quite noon but I never let the time of day stop me from celebrating with a cocktail or two—if that's your thing, of course."

"What kinda whiskey do you have?"

Lisa darted her partner a sidelong glance.

Their host chuckled. "Whiskey, huh? You have good taste. There's a great bottle of Glenlivet over here somewhere."

Johnny slung the duffel bag onto the floor and sat in one of the chairs. "I'm good."

"Are you sure? It's excellent."

"I have specific tastes." Johnny shrugged. "Nothin' against you."

If he got suspicious enough to vet either of us, he would have already decided I'd say no. Or he's still playin'.

The shifter smirked. "No, of course not. Trust me, I'm not offended. That merely leaves more for me. Lisa?"

"No, thank you." She took one of the evenly spaced chairs for herself and crossed one leg over the other.

"Okay, then." Kaiser selected a bottle of beer from the mini-fridge, cracked the cap with one twist of his bare hand, and tossed it in the trash before he joined them. Once he'd sat, he took a long pull from the beer before he released a satisfied sigh and smacked his lips. "There's nothing like a cold one on a hot day in the San Juan Valley. The summer sun doesn't care what time of day it is either."

"Uh-huh." Johnny folded his arms and waited for him to finish another long swallow.

"So." The shifter placed his half-empty beer on the floor beside his chair and folded his hands in his lap. "It looks like you're ready to move forward with our agreement."

"We're good to go, sure. As long as nothin' has changed."

Kaiser chuckled and regarded him speculatively. "Why would it?"

"No reason I can think of. I'm merely makin' sure we're on the same page."

"As far as I know." Kaiser held the dwarf's gaze a moment longer, then glanced at the duffel bag. "I assume that's your deposit."

"Half up front like you said. For the whole fifty that ain't been spoken for yet."

"Good."

"I have a question about that," Lisa interjected.

"Please. Feel free to ask anything." The shifter seemed unperturbed. "That's the point of these little sit-downs after all."

She cleared her throat. "Not that I expect anything to go wrong here. It certainly looks like you have your ducks in a row with most things."

"Oh?" He raised his eyebrows. "If something doesn't sit right with you, I want to hear about it."

"Uh-huh." Johnny fixed her with a dubious frown. "Me too."

"No, I only mean…" She looked quickly from one to the other. "I'm only saying that everything else seems fairly legitimate—for as much as I know about…all this. But legitimacy doesn't mean much if all the operations take place on an unregistered, off-the-radar property and DIY utilities skirt around the gas and electric companies for the county. I'm assuming, of course, that you gave us all the facts the last time we were here."

Kaiser's smile widened and he studied the half-Light Elf thoughtfully.

Johnny's mustache bristled as he wrinkled his nose.

What the hell is she tryin' to pull? This ain't the plan.

Finally, the shifter laughed and leaned back in his chair. "I guess I should have expected questions like this from someone so freshly off the FBI's payroll. Old habits, right?"

"I'm simply sharing an observation."

"Of course, and I appreciate your unique perspective. Not everyone in my line of work has the advantage of having their business practices picked apart by someone so experienced in bringing down entire operations like this one."

"We ain't trying to bring anythin' down," Johnny muttered.

"I never said you were and neither did your partner." Kaiser's smile widened. "Your assessment's completely accurate, Lisa. What we do here is completely legal and legitimate, excluding the lack of licensing and putting this place on the map. I hope that's not a deal-breaker for you."

"Not for us, no." She shrugged and glanced at the duffel bag. "We said we were ready to move forward with this, and the proof of it is right there in that bag. I'm merely wondering about assurances."

"What kind of assurances?"

"If something were to happen. For example, if anyone found out about those few tiny details that don't quite add up or your property was seized before the harvest season was over and before we had a chance to return with the second half to collect on our deposit." She folded her arms. "What happens to our money?"

He stared at her, then threw his head back with a wild laugh that startled both his guests. The shifter laughed so hard and for so long that Lisa leaned forward in her seat and prepared to help him if he didn't catch his breath soon.

Johnny simply glared at him.

Finally, after a sharp gasp and another round of gut-splitting laughter, Kaiser puffed his cheeks out and wiped the tears from his eyes. "Sorry. I'm so sorry. It's only—ha! I didn't expect you to be so shrewd about this."

"Why's that?"

"Oh, because you're so new to the game." The shifter sighed and grinned at them. "Most first-timers are more focused on getting in and out quickly before they have an opportunity to make a wrong move. They don't trust themselves enough to dive in deeply but you are not afraid to ask the questions on everyone's minds, even if they don't slow down long enough to ask them."

She gave him a tight-lipped smile in return. "I guess not. Although I hope you have an answer."

"I completely understand." Kaiser cleared his throat and shifted in his chair. "So let's put it all out there in the open, shall we?"

"That's exactly why we're here," Johnny agreed.

The man looked pointedly at him for a moment, then nodded. "Absolutely. I'll put it this way. Your down payment today covers so much more than merely holding your place in line for the finished product. Like I said the last time you were here, our partners buy into a kind of co-op if you will.

"If we move forward with this—and it looks like we will—the two of you have access to all our resources. There's no need to make an appointment or call ahead. You can come here any time you like, check on the status of things, and even join the transient workers when they arrive if that interests you. I also have certain protections in place should anything unfortunate happen as a result of those few...minor details that don't quite add up."

"Like what?" Johnny asked.

"Well, for one, you would unequivocally get your money back. So don't worry, Lisa. You won't throw your money away if we can't deliver on our part of the agreement."

"That's good to know."

Kaiser nodded. "I think I already mentioned certain networking advantages of doing business together, didn't I?"

"You did. Last time we were here."

"You mentioned someone who could help us with a client base," the bounty hunter added.

"Exactly." The shifter pointed at him and his grin widened. "And I said you'd have a chance to meet. Give me a second. Let me make a quick call."

He didn't wait for his guests' permission before he took his cell phone from his back pocket and dialed a number, but they would have given it anyway. Their host smiled distractedly at them as the line rang in his ear.

"Hey. Are you busy? Good. Why don't you come up here for a minute to meet our new partners? They might have a few questions for you too if you don't mind. Great. Yeah, we'll wait."

"That sounded easy," Johnny commented.

"It'll be only a few minutes." Kaiser slipped his phone into his pocket and crossed one ankle over the opposite knee. "You'll love this. Trust me. And feel free to ask any questions that might occur to you. We want everyone working with us to feel like they have as much access to the details as we do so everyone feels good about the decisions."

Lisa nodded. "That's the best way to do business, isn't it? Customer satisfaction."

"Oh, this goes so much deeper than a customer-seller relationship." He looked from one to the other with a growing glint of amusement and anticipation in his eyes. "You'll see."

The dwarf studied the shifter's mad-looking smile and narrowed his eyes.

That's the look of a guy who has somethin' big hidden up his sleeve. This is the part where we gotta be ready for anythin'.

CHAPTER NINE

They waited in expectant silence for almost five minutes before a swift knock came at the office door.

"It's open," Kaiser called. "Come on in."

Johnny and Lisa turned in their chairs as the door opened slowly and neither one of them could think of anything to say when the petite crimson-haired witch in her black trench coat stepped into the office.

"Agnes." Their host waved her forward. "Please. Come in and join us. Can I get you a chair?"

"I'll stand." The witch crossed the room slowly and studied Johnny the whole time before she stopped beside her boss' chair and slipped her hands into her jacket pockets.

The bounty hunter's eye twitched.

I'll be damned if this ain't his way of givin' us a warnin'. He's actin' like we ain't already seen her out there kidnappin' drunken shifters. No way she didn't tell him we were there.

"Agnes." Lisa looked at the shifter and his witch in turn, although she made a point to not look at her partner and risk giving anything away. "Kaiser mentioned you last time we were here."

"I did mention her, yes," Kaiser added. "But this isn't the first time you've seen each other, is it?"

The office fell incredibly silent.

There it is. The ace up his sleeve.

Lisa swallowed and summoned a mostly convincing smile. "No, it's not. We saw you last time we were here—right before we left. I guess we didn't have the time to stop and introduce ourselves."

Agnes shrugged, her expression completely unreadable. "I was busy."

The shifter chuckled. "You have an excellent memory, Lisa."

"It ain't all that hard to remember someone like her," Johnny said and gestured toward the woman. "Especially when she's the only witch on a pot farm run by nothin' but shifters."

"Ah. I realize that might cause a little confusion," Kaiser said. "But believe me when I tell you that Agnes is necessary to our work. She's one of the most effective safeguards we have here. Trust me, if you knew what she can do, you'd understand exactly why no one wants to get on her bad side."

"Uh-huh." As he studied the witch carefully, Johnny didn't know if he was more concerned by all the hidden messages in the shifter's seemingly pleasant conversation or the complete lack of any emotion whatsoever on her face. "It sounds like exactly the kinda magical you wanna keep around."

"Absolutely. And the kind I prefer to send out on personal errands for me from time to time. Not the meaningless stuff, of course, but the errands I don't trust anyone else to successfully carry out for me." Kaiser focused his gaze on him. "Do you have anyone like that?"

He's tryin' to get at somethin' here. If he says anything about Charlie, I'll blow this place sky high and take my money with me.

"Naw," he muttered. "We prefer doin' all our own personal business—personally."

"You know, that's exactly how I felt before Agnes and I met."

The shifter looked at his tracker witch and smiled. "She's been incredibly helpful since then. I hope the two of you find that invaluable third addition to your team."

"Uh-huh."

"So, Agnes," Lisa said and tried to sound casual as she shifted her position in her chair. "What exactly would you say your job is here?"

The witch inclined her head toward Kaiser. "He told you what I do."

"No, I know. I only mean, like, if you had to give yourself a title."

The witch stared at her for so long that she thought she wouldn't answer. Finally, she drew a sharp breath and muttered, "Security."

Their host chuckled. "There you have it. Simple and straightforward. And security has a multitude of definitions here when we're talking about Agnes. She's my eyes and ears in the outside world and she tells me *everything*."

A tense silence filled the office again as the shifter boss regarded his guests with a terrifyingly growing smile.

Well, that right there is an invitation to lay all cards on the table if I ever heard one.

"So before we make this little deal of ours official," the man continued, "I'd like to ask you now if there's anything you'd like to tell me. You know, so we're all on the same page from the get-go. I don't want anything to stand in the way or make us start this new partnership on the wrong foot."

Lisa turned slowly to look at her partner. "Johnny?"

"Yeah." He jerked his chin at the shifter. "But I think you already know what we'd have to say. And I ain't a fan of bein' played like I ain't got the brains to pick up what you're puttin' down, Kaiser."

"No, no. Johnny, if I offended you, I'm sorry."

"You ain't done nothin' to either of us. We have nothin'

against you and certainly nothin' to get in the way of what we came here to do."

The shifter looked at Agnes with the infuriatingly playful smirk still on his lips. "What's your opinion of all this?"

"Knowing what we know of them already?" The witch shrugged. "I'd say we've already reached an understanding or they would have tried something by now."

"Tried something?" Lisa laughed and managed to make it sound genuinely light but also confused. "Like what?"

"You two have a reputation for knocking doors down and making more trouble than any single case ever needs."

"Ha!" Kaiser slapped his thigh. "And you aren't on a case this time. You don't plan to make any trouble here either, do you?"

Johnny narrowed his eyes at the shifter and shrugged.

He's askin' straight up. I might as well make this is clear as I can without givin' anythin' else away.

"Our business with you is about paying for what's out there in those grow houses with what's right here in this bag." He pointed at the duffel bag but didn't look away from the shifter's antagonizing smile. "If you have a witch on a shifter crew to handle your personal errands for you, that's your business. It doesn't matter what we do or don't see on this property or anywhere else."

"That's very good to hear, Johnny."

"Yeah. You know what else would be good to hear?" The bounty hunter spread his arms in a gesture that suggested irritation. "Why you're runnin' us through the wringer like this when you clearly already made your mind up before we got here."

Kaiser's eyes widened briefly with another flash of amusement. "I wanted to hear it from you and to gauge how you'd react. Of course, I wouldn't have expected you to bring anything up on your own but I'm also pleasantly surprised to find you so open to discussion. Whatever you may or may not have seen, the only thing that matters is that you chose to not step in and do something about it."

"It ain't my place to handle someone else's personal business —unless they're payin' me my regular fee."

"Excellent. I hoped you'd say something along those lines and I don't see any reason why we can't put our differences aside, professional or otherwise, and move forward. Do you?"

"Not a one." He turned to Lisa. "You?"

She shook her head.

"Then let's do business." The shifter stood.

Johnny pushed to his feet, grasped the duffel bag with one hand, and held it out toward their host. "Feel free to count it."

"That's all right, Johnny. I trust you."

Agnes stepped forward to take it instead and fixed him with a hard, unyielding expression until he released the strap. She whirled and took the few steps needed to thunk it on the desk. They waited in silence while she scribbled a receipt and handed it to the bounty hunter.

The man extended his hand and when Johnny took it, he almost expected to be jerked off his feet and accosted now that the money had been paid. He fought the urge to tense in readiness but Kaiser merely his hand grasped even tighter than before and looked completely insane when he flashed a wide grin. "Welcome to the club."

"Uh-huh."

With a laugh, the man released him and suddenly looked much saner as he turned to Lisa to shake her hand as well. "You'll be very happy with the way this works out, despite the minor illegitimacy details."

"I guess only time will tell, right?"

"You have a good head on your shoulders, Lisa." He winked at her and turned slightly. "Agnes, give them a card."

The witch rejoined them and produced a slightly bent business card from her jacket pocket. Lisa took it and stared at the frayed edges and the smear of what could have been either coffee or old, dried blood.

"That's her direct line. If you need anything, give her a call. Ninety-nine percent of the time, she'll get it for you, no questions asked."

"What falls under the one percent?" she asked.

"Ha! If she tells you it can't be done, you'll know." The shifter clapped and rubbed his hands together. "I was looking forward to this and I'm happy to say you two did not disappoint. While I'm sorry to cut the celebration short, I have to get going. I'm heading out for a couple of days and need to prepare a few things before then. Please, make yourselves at home here. Have a look at the warehouses if you want. Feel free to introduce yourself—get to know the great young minds behind the best product you can find out here in these mountains. Probably along the entire west coast, come to think of it."

"We gotta get goin' ourselves." Johnny schooled his expression into relaxed but curious. "Does callin' Agnes for anythin' we might think of if you're outta town make a difference?"

"Most certainly not. If she has to, she'll give me a call but she's perfectly capable of handling things while I'm away. She has been for quite some time. Agnes, would you show them out?"

She glanced expressionlessly at him before she moved across the office.

"Naw, that's all right." The bounty hunter waved her off and nodded at their oddly excited host. "Given that we showed ourselves in, I think we can find the way out easily enough. We might come in a couple of weeks to see how everythin' is comin' along. How often are you up here?"

"It depends on the week, honestly. But don't feel like you can't come through when I'm not here. Stop by whenever you like. You own a good portion of what's on this property now and I want you to feel like it."

"Well, all right." With another fleeting glance at Agnes, the dwarf turned and strode to the door. "Nice doin' business with ya."

"You too, Johnny," Kaiser called over his shoulder as he returned to the desk. "I look forward to saying it again in the very near future."

Lisa pocketed the stained business card and nodded at the crimson-haired witch. "Thanks."

Agnes didn't respond. She didn't move again either until both Kaiser's guests had disappeared down the hall toward the back stairwell.

The two partners didn't say anything to one another as they hurried through the main house and out to the field between the stronghold and their rental vehicle.

The hounds bounded around the side of the house at the sound of their master's piercing whistle.

"All right, Johnny!"

"We're here. We're here! Time to ride."

"Oh, yeah. Hey. How'd it go with—"

"Git on, boys." He held the back door open for them and swept his gaze across the property. None of the young shifters had come to see them. "Quietly, now."

"Yeah, sure," Rex whispered and leapt onto the back seat.

"We can be quiet, Johnny. Hey, Rex, why are we whispering?"

"Seriously?"

"Yeah, but shouldn't we tell Johnny what we—"

The dwarf shut the door abruptly and rapped on the tinted window. Both hounds whipped their heads toward him and he raised a finger to his lips.

Whatever they found, they ain't sayin' a thing until we get far enough away and outta shifter hearin'. I still ain't sure this visit worked out in our favor.

CHAPTER TEN

Neither of the partners said a word until Johnny guided the bouncing, jostling SUV over the final stretch of dry grass and lumpy terrain and swerved sharply onto the frontage road through the mountains. Lisa sighed heavily and shook her head. "I would love to know what all that was about back there."

He glanced at her from behind his black sunglasses. "It was a couple of new business partners sizin' each other up, darlin'."

"Yeah, you both sure talked a lot but neither of you said anything."

"We said what was needed. That shifter has a calculatin' head on his shoulders, I tell you what."

"Do you care to explain?"

The bounty hunter glanced in the rearview mirror at the hounds seated on their haunches in the back seat. Both panted heavily despite the car's AC turned on at full blast. "Scratch the notion of a shifter crime boss meetin' with a dwarf bounty hunter. Look at it this way. Two alpha hounds cross paths somewhere that ain't either one of their territories—like wherever hounds go to do whatever they do in public."

"You mean like a dog park?"

"Wait, what?" Luther let out an excited whine. "Did she say dog park?"

"Johnny." Rex chuffed. "Is she saying there are parks out there that are only for hounds? And why haven't we heard of this before?"

"Y'all can hear me and I can hear y'all too," he grumbled. "We don't own leashes. The whole damn world is your dog park. I ain't takin' you to a fenced-in field so y'all can do what you already do while I gotta sit there and listen to y'all sniffin' every other hound that comes your way."

"Aw, come on—"

"Y'all hush. We'll get to the part where you can talk in a minute." He pulled his sunglasses down the bridge of his nose to fix the hounds with a warning gaze in the rearview mirror.

Rex slumped on the seat. Luther whined again and licked his muzzle.

"Call it whatever you want, darlin'," he continued, "but there are places out there where bein' an alpha don't always mean snarlin' and snappin' at the other guy 'cause he's flexin' in your face too much and vice versa. A hound at the top of the totem pole still knows his place, even if means he has to share it with someone else at the top of another pole.

"Sure, neither of 'em will roll over but they ain't gotta. The other hounds know who's who and sometimes, the best way to stay at the top is to get along with another top hound to prevent the others from losin' it. Maybe even from recognizin' that one's stronger than the other."

Lisa shifted in her seat to face him and raised an eyebrow. "I have no idea what you're talking about."

"Me and Kaiser? We're the alphas."

"Johnny, I don't care how much open space there was. That farm is not a dog park."

"It's not like the actual hounds would know," Luther muttered.

"Hush." The bounty hunter adjusted his grasp on the steering wheel. "I'm talkin' about neutral ground, darlin'."

"Kaiser owns the property."

"Sure, but it ain't his home. He ain't usin' his real name, and I reckon neither is any of the young guys he has out there helpin' him run his operation. He ain't even there all the time. It's as neutral ground as we're likely to get from him, seein' as he sends his shifter brute Veron and that no-nonsense dark witch of his to do all his dirty work for him."

"I don't like her." Lisa shook her head. "There's something off about her. Yeah, there's something off about anyone who uses dark magic and who would willingly align themselves with a guy killing magicals of his own race merely because they won't join him in his crusade. But she's…I don't know. It's like she's lobotomized or something."

"Body what?" Rex snorted. "She's tiny. We could take that two-legs, Johnny."

"Bet she tastes like mud," Luther muttered.

"She ain't that dead inside," Johnny said and ignored the hounds. "It might seem like it on the outside but there's way more goin' on in that head of hers than anyone's likely to notice —except Kaiser."

"And yet we walked in there, had a conversation about nothing, handed him almost sixty-three grand, and walked out again." she folded her arms. "With no threats, no explosions, and not even the slightest interrogation. And yes, I'm referring to both our vastly different definitions of interrogation."

He smirked. "If he'd showed up in the Glades lookin' for a little sit-down or if we'd found out who he is and brought our business to his home, yeah. There would have been all that and more. It's a territory thing, darlin'."

"Because you're both alpha dogs."

"It's all metaphor."

"I understand what metaphors are, Johnny." She snorted. "But you still haven't said what the metaphor means. I don't doubt that Agnes saw us at the bar the other night and told Kaiser about it."

"Yep. He brought her in to see how we'd react."

"They could have started a fight then and there and we would have been completely unprepared for it."

"But they didn't." The dwarf looked into the rearview mirror again and nodded when neither of the hounds thought it was the right moment to pitch in again. "Kaiser might own that property but it ain't his to do whatever he wants on. He has other investors to keep happy—other partners we've now joined the ranks of.

"I'm sure that most if not all of his hired hands out there ain't got a clue about where he sends Veron and Agnes on their not-so-secret missions. The guy has a bubble of focus and completely different goals around him on that farm. It might be that the young shifters grateful for a good-payin' job under the table ain't exactly on board with offerin' transformed life-or-death ultimatums."

"So he didn't want to start anything with us because he's trying to save face with his employees?" Lisa shook her head. "That doesn't make sense."

"It makes perfect sense, darlin'. Kaiser is living a double life inside a double life. It's like when we went after the Red Boar in Baltimore and had that joke of a filmin' crew followin' us around. Some of it was staged but most of it was real—except for the part where we didn't give a damn about who saw the show or what they thought."

Her eyes narrowed in thought, she studied the dashboard. "We were trying to draw the Red Boar out and make him come to us."

"Exactly."

"You think Kaiser's doing the same thing with his pot farm?"

"You bet. Drawin' out the transformed who believe it's best to work seasonally for a shifter who has a helluva good deal for transient workers out there in the middle of nowhere. Then, he picks 'em off. It might be he's lookin' to gauge the folks who have cash to burn and want in on a little somethin' extra too—seein' who stands with him or against him in his 'better world for shifters' campaign."

"And he thinks we stand with him."

"Naw." Johnny sniffed and shook his head. "He ain't decided one way or the other about it at all 'cause we saw his crew kidnap Hux, didn't do a thing about it, and still came to make the deal. It doesn't mean he won't be watchin' us real closely from here on out but if he ain't made a decision by now, I assume he still thinks we're safe."

"Until we have enough evidence against him to bring him down."

"Uh-huh. This will be a long game for all of us. Kaiser's as sharp as a tack. He ain't fixin' to show his hand until it's all or nothin'. And speakin' of evidence." He looked in the rearview mirror again and cleared his throat. "Boys."

"Yeah, Johnny."

"We're still here."

"What evidence?" The SUV fell silent and he grunted in irritation before he added, "That's y'all's cue. Did y'all find anythin' on that property?"

"You mean under all that skunk stink in those long sheds?" Rex snorted. "Nope."

"Didn't catch a whiff of any transformed, Johnny." Luther lowered his head to scratch vigorously behind one ear. "No screaming for help."

"No crying."

"No fear-stink."

"Tons of rabbits, though."

"Ooh, yeah. And squirrels. Hey, Rex. Did you catch anything?"

"Wouldn't you like to know?"

"Hey." The dwarf snapped his fingers. "Focus."

"We're focused, Johnny."

"Yeah, if they're still holding that shifternapped guy, it's not on the farm."

"But they are keeping Hux somewhere," Lisa muttered. "They have to be."

"Yeah, they are, but it makes perfect sense that it's not on the farm. Kaiser ain't mixin' his business and personal lives and he ain't mixin' his businesses either. The guy knows what he's doing."

"So do we." She studied him for a long moment but he fixed his gaze firmly on the road. "Right?"

"Of course we do, darlin'. We merely gotta go about it in a different way than usual."

"Okay. So we have to look for Hux somewhere else, which means we need a way to draw Veron and Agnes out into the open again too. We need to find them, tail them, and see where they go when Kaiser's not on his property and they have to deal with his transformed shifter side business."

"There might be a better way."

Lisa's eyes widened. "No, Johnny. That's going too far."

"Is it?" He wrinkled his nose. "It's fairly simple and straightforward and ain't gonna hurt anyone."

"We told them we'd protect them and find answers at the same time."

"We did?"

"Yes, and I'm drawing the line right here. We will not use Galfrey and Jake as bait, okay? They wouldn't agree to it anyway, and I won't put two innocent magicals out on a limb so we can tail the criminals who already tried and failed to kill them once—"

"Whoa, whoa. Hold up, now." The dwarf chuckled and darted her a sidelong glance. "I ain't said a word about Galfrey and Jake."

"You didn't have to. I know how you think."

"Huh. Well, that's usually the case, yeah. And it's a good idea—"

"It's a terrible idea and I'm shooting it down right now so don't even try it."

"Darlin', I ain't fixin' to put those fellas in any more danger than they already brought on their heads without anyone else's help."

Lisa sighed in exasperation. "You can't seriously blame them for trying to stand against Kaiser and stop what he's doing to other transformed. They didn't kill Addison Taylor. As far as we know, they haven't killed anyone."

"Now, listen. If I thought they were guilty of anythin', do you think I would have paid to put 'em up in the worst motel this side of the Mississippi?"

She pressed her lips together in an attempt to hide a smile and shook her head. "There are a ton of bad motels on this side of the Mississippi."

"And that one takes the blue ribbon. I tell you what."

"Okay. So if you don't plan to dangle them in front of Veron and Agnes like worms on a hook, what were you talking about?"

"We still have that card from Jasper Harford's butler."

"Wait, what?"

"We're gonna buy ourselves a few seats at the Harford gala, darlin', and see what we find when both Harfords' personal lives are open and on display for the rest of California's rich and famous society to see."

"How…" Lisa cocked her head. "How is that supposed to help us find Hux?"

"It ain't. But I bet you we'll find somethin' else about how all this relates to Addison Taylor. Bronson's girlfriend is shot by Kaiser's boys in a fight. We have two of the only three transformed to escape a skirmish like that, both of 'em scared outta their wits 'cause they believe this Tyro guy's been lookin' for 'em specifically after they mistook Addison for a confused transformed instead of Bronson's girl about to get proposed to. And we watched the third get shoved into the back of a getaway car by Kaiser's right-hand witch."

"Yes, all of those things are true. But how is a gala supposed to help us find the connection?"

Johnny grinned. "Well, I aim to find out exactly that, darlin'. That's why we're goin'."

CHAPTER ELEVEN

They stopped for a quick lunch and another grocery trip for their transformed shifter guests on the way to Gold Motel. Charlie's Harley was parked in the motel's front lot and seemed to have not moved even after the guest with the trailer had packed up and left. It made both Johnny and Lisa more optimistic about their next steps moving forward.

Galfrey and Jake were exactly where they'd left them and remained undiscovered by Kaiser's team on a shifter-hunt for the two who'd escaped his wrath.

Once they reached the second-floor landing, though, the shouts, growls, and shattering sounds that issued from their shared room didn't exactly showcase how well everything had been going until now.

"Oh, come on." Johnny stormed toward the door and pounded on it. "Open up!"

"You can't simply take whatever you want," the biker dwarf yelled.

He snorted. "I ain't got the foggiest idea what the hell you're—"

"You keep waving it around like some kinda trophy," Galfrey

shouted. "I'm fairly sure the rules apply to you too. And if they don't, this shouldn't be an issue."

"What rules, man? This isn't third grade."

"No shit. Shifter kids don't get kidnapped and murdered in third grade."

"Guys." Jake's trembling voice cut through the thumps and snarls. "Hey. Guys, cut it out. It's not that big a deal, okay?"

"What's mine is mine, asshole," Charlie retorted. "End of story."

"Oh, yeah? Like all this food your friends brought for us?"

"He's not my friend. He's my cousin."

"Hey!" Johnny pounded on the door again. "One of y'all better open up right now."

"Get lost."

"No, don't! That's—"

Another crash issued from inside and the bounty hunter moved his hand to his belt for one of his exploding disks. Only then did he remember that he'd left them in the room.

I oughtta leave 'em in the damn car. I can go unarmed into Kaiser's shifter den but don't need actual weapons until my cousin starts fightin' with the witnesses.

"Do you have the room key, darlin'?" he muttered over his shoulder as he glared at the door. The shouts and sounds of a scuffle had faded but that didn't mean anything when Charlie Walker was involved. "One of us is gettin' in there, and I reckon none of them inside will run if they see me standin' here instead of—"

The lock on the door clicked and the door opened slowly to reveal Lisa standing on the other side, one hand propped on her hip and the other resting against the doorframe. "Instead of me?"

"Well..." He cleared his throat. "Most of the time."

"Most of the time, you're the one who runs in first with threats and explosives." Lisa stepped aside and gestured toward the three transformed shifters who stood stiffly in the center of the motel room. "Sometimes, though, all it takes is a good warning look. Right?"

Galfrey and Jake stared at the floor. Charlie sneered at them, his fists clenched at his sides, then looked at Johnny. "They started it—"

"Don't. Just don't say a word." He strode into the room and noted the shattered bedside lamp, the array of socks and underwear strewn across the floor and onto the bed, and the open connecting door into his and Lisa's room. "How many socks and skivvies do y'all keep on you, anyhow?"

His partner shut the outer door with a disbelieving sigh. "That's the first question you want answered?"

"It seems outta sorts, is all."

"They're mine," Charlie said through clenched teeth. "Like everything else in my saddlebag."

Johnny snorted. "Are you ridin' a horse, now?"

"On the Harley. That's what it's called."

"So you thought you'd bring up your road-ridin' provisions and…what? Do some decoratin'?"

"He has another phone," Galfrey said. "He brought it in with the rest of his stuff."

"Yeah," Jake added. "And he did something to make it untraceable so we… Well, if no one can trace it, what's the harm in us using it, right? Only to make a few calls."

"Dammit, Charlie."

"I didn't give it to them," the mohawked dwarf muttered. "Have you ever tried to keep something from a shifter who thinks the whole world's coming after them?"

"More times than you know." The bounty hunter scowled. "Desperation makes a fella strong for the short term but that kinda thinkin' will tear you down again as soon as the fire goes out." He glanced scathingly at his cousin. "Kinda like drugs."

"What do you want us to do, huh?" Galfrey spread his arms to emphasize the scope of his frustration. "We've already spent two days cooped up in here with this guy. He eats all the food, bogart's the remote all day, and waves his untraceable cell phone around but won't hand it over."

Johnny clicked his tongue and sighed. "Where's the phone?"

"It's mine," Charlie muttered. "No one used it."

"That ain't what I asked." The bounty hunter stormed across the room and stopped two feet away from the shifters to study each one of them like they'd been lined up for a round of group interrogation.

Technically, that's what this is. And it's always my job one way or another to ask the damn questions no one wants to answer, ain't it?

"I ain't a fan of repeatin' myself," he said slowly, his voice low in warning. "So either one of y'all coughs up what you ain't meant to have or all three of y'all can say goodbye to the cozy motel room and the continental breakfasts."

No one spoke.

His cousin glanced briefly at Lisa, then shrugged. "That's not exactly a threat, 'coz. I'm more than happy to get back on the road—"

"That ain't an invitation, Charlie. This place is hell on the highway, but don't think I can't make it worse for y'all. Hand the damn phone over."

The mohawked dwarf responded with a pert smirk as he shook his head. "I would if I could, Johnny."

"Don't make me—"

"Fine." With a heavy sigh, Galfrey slid his hand into his pocket and pulled out a smartphone. He handed it to Johnny and couldn't raise his gaze any higher than the bounty hunter's chest. "I only wanted to make a few calls."

"To who?" He snatched the device and turned it in his hand to study it.

"Just...you know. People who might think we're dead by now."

"Uh-huh. Do you have kids?"

"No."

"Married?"

"Uh-uh."

"Girlfriends? Or…whatever kinda partner?"

Galfrey and Jake glanced at each other, then shook their heads slowly.

"Then there ain't a reason to call anyone." Johnny yanked his utility knife from his belt and flicked it open. The two shifters stepped back with wide eyes. Charlie stayed where he was and folded his arms. "The last thing we need is one of Kaiser's crew pickin' up calls goin' out with his name on your lips."

"Why would we talk to anyone about Kaiser over the phone?" Jake mumbled sullenly.

"We wouldn't because we're not stupid." Galfrey swallowed awkwardly. "Man, I only wanna see if we can get some help to find Hux—which you guys didn't do when you went to drink beers and get all cozy with the asshole who had him kidnapped—"

"Watch it." The bounty hunter flicked the blade of his knife toward the shifter's face and raised an eyebrow. "You don't think I know what I'm doin'?"

"What…w-what are you doing?" Galfrey responded and stared at the blade. "With that, I mean."

"Corroboratin' evidence."

"What?"

He moved the tip of his knife to the back of Charlie's second phone, quickly unscrewed the tiny screws holding it together, and slid them into his pocket before he removed the back and tossed it onto the bed.

"Oh, come on." His cousin rolled his eyes. "First, my whole bag is emptied all over the place, and now you gotta take my phone apart too?"

Johnny flicked the knife closed again, strapped it onto his belt, then stood in complete silence, his attention fully focused on examining the device's inner workings.

"Oh, no." Jake paled and stepped back. "Do you think his phone was bugged?"

"How the hell would anyone bug a phone no one knows about?" Charlie snapped. "I already told you it can't be traced. That's the dumbest—"

"Shh!" The bounty hunter didn't look up from the phone as he peered under and around the tiny components. "Did you pay someone else to scramble it for you or did you do it yourself?"

"I paid someone." The dwarf shifter frowned. "A buddy in Illinois. He does this kinda thing all the time and we're cool so he gave me a discount."

"Uh-huh. The moron discount." He tossed the phone to his cousin, who fumbled to catch it before he stared at him with wide eyes.

"What?"

"Your buddy must have felt sorry for your dumb ass and thought he'd feel better about rippin' you off if he didn't make you pay full price for it." He pointed at the partially disassembled phone. "That ain't untraceable."

"No way." Charlie gaped at the open back of his device. "No way. He gave me a guarantee."

"If it ain't in writin', it ain't worth a cent of what you paid for it."

"Wait, so someone's coming after us now?" Jake muttered. "They know where we are? Oh shit, man. We gotta go—"

"No, we don't." Lisa finally looked away from the staring contest between the Walker cousins and nodded at the panicked shifter. "But you'll probably feel a little better if you sit and take a deep breath."

The man heaved a somewhat jerky sigh before he settled into a crouch between one of the beds and the attached bathroom. Finally, he sat and drew his knees to his chest.

Galfrey looked at his friend with an uncomfortable grimace.

"Who did you call with that?" Johnny nodded at the phone resting in his cousin's open palm.

"Just…people."

"Charlie. Who the hell did you call on that phone you thought was so safe?"

"Friends, Johnny. Okay? And…business associates."

"That's what you're callin' 'em now? The scum who don't care one way or the other what happens to you are your business associates?"

The biker dwarf looked slowly at his cousin and his frown was filled with way more than merely frustration and anger.

Aw, now the shifter dwarf biker got his feeling hurt. It ain't my problem and it ain't my fault.

"I told you I was good, okay?" Charlie glanced around the room. Galfrey had sat on the bed closest to the door, Jake remained close to the bathroom with his arms wrapped around his knees, and Lisa leaned against the exterior door with her arms folded and merely watched impassively. "Straight and narrow, Johnny. Promise."

"Straight and narrow with a secret phone you thought was scrambled well and good by some clown callin' himself a professional. Yeah. It sounds right up your alley." He folded his arms. "Do you feel that, Charlie? It feels like déjà vu, doesn't it?"

"No, because I'm not—" The mohawked dwarf glanced at Lisa, then turned his back toward her and lowered his voice. "Can we talk about this later? Like, in private?"

"When did you make the last call?"

"Seriously, Johnny. It's not like that."

"There's a sayin' for shit like this." He turned toward Lisa and snapped his fingers three times as he tried to recall the words to memory. "How does it go, darlin'? Fool me once…"

"Shame on you," she replied. "Fool me twice, shame on me."

"That's it." He pointed at his cousin. "Most folks don't know the third line. Have you heard it?"

The other dwarf gritted his teeth and glared at him with renewed anger.

"It goes like this, Charlie. Fool yourself for over half a goddamn century, shame on everyone and everythin' but you. Ain't that right?"

For a long, tense moment, the dwarves stared at each other before Charlie narrowed his eyes and snarled. "Go to hell."

He threw the phone at his cousin, but the bounty hunter sidestepped and the open-backed device careened into the wall above the dresser, Hundreds of tiny microprocessor parts rained onto the floor. The biker dwarf stormed not toward Lisa, who still blocked the exit, but through the open door into the adjoining room.

"If you leave now, Charlie," Johnny called after him without moving an inch from where he stood, "you're leavin' forever. You understand that, don'tcha?"

The exterior door to the adjoining room opened with a creak and slammed shut again two seconds later. The dwarf's footsteps pounded away down the second-story walkway.

Rex padded slowly toward the door, sniffed the air, and sat in the opening. "Uh...what was that about?"

"Johnny," Luther added, "if everyone can come into our room whenever they want, why is there a door?"

I ain't about to explain my cousin's broken choice-maker to a couple of hounds.

He hooked his thumbs through his belt loops, turned to face the other two shifters in the room, and cleared his throat. "Now. Y'all gotta put this idea of callin' folks outta your minds, understand?"

"Got it," Galfrey muttered. "Unless you have a phone that's truly untraceable."

"I wouldn't tell ya if I did."

"What kind of trouble is he in?" Jake asked and nodded toward the adjoining door. "Charlie. What did he do?"

"That's a story for a different day and I ain't the one to tell it." The bounty hunter turned toward Lisa, who raised her eyebrows and remained silent. "If y'all are worried about somethin' he did comin' back on any of us, don't be. Whatever he's gotten into, it has nothin' to do with how we handle this movin' forward or what we're plannin'.

"The best thing for everyone is to keep the two of y'all in here until we find out exactly where Hux is and how to rescue him. Again, if y'all can't handle a few more days in this room, I don't blame ya. Say the word, tell me you mean it, and I'll give you your things. We ain't into holdin' prisoners."

"We can…" Jake looked at his friend, then scrunched his face in confusion. "We can go whenever we want?"

"Yep. But I can't promise anythin' if you do. We didn't go lookin' to find you at that bar the other night, but Veron and Kaiser's witch saw their opportunity and pounced on it. Fortunately, not on you, so I'd call that a stroke of luck for all of us here."

Galfrey chuckled bitterly. "And how long do you think that luck will last?"

"A long as y'all stay here and quit stealin' cell phones from the folks tryin' to help."

The goateed shifter ruffled his hair and sighed heavily. "Sorry. I got carried away."

"Yep."

"Okay, so what are we talking, here?" Jake asked. "Days? Weeks? Months? Because honestly, I don't think Hux has anywhere near that long. And I don't think I can handle staying in here for weeks—not only this room but, like, anywhere. Not like this."

"We'll know much more in a few days," Lisa said and finally stepped away from the door. "One thing we could confirm was that Hux isn't on Kaiser's property, which means he's being held somewhere else. We have to be careful with how we go about it, but our next step is to determine the most likely location and follow it up until we're sure."

"A process of elimination." Galfrey grimaced. "That's all you have to go on?"

"It doesn't seem like much in this particular instance." She shrugged. "But that's how all cases are solved. You take what you have and check every box on the list. Usually, the box that isn't checked will be the one to point you in the right direction."

"Usually." The shifter scoffed and shook his head. "That doesn't include how to make your clients feel better about the whole situation."

"Y'all ain't clients. You're witnesses."

"They tried to kill us. They still are!"

"Well hell, if you want me to call y'all victims instead, fine. It doesn't change how Lisa and I do our jobs. So can y'all hold out a few more days while we follow up on our other…checkboxes, or what?"

"Fine." Galfrey nodded. "Yeah, we can wait."

"Jake?"

The other shifter looked at him from the floor, his eyes glazed with disbelief. "I'm not going anywhere."

"Good. After tomorrow night, if everythin' goes the way I think it will, we'll have more info. For now, hang tight." Johnny scanned the room and picked up the remote from the top of the dresser on which the older-model TV with a dent in the corner of the screen stood. He tossed it onto the bed beside Galfrey and nodded. "Now y'all can watch whatever you want. The third wheel in here ain't comin' back."

With that, he turned and retreated into the adjoining room. The hounds scrambled out of the way but converged around the open doorway to study the disheartened shifters who simply sat and stared at nothing.

"We gonna leave them in there, Johnny?" Rex whispered.

"Yeah, they look…sad."

"There ain't a whole lotta reasons to be particularly happy about somethin' just now." He sat on the bed, propped himself against the pile of lumpy, misshapen pillows, and crossed one ankle over the other. "Let 'em have their thinkin' space, boys."

The hounds slunk away from the door but cast heavy-hearted glances over their shoulders. They sat and watched Lisa haul the most recent grocery load into the other room to set everything out on the small table again.

"Hey, Johnny. What about the pirate dwarf?"

The bounty hunter squinted at Luther. "I thought I told you to stop callin' him that."

"Fine. The biker. Your cousin. You know, the other dwarf who got turned into a shifter and now has—"

Rex snapped at his brother's muzzle and uttered a low, warning growl. "He knows who you mean, bro. We all know."

"Okay, jeez. I'm only saying—"

"Charlie made his decision. It's crystal-clear what he wants more than anythin' he knows is good for him. The bottom line is it ain't my job to worry about him if he ain't gonna worry about himself."

Lisa stepped into their room, closed the adjoining door behind her, and dusted her hands off. She fixed her partner with a speculative look but remained silent.

CHAPTER TWELVE

After a minute of feeling her gaze on him, Johnny finally looked at her and shrugged. "What?"

She sat on the other bed and drew a deep breath. "I understand that you don't want to revisit the past. You have good reasons for feeling the way you feel about Charlie, and I'm not saying you handled things the wrong way or the right way. Honestly, you're the only one who can make a call on that one. But now feels like a very good time to at least tell me what all that was about—besides you bursting his bubble about the still-traceable cell."

He wrinkled his nose. "See, you're tellin' me two different things there, darlin'. One is that I have reasons to not talk, and the other is you givin' me a reason to talk. I can't do both."

"I'm not telling you to scream it from the rooftops, Johnny. I'm asking you to talk to me. Whatever it is, it's a big deal to both of you."

The bounty hunter regarded her for a long moment before he scowled and shook his head. "You ain't gotta take this on."

"This isn't because I want to take your issues on. Even though we're partners and that's something partners do."

"Then why's it so important to know?"

She gestured toward the door. "Well, in case he comes back and I find myself in a situation that could have benefited from more insight than I have right now. Honestly, it would be nice to have that insight from the start."

"You mean if you are left in a room with him or somethin'."

"Yeah. Sure, as unlikely as that is. I only want to be informed, okay?"

"Sure. I get it. But he ain't comin' back."

With a frown, she folded her arms and tilted her head challengingly. "Why not? You didn't tell him to not come back."

"Nope. Charlie knows full well he ain't welcome if he chooses to disappear all over again."

"You do realize that sounds like you were trying to hold him prisoner here, right?"

"It has nothin' to do with where he's stayin'. It's about trust and honesty and I ain't got a speck left for my cousin."

"Hmm." Lisa pulled her legs onto the bed and crossed them beneath her. "Whatever he did must have been bad."

Johnny snorted. "I'll tell you this much, darlin'. I can count on one hand the number of times I've given second chances, except for when it comes to my cousin. There ain't enough fingers and toes in this hellhole of a motel to count how many things I forgave and how many promises he broke. And he added another one to the list earlier."

Rex sniffed his forepaw and looked at his master. "Are you including our toes, Johnny?"

"Yeah, don't forget about us. Wait..." Luther stretched his head toward his brother's paws and sniffed warily. "We have toes? Since when?"

Lisa chuckled and shook her head. "I'm very sure he's exaggerating, boys."

"Wanna bet?" He frowned at the hounds, who were busy counting the digits on each of their paws in confused whispers.

With a snort, he stood to rifle through his bag and his jeans from the start of their trip to California. "If you still wanna hear all about it in a few days, darlin', ask me again then. Right now, I'm more likely to break somethin' than say anythin' that makes sense."

"Okay. But don't act surprised when I remind you of that offer."

"Naw. I won't."

"What are you looking for?"

"That damn—ha." He jerked a piece of paper from the pocket of his second pair of black Levi's and turned to hold it toward her. "This."

Lisa squinted at it. "Is that the card Jasper's butler gave you?"

"Damn right it is. It still has the fancy gold letterin' and everythin'."

She forced a cough to cover her laughter. "I'm very sure business cards don't change after a few days in a pair of worn pants."

"Of course not. Most of 'em, anyway."

"What?"

"Never mind." The bounty hunter retrieved his phone, flipped the thick piece of embossed cardstock in his hand, and found the number he wanted. "The direct line for Jasper Harford's personal guests, all of 'em fallin' all over themselves to call in and spend a fortune on one night in a stuffy ballroom listenin' to speeches about charity."

"Yeah, at fifteen thousand a head."

"It's less than the price of a down payment on fifty pounds of marijuana, though."

"Oh, jeez." Lisa rolled her eyes. "But that's money we plan to get back."

"It is?"

"He's expecting the second half of our so-called investment in November. That's three months from now. We still have to find Hux, gather enough evidence against Kaiser to officially put him away or at the very least stop him, and discover who this Tyro guy is before he murders even more transformed shifters whenever he feels like it. If it takes us longer than a few weeks to get all that done, we're not doing our jobs."

Johnny smirked. "I'm messin' with ya, darlin'. 'Course we're getting' that money back. I'm fine spendin' half that much for a night with high-society shifters if it means we get more information about what's goin' on with the Harford family and how it's all connected. Hell, thirty grand didn't even cover a fifth of the houseboat."

"Which you didn't have to pay for."

"Exactly. It means I got a little extra to spare." He looked quickly at the business card and his phone to type in the number for gala guests to make what Jasper Harford had called "participant donations."

It's the biggest donation I ever made in my life but it's still for a good cause.

The line rang four times before it was answered.

"Thank you for calling the Harford Foundation. This is Meryl. How can I help you?"

"Yeah, hey." Johnny cleared his throat. "Do y'all have any tickets left for the charity gala Thursday?"

"I'm sorry. We're running extremely low on available seating at the event. Have you previously reserved anything with us?"

"Uh…no. I was given the number by Jasper Harford."

"Oh, of course." The woman on the other end of the line sounded as if she'd perked up considerably. "May I have your name?"

"Johnny Walker and Lisa Breyer."

"May I put you on hold for a moment?"

"Yep."

"Thank you." A click was followed by complete silence for ten seconds before the woman returned with another click. "You're in luck, Mr. Walker. Two seats have already been reserved for you and Ms. Breyer. Would you like to make a donation today to secure those?"

Johnny looked at Lisa, who watched him intently, and smirked. "I guess I oughtta. There ain't already been a donation in my name too, huh?"

"Well, no. These seats were only marked as reserved for you should you call in and decide to attend the event. You're aware of the minimum donation limit?"

He sniggered. "You bet. Do y'all take a credit card?"

Meryl chuckled. "Absolutely, Mr. Walker. Visa, Mastercard, and American Express."

"All right, then." He retrieved his wallet and read his information to her so he could put thirty thousand dollars' worth of charitable donations on it, made out to the Harford Foundation.

At least we ain't gotta run all over town for another damn cashier's check.

Once he'd finished paying for the tickets, he thanked the bubbly receptionist and ended the call. "It's ridiculous."

"Which part?" Lisa asked with a small smile. "Paying with a credit card over the phone?"

"Well, yeah, that's part of it." The dwarf tossed the device onto the bed and rubbed his mouth. "But I'm talkin' about the fact that we walked onto Harford's estate without an appointment or any other kind of information for a little chat and the man's expensive-ass coffee. Now here we are, shellin' out thirty grand to get inside the same place in a situation in which we ain't as likely to get two words in edgewise with Harford Senior."

"That's the point of these galas, Johnny. Exclusivity."

"Uh-huh. It ain't my cup of tea, I tell you what."

Luther sniggered and raised his head from where he lay on his side. "You mean your cup of shit coffee?"

Rex howled with laughter and rolled onto his back. He wiggled wildly and his tail thumped against the carpet and his tongue lolled from his open mouth.

Johnny pointed at the smaller hound. "It was a damn fine cup. Y'all would have said the same thing if I had a mind to share that particular drink with a couple of hounds."

"Yeah, but we're—" Rex laughed even harder and snorted violently. "But we're the hounds, Johnny. The only—ha! The only ones who are supposed to like the flavor."

"Huh?" Luther stared at his brother, then erupted in an explosion of giggles. "Oh, yeah. 'Cause we eat—hey. Do you hear that?"

Johnny sat on the edge of the bed and raised an eyebrow at his hounds. "I assume you're fixin' to tell me what it is."

The two hounds stopped laughing and pricked their ears. Rex rolled onto his belly and whipped his head toward the door. "Hey, Johnny. Remember when you said he wasn't coming back?"

"Who?"

"You," Luther added. "You said it."

"No, I mean…" The bounty hunter rolled his eyes. "Are you talkin' about Charlie?"

"Yup." Rex bounded to his feet and pointed his nose at the motel room door. His tail stuck out straight behind him and twitched from side to side. "That's him."

"Aw, come on, now." Johnny stood. "He thinks he can storm off and walk in again like nothin' happened?"

"Probably." Luther sniffed the bottom edge of the door. "Johnny, he never left."

"Say what, now?"

A brisk knock sounded at the door and both hounds yipped once.

"That's him, Johnny."

"Oh, yeah. That's the shifter dwarf, all right."

"Johnny?" His cousin's voice was muffled and sounded soft and embarrassed. "Come on, 'coz. Open the door."

The bounty hunter folded his arms and scowled but said nothing in reply.

I ain't givin' into his crap again. That's for damn sure.

"Johnny," Rex whispered. "Johnny, he's right outside."

"Yeah, he wants in." Luther lowered his head to scratch behind one ear and his hind paw thumped rhythmically on the carpet. "You know what they say about letting strays in."

"The worst decision ever made?" he grumbled.

"What?" Rex sniggered. "No one ever says that, Johnny."

Lisa gave her partner one of her wordless looks that said everything without saying a thing.

He pointed at her. "Don't even think about it."

"About what, exactly?"

"Johnny, it's like this," Luther continued. "Once you let a stray in—"

"They're not a stray anymore," Rex finished. "They're your pal for life."

"He ain't a stray," Johnny muttered. "And he ain't my pal."

"Come on, Johnny," Charlie said as he knocked again. "I can hear all of you in there. You know that, right?"

Rex barked. "Hey, shifter dwarf. How's it hanging?"

"Hey." The bounty hunter snapped his fingers. "Y'all hush."

A tense silence filled the motel room, punctuated by the low murmur of the TV coming through the wall of the adjacent room and a heavy sigh from outside the door.

Lisa widened her eyes. "At least go see what he wants."

"I know exactly what he wants."

"Johnny?" Something rustled in the hallway before Charlie spoke again, this time more muffled but a little louder as if he'd pressed his mouth directly against the doorframe. "Come on, 'coz. I only needed some air."

After another long moment during which her partner scowled at the door without moving an inch, Lisa pushed from the bed and crossed the room.

"Lisa."

"He's standing right there. If you won't, I will."

"Don't you—" He growled his disapproval when she opened

the door to reveal a red-faced, sheepish-looking dwarf on the other side.

"Hey, Charlie." Lisa flashed him a warm smile. "Is everything okay?"

He responded with a bitter laugh. "Not really. But you probably guessed that already." The mohawked dwarf peered past her into the room. "Johnny, can I—"

"Just 'cause you walked through this room don't mean you can walk back into it whenever you please."

Lisa glared warningly at her partner.

Charlie shook his head. "I'm not trying to get into your room. I, uh…" He jerked a thumb over his shoulder. "I only wanna talk —you know, in private. There's an empty lot out back. Well, it's not completely empty and is full of trash and everything, but no one's—"

"I saw it. What do you want?"

The cousins stared at each other until the biker dwarf cleared his throat and lowered his gaze. "Only a few minutes, Johnny. Please."

Johnny grunted but volunteered no verbal response.

Lisa sighed in frustration. "I'm not exactly a fan of getting in the middle of family issues, but I'll say this one more time, Johnny. If you don't—"

"The hell you will." He strode across the motel room and pointed at his cousin. "Five minutes. That's all you get."

"Sure. Yeah." Charlie's eyes widened hopefully. "Five minutes is great. I get it."

"And everyone else stays here. I'm the one who does the listenin'. It ain't the other way around."

She stepped aside to let him through the open door. "We'll wait here."

The shifter dwarf moved slowly down the outer walkway to give his cousin space.

Johnny paused halfway through the door and leaned toward

his partner to mutter, "If I ain't back in five minutes, grab my belt and—"

"I will not bring your homemade bombs to a family discussion behind a motel, Johnny." She smirked. "Even this motel. You can deal with this one all on your own."

His nose wrinkled, he stepped onto the walkway. "Darlin', there are some things that—"

The door shut swiftly in his face with a gentle click, followed by the jingle and clack of the chain lock being slid into place.

"You got this, Johnny," Rex whispered inside.

"Yeah, if you guys have to fight," Luther added, "we'll put all our money on you."

"If we had money."

"Right. We'll put your money on you, Johnny."

The bounty hunter rolled his eyes, turned stiffly away from the hotel room he'd paid for but had been locked out of, and grunted.

Charlie stared at him with wide eyes. "Thanks."

"You'd best get to talkin', 'coz."

"Out back, though? Just, you know…for some privacy."

He sniffed and stormed down the walkway to brush roughly past his cousin as he reached the stairs. "Five minutes starts when we're standin' next to the pile o' junk."

"That works for me."

CHAPTER THIRTEEN

"Okay." Charlie kicked a crumpled plastic water bottle across the wrecked asphalt of the motel's back lot. It skittered toward the pile of junk and loose trash. "First, let me—"

"I ain't lettin' you do a thing, Charlie." Johnny glared at him. "You're a grown-ass dwarf. It's about time you realized that and started takin' responsibility for it. Unless you're still tryin' to pull the wool over my eyes and everyone else's."

His cousin gritted his teeth and exhaled heavily through them. "I'm trying to apologize, okay?"

The bounty hunter stared at him in disbelief. "Apologize."

"Yeah. For real. I'm sorry, Johnny. Truly I am."

"Huh. That's a first—if it were true."

"Come on, man. I know I've said it a million times before but I mean it this time. For real. I'm not trying to pull anything."

"You know what? I'll believe that giant load of crap when I see it swept up and cleared out with my own two eyes."

"Johnny—"

"I told you if you walked out, you were walkin' out." He pointed at the biker dwarf to emphasize his point. "And now you think you can walk in again, actin' all sorry, and that'll fix everythin'. It ain't gonna happen like that."

"I didn't walk out. I told you I only needed some air—"

"You got up on that eyesore on wheels, spun outta here, and… what? Had a change of heart halfway across the country before rollin' back? That ain't—"

"Jesus, Johnny. I didn't leave, okay? I didn't even touch the bike. Do you need proof?"

Johnny folded his arms. "That'd be a good start. I ain't seen it in over sixty years."

"Then go look at the damn bike, Johnny." Charlie snarled and his green eyes flashed with silver light as he threw his arm out to gesture toward the front of the motel. "Go check the thing for… whatever you need to see. I've been here the whole time and I'm trying to apologize here. So maybe get your head out of your ass and give me a chance to explain!"

The bounty hunter narrowed his eyes, sniffed and glanced briefly at the tunnel that led from the back of the motel to the front parking lot. "If you're lyin' to my face again, Charlie, don't think I won't find out."

"I know you will." The mohawked dwarf clenched his fists, folded his arms, and stepped away. "You always do."

"Uh-huh. So tell me why this time is any different than the others, huh? Why does this apology mean somethin'?"

"Because I'm trying this time!" Charlie's rough shout echoed around the junk-filled lot. The pile of rubble beside them shifted and triggered a cascade of empty bottles and chips of asphalt that slid down the sides. Pebbles rolled toward the dwarves' boots, and Johnny glared at the huge mound in disgust before he shook his head.

"You now have two minutes, 'coz."

The biker dwarf sighed. "Okay, listen. I don't even care about the phone."

"No shit. You tried to give me a new face with it."

"That's not what I mean." With another heavy sigh, the mohawked dwarf took a step back and raised both hands in supplication. "I didn't get to answer your question before. About the last time I used the phone."

"Oh, so now it's my fault you can't manage to say the right thing at the right time."

"No, listen. I got the phone six months ago, okay?"

"Uh-huh. And what kinda untraceable calls are you fixin' to make?"

Charlie narrowed his eyes. "You don't have to ask me that."

"Uh-huh. And how many of 'em did you make?"

"None, Johnny. Zero. I…thought about it but I didn't. I haven't used the phone even once. You can check that too."

"Oh, yeah? I can check a phone lyin' in pieces on the motel room floor?"

"We both know you'd find a way to put it back together if you wanted to."

"That's beside the point." Johnny glanced meaningfully at his watch and shrugged. "Six minutes, Charlie. You got an extra one in there and now, your time's up."

He turned and walked toward the building and his cousin lurched after him.

"Hold on a second."

"I said five minutes."

"And you spent five minutes not even listening to me." The biker dwarf darted in front of him and grasped his arm. "Hear me out."

He looked down at the hand on his arm and drew a slow breath. "Hands off."

"Oh, come on. I didn't even try to fight back when you clocked me in the face."

"And I didn't even try to make it hurt." He jerked his arm away and stormed past his cousin again. "We're done."

"What do you want me to do, Johnny, huh?" Charlie shouted.

"Do you want me to take a drug test? Fine. Do you want me to go up to that room and lay it all out for Lisa? Be completely honest with her? Put all my cards on the table so you can burn them all and call it even?"

The bounty hunter whirled to face him again with a snarl. "This ain't about gettin' even! Dammit, Charlie. We ain't never gonna be even! How long is it gonna take you to get that through your thick-ass head?"

His cousin stepped back and shook his head quickly. "Forever. Probably."

"Damn straight. So go do it on your own time, not mine."

"So that's it? Hey, I'm willing to do all these things, Johnny. Whatever you want, I'll do it, but give me a chance."

"After all the other chances you've blown?" He sucked in a breath to calm himself, then pointed at the other dwarf. "I ain't got nothin' left, Charlie. Not for you. And I ain't gonna tell someone in your shoes to give it up and go blow the rest of your chances somewhere else but I ain't tryin' to stop you anymore. Understand?"

"Yeah. Yeah, I get it." When he tried to storm away, Charlie darted in front of him again. "Please, Johnny…just hear me out one more time, okay?"

"I have shit to do."

"Goddammit!" His cousin lunged forward to grasp his shoulders and snarled like a rabid dog.

Johnny blocked the attempt with his forearms, shoved Charlie's arms out to the side, and punched him in the jaw. "I said we're done!"

"The hell we are!" With another snarl, the mohawked dwarf leapt forward and his eyes flashed silver again before he barreled into him and tackled him to the asphalt.

They landed hard. The bounty hunter scrambled out from beneath his cousin and moved quickly to grasp him in a rear mount. Charlie snarled again, clapped his hands around Johnny's forearms, and sprang to his feet with more strength than a dwarf should have been able to muster with someone his size clinging to his back.

"What the—"

With a roar, he ducked and lurched forward to fling him over his shoulder.

The bounty hunter's back met the asphalt with a solid thump. The next thing he knew, his cousin had straddled his chest. One hand pressed against his throat while the other swung back to prepare for a solid blow to his face.

Suddenly, Charlie froze. Breathing heavily and with his fist still raised, the mohawked dwarf glared at his younger cousin and growled again. "I'm trying to be better, Johnny. That's fucking hard to do if you won't let me."

He coughed beneath the pressure around his throat but didn't raise a hand to stop his cousin. Instead, he sneered at him and held his gaze. "You ain't my responsibility."

"I know that."

"Then show me you have what it takes on your own, dammit!" He coughed again and the hand loosened around his throat a little. "It's your choice, Charlie."

"What the hell are you talking about?"

"Go ahead. Beat the livin' shit outta me to make your point. Now's your chance."

The shifter dwarf's eyes flashed with silver light again and another snarl escaped him as he leaned closer to his cousin's face. "I could kill you."

"Sure. It won't be as easy as killin' yourself one damn fix at a time, though. But I ain't gonna stop you." Johnny glanced at his cousin's raised fist, which was completely white now and trembled. His head felt like it was about to pop off his bruised neck and careen across the lot.

If I ain't right, I'm spendin' my last few minutes lyin' on my back behind the worst motel on the planet.

"Go on," he rasped and tried to swallow. "Show me what you have. Now's your chance."

With another low snarl, Charlie whipped his hand away from his cousin's throat and rolled away.

The bounty hunter wasted no time. He lurched off the asphalt and punched the other dwarf in the face again before a fit of wracking coughs overtook him.

"Jesus!" The shifter dwarf fell onto his side with a grunt, rolled onto his back, and clapped a hand to his nose. "I didn't even—"

"That was—" Johnny coughed and sucked in searing breaths as he sat fully and shook his head. "That was for takin' so damn long."

"Shit." Charlie groaned and pulled his hand away. Blood pooled in his palm, ran from between his fingers, and spilled down his nose and mouth to drip onto his riding leathers. "You had to break my nose for it?"

"It ain't the first time." He rubbed his throat gingerly and Johnny looked at his bloodstained face and smirked. "Do you want me to set it for ya?"

"Hell no. You'll screw it up."

"Even more than it is? Naw."

They regarded one another in silence before Charlie laughed. "Exactly like old times, right?"

"I sure as hell hope not. It's the first time you pinned me down like that since I was half your size."

The mohawked dwarf grinned through a mouthful of blood. "One of the perks of being made a shifter against my will."

"Uh-huh."

Charlie spat a bloody glob onto the asphalt and flicked even more blood off his hand. "Listen, Johnny. I'm serious about this. However you want me to prove it, I'll prove it."

"Naw. You already did." Johnny stood and offered his cousin a hand.

More blood spattered the crumbled asphalt but the shifter dwarf stared at him as if he hadn't been on the receiving end of his right hook. "What?"

"If you could get me on my back and choose to not give me a makeover, I think you have some kinda willpower goin' for ya."

"Willpower."

"Yeah. Put that to use everywhere else and you might be headin' down the right path." He scrutinized his cousin from head to toe and snorted. "You look like shit."

"You know, I heard somewhere that's part of the process."

"Uh-huh. Lemme ask you one thing."

Charlie spat on the ground again and glanced at his blood-stained leathers. "What?"

"Are you truly serious?"

"I just said—"

"I mean how long has it been?"

The biker dwarf frowned in surprise and shrugged. "Almost six months. Right after I bought the other phone."

"The phone you kept on you to call all the wrong folks but never used."

"Right. You know, as a…" His face assumed another bloody grin. "A kinda safety net, I guess."

"Uh-huh. It's a good thing you crushed it, then." Johnny thumped his cousin on the shoulder before he strode through the alley to the motel stairs. "Come on. I know a half-Light Elf who has a way with patchin' up most anythin' that bleeds."

"I'm good, Johnny. Shifter healing, remember?"

The bounty hunter chuckled. "Suit yourself. If you're fixin' to have that nose set crooked all on its own."

Charlie swiped under his nose, which still bled although not as freely. "Shit. Yeah, okay. Wait up."

CHAPTER FOURTEEN

When the knock came on the motel room door, Lisa looked up from the book she'd been trying to read on her tablet.

"It's us, darlin'," Johnny called. "We could use a little help if you have a minute."

"Uh-uh." Luther sniffed the air madly and trotted toward the door. "Hey, I think he's dying."

"What?" She tossed her tablet onto the bed and stood.

"Yeah, there's a whole ton of blood," Rex added, his ears pressed flat against his head.

"Johnny!" Luther uttered a bloodcurdling howl. "Johnny, don't go toward the light!"

"Yeah, but if you do, we'll bring you back!"

"Y'all hush up. There ain't no one dyin' out here."

Lisa unlocked the door and jerked it open. She stood in silence and stared at the two beaten and bruised Walker dwarves, one of them covered in blood. "Oh, my God. What happened?"

Johnny shrugged. "We had a talk."

"Yeah, with your fists." She stepped aside to let them both in. "Seriously, this is how you settle your differences? By beating each other to a bloody pulp?"

"Hey, he's the bloody one." The bounty hunter pointed at his cousin as Lisa shut the door again.

"It was a lucky shot," Charlie muttered, his voice clogged and thick through his grin. "The neck's gonna bruise like crazy, though."

"As far as I know, a broken nose doesn't bruise your neck." Lisa headed toward the shifter dwarf as he sat on the closest bed. "But I'm surprised the rest of your face isn't already purple."

Charlie laughed and shook his head.

"What? What's so funny?"

Johnny grunted and rubbed his throat again. "He's talkin' about me."

"Your neck? Johnny, what did you do?"

"It ain't what I did, darlin'. It's what my shifter-powered cousin can do now."

"Come on, 'coz. Like you didn't expect us to be better matched by now?"

"We ain't matched in nothin'. Don't you forget it."

With wide eyes, Lisa hurried into the bathroom for extra towels and when she emerged, she tossed a stack of them at Charlie. "You know what? I don't care what you two had to do to each other as long as it's over." She placed her hands on her hips and looked from one to the other, her expression one of warning. "It is over. Right?"

"That's up to him." Johnny nodded at his cousin. "For now, that's what it looks like."

"As soon as I can…uh, get my nose fixed."

"You didn't set it?" She spun toward her partner. "You broke his nose and didn't help him put it back?"

He raised both hands. "I ain't a doctor, darlin'."

"Neither am I."

Charlie poked gingerly at his nose. "Seriously, though. I don't want my face to put itself together all crooked. I'm very sure that's about to happen so…"

"Lisa?" Johnny raised his eyebrows and gestured toward his blood-smeared cousin. "Do ya mind?"

"Oh, for the love of—" She stalked toward Charlie and caught him completely off guard when she raised both hands quickly to his nose and jerked the crushed bones into place. He barely had time to shout in pain and surprise before her hands illuminated with golden light and she suffused his face none too gently with a healing spell.

The force of it knocked him back onto the mattress and he lay there in a daze and stared at the ceiling with his mouth gaping open.

The hotel room fell silent for a moment before Johnny burst out laughing.

"Whoa…" The shifter dwarf's bloody grin slid across his face again as he pressed his nose tentatively. "Holy shit."

Lisa pointed at him. "Next time, I won't bother with the extra healing."

"Hey, don't worry." Laughing, Charlie pushed into a seated position on the edge of the bed and wrinkled his nose repeatedly. "There won't be a next time."

"Good answer."

Johnny slapped his knee and continued to wheeze with laughter.

"Uh…Johnny?" Luther snuck toward his master and crouched lower to the carpet with every step. "Hey. Are you okay?"

"He's lost it, bro." Rex snorted. "All his brains. I bet the other guy knocked 'em all out down there."

"Johnny, you want us to go get your brains for you?"

Lisa folded her arms and stared at her partner, although she couldn't help a small smile. "I'm glad to see you're enjoying yourself."

"Don't take it—" He laughed again before he straightened with a deep breath and wiped a tear from the corner of his eye.

"Don't take it the wrong way, darlin'. I'm simply… Whew. I'm enjoyin' the irony."

"Oh, yeah?" Charlie finished wiping his face with the towels before he flung them into a bloody pile on the floor. "This feels ironic to you?"

"I have a right to keep that to myself." With a broad grin, the bounty hunter pointed at the bloody towels. "Get rid of these, though, huh? It looks like we're livin' in a crime scene."

"You mean the kind that would get you two arrested for aggravated assault?" Lisa looked at each of them in turn. "Does anyone feel like telling me what all this is about?"

"Not really." The shifter dwarf leapt off the bed and stooped to collect the towels. "Do you think management would have an issue with me burning these out back?"

"Don't you dare."

"I'm kidding." He grinned, turned to walk backward with the pile of bloody towels in his arms, and nodded. "I'm kidding, Lisa. I'll make sure they don't find out."

"Charlie—"

"Let him go, darlin'." Johnny stepped toward her and placed a hand on her shoulder as his cousin slipped through the door. "He'll take care of it."

"And add arson to the list."

"Are you still a fed?"

She rolled her eyes. "That has nothing to do with it."

He chuckled and led her to the closest twin-sized bed. "Come here. Come on. Sit with me for a minute."

After glaring at the door for a moment longer, Lisa sighed and finally moved to join him. "I guess it could be worse, right?"

"Oh, yeah?"

"It could've been two dead dwarves behind the motel instead of one covered in blood and the other who sounds like he swallowed a shovelful of sand."

Johnny snorted and rubbed his throat. "I'll be all right."

"Please tell me you two weren't trying to kill each other."

"Well…it might have started out that way."

"Johnny—"

"But it turned out fine, darlin'." He scratched the side of his head and sighed. "We're all right."

"Uh-huh. And I take it you didn't particularly like whatever your cousin had to say."

"Only 'cause it wasn't anythin' I ain't heard from him before over and over again. But…hell, he might be fixin' to shape up this time." He looked at her and shrugged. "My cousin has a long history with getting' hooked on the wrong vices."

"Hmm. Is it something that runs in the family?"

"Not like this." He glanced at the adjoining door between their rooms, but Charlie still hadn't returned from wherever he'd gone to dispose of the bloody evidence. "It seems he's six months into turnin' his life around. I'm not sure if he can call it recovery, exactly, but at least it's somethin'."

"Recovery?" Lisa looked startled. "You mean all this is about…" She lowered her voice. "Johnny, you could have simply told me that from the beginning. Here I was thinking he'd killed someone or…I don't know, robbed a string of banks or something. Or you."

"Well, he's done that too, believe you me." The bounty hunter ran his hand through his hair and paused when his partner fixed him with a look of disbelief and shock. "Not the bank part, darlin'. Only the robbin'."

"And?" She leaned closer. "He didn't kill someone, did he?"

"What? No. Not as far as I know, anyhow."

"Oh, jeez."

"Look, that ain't my business. He knows I'd kick his ass into the next decade if he got himself into that kinda trouble."

"Which you don't think he did."

"No. Mostly, although the guy does ride cross-country like he's runnin' from somethin'. Then again, it's as likely that it's merely old habits dyin' hard."

Lisa sighed and shook her head. "Okay. Well, if you think we can trust him, we'll trust him."

"Sure. As long as he doesn't give us any more reason not to." Johnny coughed again and rubbed his throat. "Man. I think he's right about all the bruisin'. He damn near crushed my windpipe."

She leaned away from him with a playful frown. "And you let him?"

"Now what kinda question is that, huh?"

"I'm only saying that Johnny Walker doesn't usually let anyone get close enough to crush much of anything."

"Yeah, well, tell that to the bastards who turned my cousin into half a shifter thirty years ago."

They sat in silence on the bed for another moment before she took his hand. "I'm glad you guys worked it out. Hopefully, you won't have to keep fighting each other while we're trying to finish this case."

"He ain't comin' with us for the rest of it. It sounds doable enough to me."

"Okay, good. So I guess our next move is the gala, then."

"Yep."

"I heard Nevada City has some fairly decent shopping. Otherwise, we might have to wait until Thursday and head to San Francisco a little earlier than—"

"Shoppin'?" Johnny snorted. "We have a shifter kidnapped by Kaiser, two of his buddies holed up in the room next to ours, my damn cousin out there tryin' to prove he's turnin' around, and shoppin's at the top of your list?"

"For the gala, Johnny." Lisa raised an eyebrow. "Neither of us will get into the Harford estate again looking like we did the first time we arrived."

"Aw, hell." He rolled his eyes. "Is this gonna be like the Monster's Ball all over again?"

"I'd say probably even a little more on the formal side. Will that be an issue for you?"

Johnny scrutinized her from head to toe with a broad grin on his face. "Not if you're wearin' the same kinda dress."

With a laugh, she shoved him away from her and stood to retrieve her tablet from the other mattress.

"What? You can't blame a guy for sayin' what's on his mind."

"Well, I have to get a new dress anyway."

"Why? 'Cause you already wore it once? I didn't take you for the kinda woman who can't stand the same outfit two years in a row."

"Johnny, the dress I wore at the Monster's Ball is in a dump somewhere by now."

"You threw it away?"

"You sound insulted."

"Darlin', if I wore suits on the regular, I'd have kept the one I was wearin' on our first real bust together."

She laughed and sat on the other bed to type on her tablet. "That was before you even recognized the fact that you had a partner."

"Well, sure. But a fella can be a little sentimental, can't he?"

"I have to get a new dress."

"No, you wanna get a new dress."

"It's both, to be honest. And I don't see why you're making such a big deal out of it."

"I liked that other dress."

She rolled her eyes, put the tablet in her lap, and met his gaze. "Well, thank you. But I'm very sure the gatekeepers at this gala won't have the same sentimental opinion."

"Who cares what anyone else thinks? I would have had someone ship it to us—"

"Johnny, the dress I wore that night was slashed by a knife and covered in plaster. I think the edge of it might even have been singed by…oh, I don't know. A few explosions."

The bounty hunter stared at his partner and cleared his throat. "Right. Go ahead and look for a place where I can get a new suit while you're at it."

"I'm already on it."

CHAPTER FIFTEEN

After three more days of staying in the motel, Johnny didn't think he'd make it another hour without a real body being left out back. He and Lisa had been able to leave more often than Charlie, Galfrey, and Jake to continuously stock up on groceries they couldn't put in the motel mini-fridges that didn't exist. They also walked the hounds up and down the shoulder of the highway when they got too rowdy. Despite these moments of freedom, Thursday couldn't come soon enough.

When the morning finally arrived, the two partners hurried to the rental. He made sure to bring his utility belt equipped with exploding disks and a few other goodies he'd packed for their trip to California.

I thought we'd be outta here a helluva lot sooner than this but we ain't even worked out half of what we need to know.

Charlie hurried down the stairs as the hounds bounded down on either side of him.

"Johnny! Hey, Johnny! Wait up!"

"Yeah, aren't you forgetting something?"

Rex and Luther sat at their master's feet and stared at him, their tails thumping against the asphalt.

The bounty hunter took one look at them and sniffed. "Nope."

"Wait, what?"

"He's playing hard to get, bro."

Luther's tongue flopped out of his mouth as he panted. "Okay, fine. I'll give you a hint. It's us, Johnny. You're forgetting us."

"Nope." Johnny nodded at his cousin as Charlie joined them in the parking lot. "I can't say when exactly we'll be back. It might even be tomorrow mornin' if this goes real late."

"Sure. No problem. The same old thing is going on around here, right?"

"Yep. Except you'll be keepin' an eye on the hounds for me too."

Luther whined. "What?"

Rex gasped. "Johnny—"

"Sorry, boys." Lisa placed her purse on the floor of the front passenger seat, then turned to scratch the hounds behind the ears. Neither one of them paid her any attention. "This is not a canine-friendly event, remember?"

"Yes, but that doesn't apply to us."

"It applies to everyone with four paws who can't turn into somethin' resemblin' a person on two legs," Johnny corrected.

Rex crouched closer to the asphalt and backed away. "Aw, man…"

"Wait. Hold on." Charlie chuckled nervously and looked warily at the hounds before he settled a slightly panicked gaze on his cousin. "You want me to watch two shifters on lockdown and two coonhounds while you guys go have fun at a fancy party?"

"Maybe in not so many words," the bounty hunter replied, "but yeah. That's the gist of it."

"Johnny, I can't babysit everyone at the same time."

"You can if you wanna stay in on this. And you will." He clapped the shifter dwarf on the back and gave him a little shake. "Don't make me regret it."

"I'm not trying to. Believe me. But it's… I mean…"

"You don't think you can hold your own here without your little cousin to help clean up?"

Charlie snorted. "No. But you could at least give a guy a little incentive."

"How about I let you stay in the rooms I paid for, huh? Is that incentive enough?"

"Oh, come on. Fifteen-year-old girls watching a toddler for four hours get paid more than that." Charlie followed him around the front of the SUV and held the driver's door open while Johnny slipped behind the wheel. "You gotta give me something, 'coz."

He shook his head. "There's a hundred bucks on the bed—and no, you can't sleep in our room. I'll give you another hundred when we get back if you ain't burned the place down by then."

"Two hundred."

With a snort, he jerked the door out of his cousin's hand. "How about fifty?"

The car door slammed shut, but when Charlie continued to rap urgently on the window, Johnny had no choice but to start the engine and roll the window down to get him to stop. "What?"

"Another hundred's fine, Johnny."

"Great."

"You know what would be an even better deal, though?"

He rolled his eyes and slumped against the back of the seat. Lisa chuckled as she closed her door and buckled up. "You're gonna tell me whether I wanna know or not."

"You guys went and put that money down as a deposit at Kaiser's farm, right?"

"Dammit, Charlie."

"No, no. Hey. Not for me. I'm only saying if you need anyone to move all that—"

"Ask me again and I'll make sure that nose of yours heals sideways and stays that way for the rest of your life."

The shifter dwarf frowned and retreated a few steps. "It's already healed."

"It won't be if I knock it sideways again." Johnny snapped his fingers and pointed at the hounds, who milled around Charlie's feet and sniffed dubiously at their new temporary caretaker. "Y'all make sure he stays outta trouble—and those two upstairs. Understand?"

"Yeah, yeah. We got it, Johnny." Luther sat on the sidewalk and chuffed. "Doesn't mean we have to like it."

"Yeah, how come we have to stay behind every time you two-legs go out and do something fun, huh?"

Charlie sniggered. "I thought I was supposed to keep an eye on them."

"You keep thinkin' that."

Johnny rolled the window up but the hounds' voices still rang clearly in his and Lisa's minds.

"You keep an eye on us, all right," Luther said as he sniffed Charlie's riding boots.

"Yeah, watch us real close," Rex added. "Otherwise, you'll never see us coming. One wrong move, shifter dwarf. That's all it takes."

Charlie laughed and folded his arms.

The bounty hunter pulled away from the sidewalk, turned the SUV, and headed quickly onto the frontage road.

Lisa glanced at him and drummed her fingers on her armrest. "I know you don't like leaving them behind."

"Are you kiddin'? After bein' cooped up in that dump for the last few days without a second of quiet all to myself?" He ended the statement with a bitter laugh and shook his head. "I've been fixin' to get rid of the whole shebang since we stepped into that room for the first time."

"Fair enough." She brushed her hair away from her face and closed her eyes. "I'm merely looking forward to a shower I don't have to share with four grown men every twenty-four hours."

He thumped a hand onto the steering wheel and looked at her. "Sharin' what with who now?"

"The shower."

"You been showerin' all on your lonesome, darlin', and takin' damn fast ones, too."

"Johnny." She pulled her aviator sunglasses out of her purse, slipped them on, and stared at him through the darkened lenses. "The shower in our motel room smells like the swamp."

"And?"

"And we've shared a single shower between the five of us during the last few days. I think I've earned a nice long one all to myself where I don't have to imagine whatever was left behind by the last four magicals to use it before me."

"Oh, yeah? And where were you plannin' to get that luxurious shower? The Harford estate?"

She laughed. "I booked us a room at the Ritz-Carlton."

"You did what now?"

"We need a place to get ready and maybe even to stay the night if the gala runs late like you said. And I need at least thirty minutes under hot water that doesn't feel like it's been heated by one of those faulty coffeemakers."

"Huh." He sniffed, adjusted his grasp on the steering wheel, and glanced at her purse. "That's a first."

"What is?"

"Usually, I'm the one bookin' rooms and accommodations."

She smirked. "You still are. I put the reservation in your name."

"'Course you did."

"Of course I did."

For Johnny, the two-and-a-half-hour drive to San Francisco from Yuba City was the fastest part of their afternoon. They spent two hours shopping for acceptable gala attire, another hour and a half for lunch at a swanky seafood restaurant—not including the half-hour wait to be seated—and another three hours in the hotel room. One of those he spent stretched on the bed, flipping through channels on the TV while Lisa spent a full sixty minutes in the shower. Eventually, he had to check on her and earned a quick reprimand for his trouble.

"I said a shower to myself, Johnny. Is that too much to ask?"

"You've already been in there twice as long as you said, darlin'."

"And we still have more than enough time. I'll be out when I'm finished."

"You, uh…" He stepped farther into the steam-filled bathroom and tried to sneak a glance around the edge of the shower curtain. "Do you need anyone to—"

The wet washcloth that smacked against his face was all the answer he needed.

"Christ." He tossed the soggy cloth into the sink and wiped hot water and a thin spray of soap off his mustache.

"Privacy, Johnny."

"Yeah, I heard you loud and clear." With a grunt, he hurried out of the bathroom. "It's like we're startin' all over again."

Before he shut the door, her stifled laughter followed him out and brought a smirk to his lips.

The water turned off soon after that but she spent another hour in the bathroom with the door slightly open and the roar of the installed blow dryer turning on and off every ten minutes.

After the fifth time, he finally gave up on trying to find anything on TV and tossed the remote beside him on the king-sized mattress. "Did that shower make you grow a whole other head o' hair in there or what?"

"I'm almost finished. And you're being way too impatient."

"I'm merely tryin' to decide what all the damn fuss is about. That's all."

"The fuss?" The hair dryer clicked into its cradle on the bathroom wall, followed by the light spritz of either hairspray or perfume.

The hounds would be able to tell me if they were here.

"We're going to a ridiculously expensive event as ourselves, Johnny." The bathroom door squeaked a little as it opened. "No, we don't exactly have to try to disguise ourselves to look like we fit in with New York's finest crime lords, but this is still a little important, don't you think?"

"Sure." Johnny shifted on the bed to face her. "But it ain't like we gotta—"

Lisa stood with her arms wide and the pastel-green gown cascaded down her body to her feet. She'd done her hair in the same loose coils as the first time he'd seen her dress for an occasion even remotely like this one, and the thin silver-drop earrings dangling from her ears winked under the room's bright lighting.

She inclined her head and chuckled. "Okay, what's that saying? Something about your mouth not being a birdhouse?"

Johnny shut his mouth with an audible click and cleared his throat. "All right. I take it back. You go on fussin' as much as you like."

"Oh, now it makes sense."

"Well, when you won't let me open the door to talk to ya, how am I supposed to know what you're getting' up to in there?"

"I'm not getting up to anything." She tried and failed to hide a smile as she crossed to the shoebox on the small table on the other side of the room and pointed at the garment bag hanging on a hook beside the closet. "But you should probably open that and start getting ready yourself. What have you been doing in here this whole time?"

"Waitin' for you." He chuckled as he stood from the bed and strode toward her. "I think I been waitin' for you my whole life, darlin.'"

She turned and flashed him a dazzling grin. "You're laying it on thick."

"Well, when you look like that…" He shrugged

"It's almost time to go." She snatched the hanger with his suit off the hook and pushed it into his arms. "So I suggest you start fussing over yourself."

"Uh-huh." Johnny took the suit, hung it over the armchair, then slid an arm around her waist and pulled her close. "I think there'll be even more fussin' over you at that estate. Do you think you can still take care of yourself when all those west-coast high-society types start throwin' out their ridiculous offers hopin' you don't refuse?"

She laughed, took his face in both hands, and planted a quick kiss on his lips. "We're not going for offers, remember?"

"Hell, I know that—"

"And yes, I can still take care of myself although I like having you around sometimes. Especially if you put that suit on so we can get out of here."

"Oh, I get it. It's a nice way to pressure a guy into takin' his clothes off."

She laughed and wriggled out of his grasp. "Get changed. I don't want to miss out on the hors d'oeuvres because you decided to keep fussing."

"Or we could simply stay here, order room service, and have a party with only the two of us. What d'ya say?"

Lisa took one of her silver satin shoes from the box and pointed it at him, stiletto heel first. "Remember what I did with the last pair of heels like this I wore for a fancy soiree with you?"

Johnny exaggerated a gulp and backed away as he raised both hands. "Easy now, darlin'. That's as dangerous as a gun in the wrong hands."

She sat to strap the shoes on as she smirked and shook her head. "Put the suit on, Johnny."

CHAPTER SIXTEEN

Trying to drive into Sausalito on a Thursday night for one of the San Francisco Bay Area's most anticipated events of the year would have been an exercise in severe frustration. To avoid this, they took a cab from the Ritz-Carlton and reached the front gates of the Harford estate at 8:12 pm.

"We aren't too late," Lisa said cheerfully as she handed the cab driver a ten-dollar tip. "Fashionably late has its perks."

"It looks like we're right on time." Johnny thanked the cabbie again and slid out first to open the door for his partner.

The cab accelerated away as soon as they were out and wove through the somewhat heavy traffic on the road that ran past the home of the Harford family and this evening's venue. Most of the other vehicles dropping their high-society passengers were town cars or Lexuses with private drivers or limousines.

"At least we ain't payin' for a valet," the dwarf muttered as they followed the thick but rapidly moving crowd toward the estate's huge wrought iron front gates.

"After the cost of getting a seat for this?" Lisa smirked at him. "A valet would have been a drop in the bucket."

"Oh, sure. Do you think we should have hired one of those stretch limos for only the two of us?"

"No one will know we took a cab and no one cares."

"That's what I thought."

Light conversation and laughter filled the front area of the estate where the top society business moguls, charity founders, and old-money representatives of California—all dressed in their finest attire at the end of the summer—had gathered to wait. The line ahead of them paused briefly at the entrance to the gates and a group of Jasper Harford's security team—more shifters in dark suits with walkie-talkie watches—marked the foundation's "donating participants" present on the guest list.

"At least we ain't gotta steal a golden ticket from another damn thief for this one," Johnny muttered.

"Oh, come on." Lisa elbowed him subtly in the arm. "This is so much better than having to steal and lie our way into a fancy event."

"Uh-huh. You ain't the one coughin' up for so-called donations."

"I wasn't the one who enjoyed blasting a supply warehouse to smithereens to get our hands on the Monster's Ball ticket either." She adjusted her hold on her silver handbag and studied him boldly from the corner of her eye. "But I like this suit on you better than the last one."

He spread his arms somewhat sheepishly and glanced down at himself. "It's white."

"Off-white. You look like you fit right in."

"I look like I'm tryin' to play a Jasper Harford knock-off." The dwarf snorted. "Look at this. All the fellas playin' the same game in suits that look like they've been dipped in milk."

"Until Labor Day, Johnny, white's the way to go. I told you that when we chose your suit."

"It feels like a reverse funeral."

Her peal of laughter made several of the estate's guests in

front of them turn to cast her approving glances and gracious smiles.

Johnny wiped his mouth with the back of his hand and tried to hook his thumbs through his belt loops. It took a moment to recall that his belt was blocked from his immediate reach by the tails of his dinner jacket that were slightly longer than he was accustomed to.

I ain't accustomed to wearin' nothin' over my damn clothes.

He shoved his hands into the pockets of his slacks instead.

When they reached the guards stationed at the gate, the bounty hunter cracked a crooked smile and nodded at the shifter who held an incredibly thin tablet onto which the guest list had been uploaded. "Hercules. How ya doin'?"

"I'm fine, sir. Thank you." The shifter glanced at him and his eyes widened slightly when he noticed Lisa in her flowing pastel gown. "Name?"

"What?" Johnny snorted and glanced over his shoulder. "Come on. We were here only last week."

Hercules looked unamused. "Mr. Harford has an extensive guest list. It's my job to make sure everyone's on it tonight."

"You—do you honestly think we'd try swindlin' our way into this place simply 'cause we had ourselves a two-hour chat with the man a couple of days ago?"

The corner of the shifter's mouth quirked in slight amusement but he simply repeated, "Name?"

He's enjoyin' the hell outta bein' the literal gatekeeper, ain't he?

"Johnny Walker," Lisa answered and smiled sweetly.

The guard scrolled through the guest list and took his sweet time looking for their name. Finally, he nodded and his smile widened. "It's good to see you folks here. You've been seated at the Tiger Table tonight."

Johnny cleared his throat and searched the front of the estate grounds behind the gate, where small pockets of guests milled casually toward the front entrance of the house. "The what now?"

"The tables will be marked once you enter the ballroom." The shifter grinned. "You two enjoy yourselves tonight."

"Thank you, Hercules." Lisa nodded and stepped past the guard to head up the perfectly paved road across the grounds.

"Now lemme get this straight." Johnny pointed at the guard. "It's only been named the Tiger Table, yeah? It ain't a table for tigers."

His partner rolled her eyes, caught hold of his hand, and hauled him after her so the guests behind them could gain entry. "Are you serious right now?"

"I'm seriously wonderin' why the hell anyone would name their tables after critters that don't even live on this continent. What happened to plain old numbers?"

"They probably wanted to spice things up a little." She finally released his hand and shrugged. "Numbers can be boring."

"Not the kind bein' shelled out tonight."

"Stop." She swatted his shoulder playfully with her handbag, then swiped aside a loose curl hanging from the pile of them pinned on top of her head. "Can't you relax and try to enjoy yourself? We're not here to stake the place out."

"The hell we ain't. We're searchin' under every pocketbook and five-thousand-dollar pair o' leather shoes we find."

After smiling at one of the other tall, impeccably dressed women who met her gaze and nodded at her in greeting, Lisa leaned toward her partner and lowered her voice. "None of these guests are criminals, Johnny. This isn't the Monster's Ball and it's not a front for illegal activity. It's a charity gala for California's high school districts. The kids."

"Uh-huh. And there ain't a kid in sight."

She looked at him in exasperation and couldn't help but laugh. "You're the one who thought this was the next best thing after Kaiser's farm was a dead end. At least pretend to be happy we're here. You know, for a good cause and everything."

"Yeah."

The bounty hunter pressed his hands even deeper into his pockets and scrutinized the other guests. The river of California's elite in all their finery flowed swiftly down the road toward the massive house that was Jasper Harford's home.

I had a better time of it showin' up as my own damn self with my partner and two coonhounds for a private chat. I ain't one of these folks. They are all judgy and condescendin', thinkin' they're better than the rest of us who don't wear our money on our goddamn sleeves.

"Oh, my God." Lisa clutched his arm and her eyes widened. "Johnny. Is that who I think it is?"

"Where?" He looked around quickly but didn't see a single hair or button or sequin out of place. "Who are you talkin' about, darlin'?"

"Right there. Eleven o'clock—the front pagoda."

He squinted in that direction.

Half a dozen men and three women stood around a tall, trimly built man who wore a white dress suit almost identical to his, only this particular guest had chosen to complete the ensemble with white leather loafers instead of brown ones like his. The other difference was a white fedora cocked jauntily to one side on his head.

"Do you mean the guy tryin' to steal my suit?" Johnny muttered.

"He's not trying to steal your—" Lisa eyed her partner's outfit, then looked quickly at the man across the grounds who wore it with a very different style. "Oh, wow. It goes to show I have incredible taste in men's suits."

The bounty hunter snorted. "Well, I now feel like a moron."

"Seriously? You do realize how many men here are wearing white suits, right?"

"You said it was off-white."

She laughed again and lifted a hand quickly to her mouth. "Johnny, forget the suit. You know who that is, right?"

"A fella who looks a helluva lot better in that outfit than I do."

"Stop. You couldn't have pulled a fedora off anyway."

"Is that a challenge, darlin'?"

Lisa grinned at him and shook her head. "I don't think so. And you truly don't recognize him?"

"Nope."

A staff member carrying a tray of champagne flutes walked slowly around the front lawn, offered drinks, and smiled at all the guests. Lisa hurried toward him and tried to keep her footing on the grass in four-inch stilettos as she lifted her handbag subtly to catch his attention. "Excuse me. Hi."

"Champagne, ma'am?"

"I…yes. Thank you." She took the flute he offered her but didn't raise it to her lips. "I hope you can help me out here—that gentleman in the white suit at the pagoda."

"Mr. Delarou. Yes."

A surprised laugh burst from her lips. "So it is him?"

"Yes, ma'am."

"Thank you. That's all I needed to know."

"Enjoy your evening." The server turned toward another group of guests that wandered leisurely toward the front of the house and nodded. "Champagne?"

Johnny finally caught up to his partner and stood beside her as she stared at the group of guests beside the pagoda. "Do you wanna share why you're goin' all goo-goo-eyed over some fella in a white suit who ain't the one you showed up with?"

Lisa frowned teasingly at him. "I'm not goo-goo-eyed."

"Uh-huh. Keep tellin' yourself that."

"I was right." She tried to sneak another glance at the man and broke into a self-conscious grin. "That's Hank Delarou."

"Is that supposed to mean somethin'?"

"The Hollywood movie star Hank Delarou."

"Puttin' 'movie star' in front of someone's name doesn't change the name, darlin'."

She scoffed. "Johnny, he starred in three major action movies that all came out this year."

"Good for him."

"You seriously have no clue, do you?"

The dwarf shrugged, his hands still in his pockets. "Tell me why I have a reason to watch action movies when I'm livin' one every damn day."

"You'd have to live under a rock to not know who Hank Delarou is. Or the middle of nowhere in the Everglades, I guess."

"Without a TV," he agreed.

She ignored his gruffness and flashed a smile at the other guests who passed them en route to the house. "I had no idea Jasper Harford had friends in Hollywood."

"How much do you think all these folks are truly here for the kids, huh?"

"You know, if you don't want to be here tonight, feel free to go back to the hotel. I intend to enjoy myself either way."

Johnny scrutinized her with disapproval and his mustache bristled above his twitching lip. "Now see, that's exactly the kinda thing you say to a guy to get him to stick around—"

"Oh, my God. Johnny. He's coming toward us."

"Huh?"

Lisa knocked back the entire flute of champagne in one swallow and thrust the empty flute into his hands before she swiped aside the curls dangling beside her face. She shook her head a moment later and turned toward him. "Don't look and act natural."

"Are you talkin' to me or yourself?"

Her eyes widened severely in a silent warning and he glanced at the empty champagne flute with a raised eyebrow.

"No, you go on ahead," the deep voice said from close by. "I'll meet you inside. It's good to see you, Thomas."

With a chuckle, the movie star waved at the other guests who filtered away from him before he approached the two partners in the center of the lawn.

He cleared his throat. "Excuse me."

Lisa whirled toward him and grinned. "Oh. Hello."

Johnny snorted.

"I hope I'm not interrupting."

"Well, you are."

She bumped his ankle with hers, the movement thinly veiled by the flowing skirt of her dress. "Not at all. We were merely… standing here. Talking."

Great. Now I gotta deal with her bein' all starstruck for a guy wearin' my suit with a dumbass hat.

The man chuckled and turned toward Johnny. "This is a little awkward for me, I must say. Usually, I'm the one in your shoes."

Johnny looked at the man's shiny white loafers and raised an eyebrow. "Not tonight."

"Ha. No. It's a little refreshing, to be honest. And I have to ask…" He stepped closer and flashed him a quick, dazzling grin full of perfectly white, perfectly straight teeth set in a chiseled jaw. "You're Johnny Walker, right?"

"Huh?"

"What?" Lisa whispered.

"Dwarf the Bounty Hunter?" Hank laughed nervously. "Stop me if I've completely missed the mark, but I could've sworn you're—"

"That's me." He darted Lisa a sidelong glance and used every ounce of willpower he had to not burst out laughing before he extended his hand toward the movie star. "In the flesh."

"Hank Delarou." They shook and the man stroked his hairless chin and stared at him in disbelief. "I'm a huge fan of the show. That was an excellent return season last year—extremely good stuff. You had the whole world reliving old times."

"I hope not."

Hank burst out laughing. "It's great to meet you, Johnny. Can I call you Johnny?"

"I wouldn't respond to anythin' else." The dwarf looked at Lisa, who stared with wide eyes at the movie star and her mouth open in an "O" of surprise. "This is my partner, Lisa Breyer."

"Oh, I'm sorry. Yes. Lisa. Nice to meet you." The movie star extended a hand toward her and she placed hers in his for a somewhat distracted and incredibly brief shake.

"Nice to…"

When she didn't say anything else, Hank nodded at Johnny again and studied him curiously. "Nice suit. If I'd known I'd arrive here dressed like Johnny Walker, I would have chosen something else. I hope you don't hold it against me."

"Long as you return the favor, sure."

"Ha. Well, okay." The man glanced at his shoes and nodded. "Brown. I knew I should have gone with brown. Hey, enjoy your night, huh? Maybe we'll have a chance to talk again after the opening ceremony."

"I'm sure you know where to find me."

Hank laughed again and tipped his fedora. "Ms. Breyer. Johnny."

He left, walked across the lawn toward the front of the house, and raised a hand in greeting at each of the other guests he recognized. When he glanced over his shoulder with a wide grin, Lisa gasped and clutched Johnny's arm again.

"Oh, my God."

"Uh-huh."

"Oh, my God, he knows who you are."

"We already established that, darlin'."

"And he…oh, my God."

The dwarf patted the back of her hand gently where it dug into his arm and chuckled. "Are you gonna be all right? Or should we go back to the hotel so you can process the whole thing?"

"What?" When she realized he was laughing at her, she swatted him playfully with her handbag.

"You sure can handle yourself, darlin'. Hundred percent."

"Stop it."

He pried her fingers gently from the sleeve of his suit jacket and settled her hand on his forearm instead. "In case you've forgotten, there are two seats at the Tiger Table waitin' for us. Do you need me to carry you inside?"

"Feel free to shut up anytime, Johnny."

"You bet." With smirks on both their faces, they joined the other gala guests who drifted toward the entrance. "I might end up enjoyin' myself tonight after all."

"Oh, now?"

"Sure. As long as you can still keep your eyes off Mr. Movie Star and peeled for anythin' outta the ordinary."

"I'll be fine, Johnny." As they reached the bottom of the wide, curved stairs leading to the front doors, she snatched another champagne flute from the event staff stationed there and drained half of it.

Johnny watched her with a crooked smile.

Lisa didn't look at him when she muttered, "Don't say a word."

CHAPTER SEVENTEEN

The ballroom inside the Harford estate was truly a sight to behold. White curtains had been bunched and draped elegantly between each of the narrow windows that stretched from floor to ceiling around the room.

Matching satin ribbon decorated the wall sconces and hung tastefully from the three chandeliers that dangled from the ceiling. The tablecloths on every large round table were a slightly darker shade of off-white, with floating candles in glass bowls of water and the places already set and ready for dinner to be served.

A four-string quartet played in the far left-hand corner of the ballroom and took the full focus in front of the side of the stage erected for the speeches.

I'll be bored outta my damn mind halfway through the first one.

"This is incredible," Lisa whispered. "Imagine the time it must have taken to turn this into an event venue. Oh, look at that."

Along the right-hand wall beside the open bar was a table decorated with tastefully framed photos of eighty-seven teens. Below each was a short biography of each student who'd received that year's Bright Minds award—a full-ride scholarship to the college of their choice, courtesy of the Harford Foundation.

"Now that's boastin'," the bounty hunter muttered.

"Of course it is." She laughed. "Sending that many students to whatever college they want? That's a huge accomplishment."

"And you're tellin' me this gala ain't bein' held to put all those kids on display?"

"Johnny, that table there is the definition of a display. You know what? I bet those kids are honored to have received the scholarship."

"Sure. And they should be rewarded for all the hard work they put into their schoolin'. But I don't see any of 'em here."

"It's a charity fundraiser for this year's graduates."

"Uh-huh."

Lisa glanced at him with a frown and shook her head. "Why does all this rub you the wrong way?"

"It ain't all this that's botherin' me." Johnny sniffed and narrowed his eyes as he scrutinized the rest of the opulently decorated ballroom. "I'm tryin' to decide where the hell this damn Tiger Table's supposed to be."

"Okay…well, do you want to ask someone?"

He stared at her with a deadpan expression and she laughed.

"Fine. We'll simply look for it like everyone else."

"But first, I'm headin' to the bar. It's not like these folks here are likely to have what I'm drinkin' but it's worth a shot."

"Johnny—"

"You already put away two glasses of champagne, darlin'. Give a fella a chance to catch up, huh?"

They moved to the open bar and to his surprise, the shifter who mixed cocktails and uncorked bottles of wine did have a bottle of Johnny Walker Black—unopened.

The dwarf squinted at the bartender and rapped his knuckles on the portable bar. "Now tell me this. What's a swanky getup like this doin' with a bottle of that whiskey? And don't think I ain't seen you crackin' the seal. No one else is drinkin' it."

The bartender smirked. "It's for you, Mr. Walker."

"Hell, I could've told you that." Johnny snorted. "I did when I ordered it."

"My apologies for the confusion. This specific bottle was ordered and stocked at the bar tonight at Mr. Harford's request—for you alone."

"Oh." He cleared his throat and glanced at Lisa. "And how the hell did he know what I'd be drinkin' tonight?"

"Johnny, let it go and take the drink," she muttered.

"No, that's all right." The bartender poured two fingers of whiskey into a rocks glass and when Johnny nodded curtly at him, he added another two. "Mr. Harford makes it a point to provide all his esteemed guests with their preferred drinks. Call it an extra step in hospitality, if you will. And I assume the lovely woman with you tonight is Ms. Lisa Breyer, yes?"

She grinned at him. "That's a good guess."

"It ain't a guess, darlin'." Johnny sipped tentatively at his whiskey, then set it down and leaned slightly forward over the bar to squint at the shifter again. "They've been vettin' us."

"Of course." Without missing a beat, the man picked up a bottle of Hendrix gin and began to make Lisa's drink. "Extra lime, Ms. Breyer?"

"Um…" A surprised laugh escaped her. "Sure. Thank you."

"My pleasure."

Johnny didn't stop mean-mugging the bartender. "How much do y'all get paid to memorize every damn name on this list and what your boss says is the best drink to oil their gears?"

The shifter chuckled. "I imagine that would be considerably more than the current compensation." He placed Lisa's double gin and tonic on the bar and nodded. "But this is merely one of a few exclusive…benefits. The special guests at the Tiger, Snake, and Badger tables are the only ones for whom we have received special orders for tonight."

"Huh. Do all the tables have critters on 'em?"

"Yes, sir."

"Naw, cut it out with the 'sir' business."

Lisa sipped her drink, then cleared her throat. "And where exactly is the Tiger Table tonight?"

The bartender gestured toward the far end of the ballroom. "Do you see those three tables closest to the stage? You'll find the Tiger on the farthest to the right."

"Wow. That close."

"Yes, ma'am. And if you need anything else tonight, ask for Ray. That's me."

"Thank you, Ray."

Johnny rapped his knuckles on the bar again. "Yeah. Thanks, Ray."

"Absolutely. Enjoy your evening." With a perfectly hospitable smile, the bartender turned to greet the next guest waiting for their drink.

The partners moved toward their table and the bounty hunter scowled the whole time.

"We seem to be getting the VIP treatment tonight," Lisa commented.

"Uh-huh. And I take it back. The whole thing's rubbin' me the wrong way."

"Johnny, they have your drink. They know exactly what we wanted. What's not to like?"

"All of it. Jasper Harford went pryin' and I don't trust a party where I ain't gotta ask for a damn thing myself."

"What?" Lisa smiled at the other guests milling around them and brought her straw to her lips again for another sip. "When we were here last week, Jasper already knew exactly who we were and what we did. How is this any different?"

"It ain't a private chat, darlin'. When you're sittin' one-on-one with a guy, you get a read on exactly what he wants while he's lookin' you in the eye. You can't get a read on any of these high-falutin' money types."

"Well, it's not like the entire guest list knows what you drink." She clicked her tongue as they skirted a pocket of guests who had paused to chat and finally approached their assigned table. "And if they did, would that truly be such a big deal?"

"It's a breach of privacy."

"It's a drink."

They stopped beside the table, where only one other guest was currently seated. The man was in his late fifties or early sixties and wore an off-white dinner vest. His white bowtie with purple polka dots provided the only color in his attire. He looked at them with a wide smile. "Tiger Table?"

Lisa glanced at a stylized tiger's head embroidered on the white tablecloth and centered between the bowls of floating candles. "That's us."

"Then please, take a seat."

The bounty hunter narrowed his eyes and glanced around the ballroom as he pulled a chair out for his partner.

"Thank you." She sat, he grunted, and the conversation continued without him as he scanned the other guests' faces.

All I did was buy two damn tickets over the phone with my credit card. How does that put us at the special-guest table? There's no way our little chat with ol' Jasper last week left the kinda impression that warrants all this.

"Johnny? Johnny."

"Huh?"

"Mr. Abernathy was asking us what we do."

"Oh, please," the man said quickly as he stretched his hand across the table toward Johnny. "Call me Peter."

"Johnny." The dwarf finally shook the man's hand before he sat.

"I'd love to hear all about it," Peter said jovially. "What line of work are you in?"

"Private interrogation," he muttered, distracted by all the other smiling, talking, laughing guests in their gala finery.

Peter chuckled and turned to Lisa with a curious frown. "I'm sorry."

"Private investigations," she clarified and knocked her leg against her partner's beneath the table. "We run a private firm."

"Ah. How exciting. So you take personal cases from private clients, then?" The man sipped his martini and widened his eyes. "Unfaithful partners, blackmailing, tracking suspicious activity, that kind of thing?"

Lisa laughed. "No. I'm sure other firms take on cases like that, but we're more on a… Hmm. How exactly would you describe the kind of cases we take, Johnny?"

The bounty hunter grunted. "We used to work with the feds—or for the feds, in her case."

"Oh." The man exaggerated a wide-eyed look of surprise and raised one shoulder in a half-hearted shrug. "And law enforcement doesn't take issue with your firm working criminal cases?"

"They didn't when we used to take criminal cases." Lisa tried to both smile at the man and shoot Johnny quick warning glances, but he wasn't paying any attention. "Now, it's more private. Family disputes sometimes or unexplained kidnappings the local police might not have the time or the manpower for. That kind of thing."

"We had a hound as a client once," the dwarf muttered.

Peter almost choked on his martini and leaned forward. "I'm sorry?"

"A Blue Heeler named Boots."

Lisa laughed. "That was an unusual case, to say the least."

"I'll say."

"What do you do, Peter?"

"Oh, I'm retired now. Finally." The man scratched his wrinkled cheek and grinned. "My son took over running the family business a little over a year ago."

"Abernathy…" Johnny finally looked at him for the first time and cocked his head. "As in Abernathy Luxury?"

"Ha! It seems my name precedes me. Are you a fan?"

"Sure. Lisa and I were enjoyin' one of your finest a few weeks ago."

"Is that so?" Peter chuckled. "I hope you're happy with her."

Lisa choked on her next sip of gin and tonic and tried to cover it with a confused smile.

"I tell you what." Johnny smirked and raised his whiskey glass toward the man. "After a few minor upgrades, she's the best I ever stepped foot on."

"Upgrades?" This time, the man looked truly surprised. "Well, if I'd known any of our finest were in need of a few upgrades, I'd have taken a look at it myself."

"Merely the personal kind, you understand." He glanced at his partner and nodded. "But she's keepin' us happy."

"I'm sorry." Lisa set her drink down. "I think I missed something. Who, exactly, are you talking about?"

Peter threw his head back and roared with laughter. "Who are we—ha! Oh, that's good."

After another sip of his whiskey, Johnny leaned toward his partner and said, "Good ol' Pete here built our houseboat, darlin'."

"Built the—" She stared at him for a moment. "Okay."

"No, no, I didn't build it personally, of course." Peter pulled a white handkerchief from the breast pocket of his vest and dabbed his eyes as his laughter died down into sporadic chuckles. "But if it was manufactured before last May, there's a good chance I oversaw the production at some point."

"Trust me." The bounty hunter grinned. "That beauty restin' in her Miami slip was brand-new when we got her. Top-of-the-line."

And completely paid for by the FBI.

"Then you have yourself an excellent model, Johnny." Their table companion shook out his handkerchief, folded it, and chuckled again as he slid it into his pocket. "Although it must have lacked amenities somehow. I'd love to pick your brain about what exactly needed upgrading."

"There's a big difference between needin' and wantin', Pete."

"Ha! Don't I know it."

As the men jumped into a conversation about yachts and houseboats and engine parts, Lisa leaned back in her chair and sipped her drink.

If Johnny's not put off by us being at a table with the man who built the houseboat he blackmailed out of the FBI, then neither am I. It's merely a normal, high-society coincidence at a charity gala, that's it. That had better be it.

CHAPTER EIGHTEEN

Half an hour and one more trip to the bar later, a man took the stage. The two partners hadn't seen him before, but he was as impeccably dressed as the other guests and appeared to be about the same age as Jasper Harford. He grinned from ear to ear as he took his place behind the podium and the four-string quartet finished their last piece with a flourish.

"Good evening." He cleared his throat and leaned closer to the microphone. "Can everyone hear me all right? Yes? Excellent. Welcome, ladies and gentlemen, to this year's Bright Minds Charity Gala. My name is Collin Haverlin and I suppose I'm now something of a Master of Ceremonies for tonight's entertainment. I know you've been looking forward to this event for at least the last year. Maybe longer if you happened to miss last year's for whatever reason."

A round of laughter filtered politely through the ballroom. Johnny frowned and glanced at all the smiling faces.

How's that so damn funny?

"Before we begin, I'd like to extend a warm welcome to each and every one of you who have made it your focus and priority to be here tonight. I thank you. Jasper Harford thanks you, and…

Well, I suppose he'll get to that in a moment." More laughter and a lone whistle filled the air, and the man waved the noise down again, grinned, and nodded emphatically.

"Yes, yes," he continued. "Everyone loves Jasper. Most importantly, though, I know the hundreds of bright young minds who received last year's scholarship awards thank you very deeply as well. For most of them, their dreams are now becoming a reality thanks to your generous contributions and, of course, your faith in them. Your faith in what the Harford Foundation has set out to achieve."

Polite applause followed and a stream of event servers filtered through the ballroom, their arms laden with massive trays of plated meals as they moved toward the individual tables.

"Now," Collin said briskly and tugged briefly on his tie before he patted the lapel of his dinner jacket, "as we've done every year and will continue to do for as long as he'll humor us, I'll call the man of the hour up. Without further ado, ladies and gentlemen, I give you Jasper Harford."

The ballroom exploded with much more enthusiastic applause, scattered whistles, and a few hoots and shouts of encouragement as the MC stepped away from the podium and gestured toward the side of the stage.

Lisa raised her chin for a better view, although there wasn't much of a need for that from their vantage point at the Tiger Table so close to the stage. "Look at him," she muttered and leaned toward her partner. "He doesn't even look like the same man we spoke to last week."

"Sure he does." He rolled his shoulders back and tugged at the end of one white jacket sleeve. "He looks like a man who ain't comfortable gettin' all dressed up for a party in his own home."

She nudged him with her elbow and clapped with the rest of the guests as Jasper took the stage and shook Collin's hand. The men patted each other on the back and shared a private joke between them before Collin stepped down and Jasper moved to the podium.

"Well. Since everything's already been said…"

More laughter filled the room.

Johnny snorted and sipped his half-empty second glass of whiskey. "It ain't comedy hour."

"Your meal, sir."

He turned and grinned at a huge plate of steaming, blackened catfish that was placed in front of him. "Well, look at that. Do you have a southern cook in the kitchens?"

"Armand has studied with the best chefs in every region of the world," the server replied.

"Huh. Good for Armand. I'll hafta let him know what I think."

"I'm sure he'd be happy to receive your compliments, sir."

"Not before I taste it first."

The server moved around the table to place meals in front of the other guests. Lisa's eyes widened when a Cornish hen in a honey-truffle glaze settled in front of her. "Wow. And they scored another homerun on the meals."

"Okay, okay," Jasper said on the stage. "I blame Collin for the timing, here. Yes, our fabulous chef Armond Cantaroun has kicked off tonight's affair with impeccable style and taste, as always. I won't keep you any longer than necessary, so try to not completely tune me out while you eat."

The guests at the back of the ballroom who hadn't yet received their meals clapped and laughed.

Johnny took a mouthful of his catfish and almost choked.

"Are you okay?" Lisa asked.

"Yep." He swallowed and stared at his plate. "Don't say a word to Darlene about them servin' me catfish out here in Cali."

"Why? Is it that bad?"

"She sure as hell would think so." After he'd swallowed the rest of his whiskey, he took another mouthful. "It's better than hers."

She stifled a laugh and divided her focus between the meal in front of her and what Jasper Harford was saying behind the podium.

"As much as I'd like to take credit for all the incredible work being done day in and day out at the Harford Foundation," the man continued, "I must admit that I'm not fully responsible for the outcome, neither of the ongoing operations of the foundation nor tonight's event. We have a most remarkable team working for us—*with* us—and I would like to extend my sincerest gratitude to every staff member and invaluable addition to this foundation, both those who are here with us tonight and those who couldn't make it."

The clink of silverware on plates joined the next round of polite applause.

"And Collin, of course." Jasper gestured toward the other man, who'd now taken a seat at the table closest to the four-string quartet. "How long have I put up with you, Collin?"

"Not nearly as long as I've put up with you." The guests close enough to hear the response off-microphone chuckled and threw out a few cheers. "Thirty years, give or take."

"Thirty years," Jasper said into the mic for everyone to hear. "Give or take. That's more time than we deserve and yet this foundation wouldn't be what it is today without Collin Haverlin to oversee as much of it as he does."

When Jasper started a round of applause, the entire ballroom of guests followed suit. Collin blushed at the table and waved it all off.

Lisa leaned toward Johnny and kept her gaze on Collin. "Did we know Jasper had a partner in all this?"

"He might not be his partner," he mumbled through a mouthful of catfish. "Watch and see. I reckon the man will start thankin' his butler now too. Who says ol' Jeffrey couldn't use a little appreciation now and then?"

"What?"

"It's a good thing they brought the food out, darlin'. Otherwise, I'd be outta this chair and huntin' around the place merely to keep death-by-boredom at bay."

Lisa chuckled as the woman seated on her other side glanced caustically at him. "I'm so glad you're enjoying yourself," she muttered.

"It's the best damn catfish I ever had. This Armand fella knows his stuff."

She returned her attention to the stage.

That's why we're here, right? To enjoy ourselves as ourselves. If the only way he can do that is through his stomach, fine.

Jasper's laughter faded into a soft chuckle. He ran his hands along the edge of the podium as he looked out across the ballroom in his home now filled with so many guests, benefactors, and donors.

His smile faltered for a moment and he cleared his throat. "And there's someone else here I want to pay particular attention to tonight—someone who has stepped up for the occasion with unfathomable dedication and perseverance. A man who, by all accounts, has more than earned the right to stand here on this stage and address all of you, ladies and gentlemen. Even if it were not expected of him, I believe he would still be here today. That's the kind of man he is."

When Jasper paused, the entire ballroom settled into an expectant silence.

He shook his head quickly, sniffed, and gazed at the faces that stared at him. "Every year before now, you've listened to me hem and haw about this foundation and the Bright Minds awards. Your charity and devotion to this are, of course, most appreciated, and I cannot possibly thank you enough. Devotion is, naturally, what we also expect of the young minds who receive these annual awards—intelligent, dedicated, passionate, brilliant young men and women who exemplify everything we need to see so much more of in the world today. And so, it is with—" The man's voice broke and he chuckled self-consciously. "Excuse me."

Johnny finally looked up from his meal and frowned as he chewed. "Did I miss somethin'?"

"Not so far," Lisa muttered. "He's been trying to make an introduction this whole time. I think."

"Huh." Another glance around the ballroom showed the other guests looking as confused as he felt. Some of the women dabbed at the corners of their eyes with their white linen napkins as they gazed at the stage.

Jasper's chokin' everyone up, includin' himself. Who has that tight a hold over the face of old-school shifter charity?

Their host sighed into the microphone and summoned a smile. "It is with great honor and overwhelming pride, ladies and gentlemen, to share with you all a new pillar of strength within the Harford Foundation. As I'm sure many of you are aware, there has been some speculation recently as to the new direction this foundation will take in the years to come. None of us live forever, not even a Harford."

More laughter filled the room but it was subdued and hushed—almost hesitant.

No one was expectin' a speech like this one.

Johnny set his fork down and watched the reactions of the guests around them.

"Everything we look for within our award recipients are attributes I've seen in this man since the very beginning. And yes, while he is years removed from being a high-school graduate, I still see in him every Bright Minds recipient who has thrived and flourished with the help of your generosity and influence.

"This foundation would cease to exist as it is without him. I'm not sure there's much more I could say without boring you all to tears after this, so I'll simply wrap this up by introducing my successor at the Harford Foundation, who will step up as the face of our future as I step aside. My son, Bronson Harford."

The ballroom was intensely quiet for all of five seconds before a roar of applause and cheers split the air.

"Huh." Johnny studied some of the more surprised-looking guests and cocked his head. "That was a whole lotta buildup for somethin' folks could have correctly assumed all on their own."

"I'm very sure it's supposed to be symbolic," Lisa said as she clapped with the rest of them. "But here's our chance to finally see the man we've heard so much about."

"Not in this kinda settin'. Jasper said his boy rallied to set the whole event up this year. He didn't mention—"

"Pardon me, sir." Another server who'd snuck up behind Johnny placed a freshly poured glass of whiskey in front of him and removed the empty one swiftly. "Is there anything else I can get for you?"

"Nope." With wide eyes, the bounty hunter nodded at the man and picked his drink up. "Perfect timin'."

"Johnny." Lisa nudged him furtively and stared intently at the stage.

"Do you want another drink, darlin'? You know, if they're gonna refill mine and not yours, I'd say there's a problem with their—"

"Forget the drinks. Look."

He sipped his fresh whiskey and followed her wide-eyed gaze to the stage. Bronson Harford stood there with his father and mirrored Jasper's easygoing smile as the entire ballroom applauded the foundation's namesakes.

Why does he look so familiar?

"Thanks, Dad," the young shifter said loudly enough for the microphone to pick up as he grasped his father's hand. The older Harford pulled his son in for a tight hug and they both laughed.

"And now I'll turn it over to the real man of the hour," Jasper added before he left the stage.

"Wow." Bronson sighed. "That was certainly more praise than I expected, even from my father."

The guests all chuckled and a few cheers rose at the back of the ballroom.

"And I guess the cat's out of the bag now, so to speak. For some of you, it might be news that I'll take over in Jasper Harford's place—unofficially for now, of course. You all arrived at the perfect time to get the story before anyone else. I fully intend to carry on the legacy of this foundation in the same way it's been passed on to me…"

The young Harford continued his speech and Johnny squinted and leaned forward for a better look as he placed his whiskey glass slowly on the table again.

"You do see this," Lisa muttered. "Right?"

"Uh-huh. And I'm sure we've seen him before too."

"And we even saw his picture the last time we were here." She bit her bottom lip, her smile completely gone now as Bronson captured the entire room with his words. The two investigators, however, had completely stopped paying attention. "That's why we didn't recognize him."

"The kid cut all his hair off." Johnny leaned back in his chair and studied the way Bronson moved on the stage. He gestured occasionally toward someone seated in the closest row of tables and made a few well-mannered jokes suitable for the high-society audience that hung on his every word.

I wonder if Jasper knows his kid was at Kaiser's weed farm instead of off at his buddy's estate in the mountains.

CHAPTER NINETEEN

Bronson Harford's speech about the Harford Foundation, its legacy, and all the things they had planned for the future was eloquent and engaging, to say the very least. The guests' full attention was glued to his presence on the stage while their meals grew cold in front of them.

The kid has charm, I'll give him that. Johnny nursed his drink and scrutinized the young shifter's demeanor. *Even so soon after his girl was killed in a skirmish. Either he ain't as bent outta shape as we thought, or he's the cream of the lyin'-through-his-teeth crop.*

Lisa hadn't touched her food since they realized that Bronson Harford was one of the young shifters who'd been on Kaiser's farm during their first meeting with the natural-born shifter responsible for hundreds of transformed shifter deaths. She had, however, been brought a third gin and tonic, and she nursed it while Johnny sipped his drink slowly and distractedly.

"Now all that's out of the way," Bronson said and spread his arms expansively, "I want to thank you all again for being here tonight. We have some incredible music lined up for the night. And if you're interested in seeing how influential your contributions from last year have been, take a look at the recipients' table over here on my left—your right. These kids took it upon themselves to write an open letter to their gracious benefactors, and they're far better at expressing their gratitude than I am." He started to leave the stage, then stopped and leaned toward the mic. "Oh, and I know I don't have to remind you, but the bar's open all night. And whatever you do, don't leave before dessert."

A wild round of applause filled the ballroom and a grinning Bronson raised a hand in thanks before he hurried down the stairs off the stage to rejoin his father at their table.

The four-string quartet struck up another lively number as background music until the main act took the stage later, and Lisa stood quickly from her chair. She extended a hand toward her partner and plastered a smile on her face. "Johnny?"

"Yeah." He couldn't look away from the father-son duo laughing and talking to the thin trickle of guests who'd begun to make their appearances at the head table.

"It's time to mingle, don't you think?"

"Mingle. That what we're callin' it?"

"Oh, you're not leaving, are you?" Peter asked as he dabbed the corners of his mouth with a napkin. "You heard the man. No leaving before dessert."

"No, we're merely going to stretch our legs," Lisa said with a curt nod. "We'll be back. If we don't see you again, Peter, it was wonderful meeting you and sharing the Tiger Table."

The man chuckled and patted his full belly. "Likewise."

Johnny snatched his drink off the table and stood to join her in a slow stroll around the outer edge of the ballroom. The other guests now moved around more to talk, refill their glasses, or approach the recipient display table with the framed pictures of the lucky kids who'd received the Bright Minds awards.

"There's no way you had a hunch about this," Lisa murmured before she smiled sweetly at a couple in passing.

"Well, I had a hunch about somethin'," Johnny replied. "I didn't expect it to be Bronson Harford in the flesh."

"Except we met him as Carp."

"Yeah. I knew none of those shifters workin' for Kaiser were usin' their real names."

"Johnny." She placed a hand on his elbow and turned to face him. Despite her unease, she managed fairly well to look like nothing more than a guest enjoying herself at the gala. "This changes everything."

"I can't speak for that, darlin'."

He sipped his whiskey, then raised it when he noticed a group of guests standing around Hank Delarou. All of them watched him with brimming smiles and the actor laughed and raised his glass at him.

The bounty hunter turned to Lisa to resume his previous conversation. "Kaiser said all the young shifters at his farm were there for the grow work, right? So it might be that the worst thing Bronson's been involved in since Addison died is a little side gig at a pot farm where no one knows his name or who his daddy is."

"Sure. If he were anyone else." They wandered on through the crowd at the perimeter of the ballroom, nodded politely at other guests, and refused the next round of champagne carried through the room by multiple servers with drinks trays. "But to work for the guy responsible for her death? That doesn't make any sense."

"Does if the kid's tryin' to find out where things went wrong."

"Seriously? You think Bronson decided to go undercover one day and conduct the search for Addison's killer on his own? He's not a government agent or a bounty hunter with a reputation, Johnny. He's the son of a Gold Coast billionaire and doesn't have that kind of experience."

As they rounded the other side of the ballroom and circled toward the head table where the Harfords sat, Johnny nodded and cleared his throat. "I think he has more than enough experience."

Lisa turned to where Bronson stood a few yards away from

the table and shook hands with the guests, nodded, smiled, and accepted compliments and congratulations graciously.

"Look at him. Does that look like a guy grievin' his murdered fiancée?"

"No…" She frowned. "No, he looks like he's having the time of his life, to be honest."

"Uh-huh. The kid's been bred to sweep all his personal feelings under the rug and put on a good face for the high and mighty. If he can fool all these folks into thinkin' he wants to be here tonight—includin' his old man—I think he puts on a helluva show for Kaiser and the other shifters on that farm."

They watched the younger Harford for a moment longer before she tilted her head in thought. "Then again, there's still a chance that we've simply jumped to conclusions here."

"How's that?"

"Look at the way he's moving, Johnny. The kid who called himself Carp…that shifter looked like he was in a constant hurry. He apologized for the fact that he'd interrupted our tour, remember. Honestly, if we'd seen him interact with Kaiser any more than that, I bet Carp would have bent over backward to please his boss."

"That's what I'm sayin', darlin'. Bronson could give ol' Hank over there a run for his actin' money."

"Or maybe it's not the same shifter. Maybe they merely look freakishly alike and we're trying to force the pieces together anyway because we've grasped at straws through this entire case."

"Huh. Well, there's only one way to find out." He swallowed the rest of his drink and placed the glass on the mostly empty tray of a passing event server.

"What? Johnny—" Her partner either didn't hear or simply ignored her and moved purposefully toward Bronson. Lisa stood alone in a sea of California's elite and scowled at his back before she recollected where she was and schooled her features into something more appropriate. She sighed heavily, gulped what remained of her gin and tonic, and handed the empty glass to a server who seemed to materialize out of thin air. "Thank you."

She hurried after her partner as quickly as she could without losing her footing in the four-inch stiletto heels.

Bronson shook the hand of a massive man in a charcoal-gray suit and a matching bowler hat when Johnny reached him. "Thank you so much for coming, Mr. Greely. It's great to see you."

"Mr. Harford." The dwarf stepped forward when the other guest moved away and he plastered a crooked smile onto his face. "Or is that your old man? Go ahead and tell me right now and I'll call you Bronson instead. No harm done."

The young shifter locked gazes with him and his eyebrows twitched upward before a brilliant grin flashed across his face. "Well, I guess I'll have to get used to being called Mr. Harford sooner or later, right? Bronson works for now." He took Johnny's extended hand and didn't flinch when the dwarf tightened his grip a little more than was necessary. His smile widened when Lisa stepped beside her partner. "It's so good to see you here. I hope you've enjoyed yourselves. And yes, I promise all the speeches are over."

"This is all wonderful," Lisa said and was on the verge of giving the bounty hunter a hard nudge when he finally released the young shifter's hand. "You arranged a fantastic event tonight. Everything's perfect."

"Well, thank you very much." A small frown flicked across Bronson's forehead and his laugh was a perfect mixture of hospitable amusement and polite confusion. "I'm sorry. I didn't get your names."

"Johnny Walker." The dwarf placed a hand on the small of Lisa's back where the line of her dress was cut low a little above the waist. "And Lisa Breyer."

"And…" The young man chuckled again. "Forgive me. I've met

so many new faces tonight but yours seem incredibly familiar. Have we met before?"

Johnny smirked. "It's hard to say when you have so many folks movin' around your own house, right?"

"Right. Well again, thank you for coming."

"Hey, listen." Johnny stepped forward and lowered his head, which forced Bronson to lean closer so he could hear. "Is there any chance we could have a few minutes of your time? A private matter and all."

"Oh. I'm happy to discuss it with you here. Or you can call and make an appointment—"

"With Martha?" Johnny nodded and he noted the surprised look the younger Harford gave him when he realized that the dwarf already knew about his father's assistant. "Yeah, she's a gem all right. I bet she runs a tight ship on the phones. But listen. It won't be more than five minutes. Let us steal you aside, then we'll cut ya loose and get outta your hair, huh?"

Bronson glanced at the head table, where Jasper was engaged in an animated conversation with two elderly women who looked like they'd dressed in the most expensive wrapping paper on the planet. He nodded and turned to gesture toward one of the alcoves at the edge of the ballroom. "I'd be happy to give you a few minutes, Mr. Walker."

"Johnny. Just Johnny, nothin' more."

"Of course." With a smile, he led them to the most secluded area they were likely to find. "I'd invite you to step into my office but it's currently occupied by my father."

"Naw, we ain't fixin' to pull you away from your party." Amazingly, the din of so many conversations faded substantially in the recessed alcove beside one of the access doors that most likely led into the kitchens. "I'm sure someone would realize you were missin' sooner or later."

"Most likely, yeah." Still smiling, the young shifter smoothed the lapel of his suit jacket and nodded. "How can I help you?"

Johnny cleared his throat. "First of all, son, we wanted to say how sorry we were to hear about Addison."

The young shifter's smile faltered and he stopped scanning the ballroom to look him squarely in the eye. "Thank you."

"Three months ain't nearly long enough to move past that kinda loss."

"Which makes what you've done here tonight even more remarkable," Lisa added. She'd finally caught on to her partner's game but still tried to soften the blow.

If he pushes this kid too hard, we'll have a nightmare of a mess to sift through after this.

"I…" Bronson swallowed and his eyebrows drew together. "I appreciate that."

"Of course."

"Listen." The bounty hunter leaned closer. "We had a little talk with your old man the other day while chattin' over a cup of that Kopi Lewak of his."

"Ha." The shifter's smile widened but his eyes seemed particularly flat and lusterless now. "Dad and his coffee."

"That's right. It was when you were up in the mountains with your buddies. At least, that's what he told us. The conversation took a turn and of course, your fiancée came up. He said y'all didn't get much information from the police after that night."

Bronson pressed his lips together. "That's right."

"You were there, yeah?"

"I was. I'm sorry, Mr—I'm sorry, Johnny. I was under the impression you wanted to draw me aside for a business conversation."

"I did. This is merely a different kinda business." He stepped closer and turned partway to gesture toward the crowd of mingling guests. "Now I can't say any of these fine folks here have reason to take one look at you and think there's anythin' amiss. You're doin' a fine job with takin' things over. But I have some friends out in Sutter County who believe the night you and

Addison were caught up in one of them shifter skirmishes sparked more trouble than maybe you're aware of. Have you heard about any of that?"

The shifter glanced at Lisa. "I don't think—"

"We're not trying to pry," she added with a sympathetic smile. "And we are more than happy to make our contributions to the foundation tonight. We're merely wondered if there's anything you'd like to tell us about that night."

"I'm not sure what you mean."

"Yeah, your old man had the same look in his eye when we asked him too." Johnny clapped a hand on his shoulder and the young shifter looked at it without trying to shrug away. "The shifter callin' the shots that night—the one who sent out that gang of natural-borns to the docks who fired on the others caught up in the mess—goes by the name of Kaiser. Have you heard of him?"

The corners of Bronson's lips twitched into a weak smile, and he nodded when Johnny removed his hand. "My father and I have a very different understanding of what happens outside the foundation and this estate. He doesn't have a working knowledge of what other shifters are talking about. I do."

"All right. Then you know exactly what they're afraid of happenin' from here on out, aint'cha?"

"Mr. Walker." The young man straightened the front of his jacket again. "Now's not the best time to have this kind of conversation. I'm happy to meet you again another time and answer whatever questions you might have. Although unfortunately, I told the police everything I know about that night and even they didn't think it was enough to charge those criminals with Addison's death."

"Maybe the police didn't have all the facts."

Bronson swallowed but his smile morphed into its previous mask of carefree enjoyment. "Is there a reason you're trying to look into this?"

"Like we said," Lisa added, "we're looking out for some friends who don't have the same…means to get to the bottom of this situation."

"Situation? I'm sorry, Ms. Breyer. This is a charity gala, not an investigation. If you'll excuse me, I have a whole room of other guests to greet and thank for their time."

"Of course."

"And thanks for yours," Johnny said with a nod. "This is a great party you're throwin'."

"Enjoy the rest of your night. Excuse me." With a curt nod—although he didn't look at either of them again—Bronson tugged his jacket again and skirted the bounty hunter to move to another group of high-society benefactors who watched him from the closest table. "Senator Danroth. Thank you for coming. We didn't know if we'd see you here tonight…"

The partners turned to watch the younger Harford walk briskly away from them. "He's damn eloquent for a kid pushin' his grief aside."

"That was reckless," Lisa muttered.

"No, that was gettin' straight to the point." Johnny snorted and scanned the tables. "Did you see the way he tried not to twitch when Kaiser's name was mentioned?"

"Honestly, Johnny, I think starting the private chat with our condolences for his dead girlfriend probably set the mood for that one."

"Naw. He's been gettin' condolences and congratulations in spades tonight." He ran a hand through his hair and squinted into the crowd. "Bronson knows somethin'."

"Well, if nothing else, he certainly knows how to handle himself at a charity gala when Johnny Walker starts stepping on everyone's toes."

"I ain't stepped on nothin'. I told you from the start he was involved in this mess. Didn't I?"

"Just because he looked suspiciously put off by your mention of Kaiser in the wrong place at the wrong time does not mean Bronson has anything to do with those skirmishes, Addison's death, or whatever else is happening as a result of either of them. Not nearly enough to count as proof."

"Sure. But he knows more than he's lettin' on."

"Then we should call and set up a real appointment to speak to him, don't you think?"

The dwarf scratched the side of his face and turned slightly to face the head table where Jasper Harford still sat, laughing and talking with the slew of guests who stopped to sell hello, and nodded. "Or we could get real information from a guy who ain't tryin' to hide a thing."

"Johnny." Lisa rolled her eyes, hurried after him, and hastily summoned a smile to her face again to hide her irritation.

CHAPTER TWENTY

"I noticed no one's servin' coffee on a silver tray tonight."

Jasper looked up from his seat and laughed when he saw the bounty hunter. "Johnny! How good to see you. And Lisa. What a great surprise."

"Is it? 'Cause our names were on the list." With a crooked smile, the dwarf took the elder Harford's hand and gave it a genuinely friendly shake. "And in case you hadn't heard, someone told the bar to stock up on the only whiskey I drink."

"Ah, yes. I'm glad you noticed. Please, have a seat." The tycoon gestured toward the two open chairs beside him and nodded at the other guests who turned away to make room for his new visitors. "I did know you'd put your names on the list and added your contributions to the donations tonight—for which, of course, we are all incredibly grateful."

"I bet you are."

The man laughed again. "I merely didn't know whether or not you two would decide to attend. Honestly, I expected you'd be a little too busy to spend another night in Sausalito but I'm glad you managed to fit it in."

"It's a fantastic event," Lisa said as she sat beside Johnny. "Bronson did all this?"

"Absolutely. Like I said, he was adamant about pouring all his energy into this." The shifter's smile faded a little and he glanced at his fingers as they traced the outside of his drink. "To be perfectly honest, I'd expected a few other important people to make an appearance but we can't always depend on these things to turn out exactly as planned."

"Important folks, huh?" Johnny scooted his chair closer to the table. "Don't tell me y'all had the president on your guest list too."

"Ha. Important to Bronson, not necessarily the foundation."

"Like who?" Lisa asked.

Jasper took a large sip of his cocktail and sighed. "I'd heard my brother-in-law had paid his donation for tonight's event—Bronson's uncle."

Johnny snapped his fingers. "Langley, right?"

"Yes. I think Bronson truly believed the man would finally arrive when he said he would, but the disappointment there is nothing new."

Lisa looked up to see the younger Harford engaged in conversation with another group of guests, although his gaze flicked constantly toward his dad's table. "He doesn't look too terribly disappointed."

"No. He wouldn't." Jasper sighed. "He always puts a good show on for everyone else. That's part of why I wanted to postpone the gala but now that I see it in full swing… Well, it seems the night has taken some of the weight off his shoulders. For now, at least."

"You know, when we called the other day, you didn't mention you were plannin' to step down and hand over the reins."

Their host chuckled. "I made a promise to not say a word to anyone before tonight. And as much as I like you, Johnny, that promise did not include any exceptions."

"Naw, sure. I understand. It's a big night for y'all."

"Yes, it is."

"What about those buddies of his?"

The shifter looked quickly at him and widened his eyes. "I'm sorry?"

"The friends Bronson went to the mountains with last week. Are they here tonight?"

"Oh. No. Despite how much time my son spends with that group of young men, I don't think any of them are quite as enraptured by charity work as Bronson is. Don't get me wrong. They're all good kids."

"They'd have to be if they're friends with Bronson." Lisa smiled and forced herself not to look at the younger Harford again despite the fact that she sensed his gaze on them.

"That's kind of you to say."

"Is there any chance you could give us the names of those friends?"

Jasper smiled at him and seemed a little confused. "It seems an independent businessman's business is never finished, even at an event where business takes a back seat."

Johnny shrugged. "I thought I'd ask now while we had your ear for a few minutes. That time might be runnin' out fast with all the folks you have linin' up to have a word with you."

Harford leaned back to pull his phone from the pocket of his slacks. He tapped what appeared to be a message into the device and shook his head with a small smile. "I take it you two haven't yet found the answers you've been looking for since we spoke last."

"Almost." Lisa settled her handbag in her lap and glanced at his phone before he placed it on the table. "We only have a few more pieces to put together. Of course, we don't want to bother Bronson with any of that tonight but if we can speak to his friends, they might be able to give us something that helps."

"Of course. Oh, here he is. Thank you, Christian." Jasper

grasped the pen and pad of paper offered by one of the staff, who nodded and vanished quickly into the crowd again.

"Do you have employees readin' your mind, now?"

Jasper chuckled and tapped his phone with one hand as he scribbled on the pad with the other. "We have an estate-wide messaging system. I would have used the watch but it's a little loud in here to make any verbal message worth listening to." The pen clattered onto the table and he ripped the top sheet of paper off, held it out toward Johnny, and grinned. "There you are. Upstanding young shifters, all of them, I assure you. Oh, I'm sorry. Did you want their numbers? I can have someone fetch them from my study if you like."

"Naw." Johnny slid the paper into his pocket and extended his hand for another friendly shake with their host. "If the names aren't enough to help us find a couple of upstandin' citizens with nothin' to hide, Lisa and I are in the wrong line o' work."

"Ha. Indeed."

"We'll let you get back to partyin', Jasper. Congrats on the foundation and the transfer of power too, huh?" The shifter laughed and started to stand, but he put a hand on the man's shoulder and gave it a little pat. "Don't get up. Enjoy the night."

"You too. Oh, I highly recommend staying for dessert at the very least. You won't believe it."

"You bet." The bounty hunter pulled Lisa's chair back politely and helped her to her feet before he turned and settled her hand on his forearm again. "Now we have somethin' to work with."

"Very smooth, Johnny." She smirked and tucked her handbag under her arm. "You could have at least told me what you planned to weasel out of him."

"It ain't weaselin', darlin'. The guy was more than happy to give me what I asked for. Besides, I saw an openin' and had to take it." They skirted around a particularly large group of guests that laughed and chatted as they moved toward Jasper's table. "If we'd waited any longer, I'd have had to fight through the masses simply to get a word in edgewise."

"You're kidding, right?"

"'Course. No one gets away with fightin' at a charity."

She laughed and shook her head. "So what does one do during the rest of a charity gala after we've spoken privately to both Harfords?"

"One gets the hell outta Dodge." They'd almost reached the open double doors into the ballroom when another line of servers with laden trays approached the room. "I ain't stickin' around so Bronson can stare at us like we're the next charity case on his list. Ooh…hey. I'll take one of those."

He snatched a small plate of dessert from a passing server's tray. The staff member smiled and handed another to Lisa before he continued through the crowd.

She stared at the plate in her hand and looked slowly at her partner. "I won't eat cake with my hands."

"I wouldn't dream of it, darlin'." The bounty hunter stopped at the closest unoccupied table, glanced around, and pilfered two dessert forks from those that had been set while everyone was up and about. He brandished one at her and lowered his head in an awkwardly Johnny-ish mockery of proper etiquette. "Madam."

"That sounds very strange coming from you."

"Good. I ain't sayin' it again."

"Thanks for the fork."

They moved out of the ballroom and took their first mouthfuls. Johnny stopped dead in his tracks and grunted. "Dammit."

"What?"

"This Armand fella? The chef? Where the hell did he come from anyway, huh?"

"I…don't know." Lisa took another forkful. "But this is…"

"Yeah. I had better catfish out here than in my damn hometown and now, the dessert's makin' Darlene's bread puddin' taste like glue."

She snorted a laugh and covered her mouth with her free hand. "I promise I won't say a word."

"Yeah. She'd kill both of us."

———

After he'd waited patiently through the round of toasts that demanded his attention in the ballroom shortly before midnight, Bronson finally found a window of opportunity to get away for a stolen moment of peace and quiet. He moved down the hallway parallel to the ballroom toward the back of the house's first floor. Part of him hoped he'd encounter Johnny Walker trying to dig into even more of his private affairs and thinking he wouldn't be caught. But the bounty hunter, he knew, was smarter than that.

Not smart enough to keep his thoughts to himself at a charity event. Where the hell does he get off thinking it's okay to bring Addison up at something like this?

He'd seen the partners slip out of the ballroom a few hours earlier when dessert was served. According to Hercules, they had left the estate. Bronson had only heard a quick snippet of their conversation with his dad before he'd been caught up in another flurry of guests who demanded his attention with their congratulations and awful, stuffy jokes. The part he had heard didn't make him feel any better about the night—not that he'd felt amazing about the gala to begin with.

The young shifter loosened his tie and stepped through the exterior back door beside yet another entrance to the kitchen. Outside, in the cool, salty air beneath the stars, he felt like he could finally breathe again. Relief washed over him as he leaned back against the wall and gazed at the night sky.

None of this is what I wanted. Everything fell apart and now, I'm right back where I started, walking in dad's footsteps. You might as well call me a carbon copy of the man.

He jumped when his cell phone rang in his pocket and he pulled it out with a frown. It was his uncle Langley.

"Hey."

The older shifter's low chuckle came through the line. "It's not exactly the greeting I expected but I'm sure your night's been relatively taxing to say the least."

"It would have been a little easier if you'd bothered to attend like you said you would."

"Bronson…" His uncle sighed. "We've already discussed this. You know why I can't be there. At least not this year."

"So I have to wait another year for you to finally deliver on your promises?"

"I promised no such thing and you know it."

"Fine." Bronson scuffed the bottom of his shoe across the top of the manicured lawn and glanced around. "How's business?"

"The same as it always is."

"Okay. Is there a reason you called?"

"I merely wanted to check in on you. You were upset the last time we talked and I might have felt a little…responsible for parts of that."

"Right." *Oh, so now he feels bad about screwing everything up.* "I'm fine, Langley. Truly."

"Then I'll take you at your word." A long pause followed on the other end of the line before Langley cleared his throat. "I can't help but think something else is going on. Is there anything you'd like to discuss?"

"Yeah, there is." Bronson turned to scan the expanse of the back lawn that stretched in front of him. It wasn't nearly as brightly lit as the front where some of the guests had also stepped outside for fresh air, but he didn't generally need much light to see movement in the dark anyway. At least for now, he was as alone as he was likely to get tonight. "A few…interesting guests showed up tonight. They tried to grill me about Addison if you can believe it."

"Bronson, I'm sorry—"

"It's fine. I'm fine. The questions were nothing new for the most part. But I did overhear them talking to Dad too."

"Okay…"

"Yeah. And your name came up." Langley was silent for so long that the young shifter didn't know what to think. "Are you still there?"

"I'm here. Who were these guests?"

"A dwarf man and a Light Elf woman. He said his name was Johnny Walker."

"Hmm. Interesting. What did Jasper say?"

"Well, he gave them an earful about how disappointed I was to see you absent from another event. Again."

"Your father certainly has a way of painting prematurely colored pictures, doesn't he?"

"Except he wasn't wrong."

His uncle cleared his throat. "I understand that you're frustrated. That doesn't change how busy I am right now but I promise I'll make it up to you. Did the prying guests ask you about me directly?"

"No. They asked some very vague questions about…about Addison, though."

"And what did you tell them about her?"

Bronson gritted his teeth and scowled fiercely as he stared across the pristine lawn. "Nothing. I wasn't about to talk about my dead girlfriend with two gala guests I'd only just met."

"Okay. That's fine. It's good. Leave it at that for now, understand?"

"Leave it? Langley, I'm very sure these magicals attended my event simply to grill me—"

"You don't know that and you won't do anything out of turn. Am I clear?"

He sighed. "Yeah. You're clear. When will you be in town again?"

"I'll be gone another week. After that, I'm sure we'll have more time to sit and speak face to face again. You can come for the weekend if you like."

"Yeah, we'll see."

"Thank you for being so forthcoming with this information. It's unfortunate how forward people can get when they feel they have access to someone who's so successfully kept themselves out of the media over the last few months. Hang in there."

"I said I'm fine."

"I know you are. And if anything else gets out of hand, we'll deal with it then. Go enjoy your party, Bronson. You've earned it."

Langley ended the call and the young shifter sighed before he shoved his phone into his pocket.

I've earned it, huh? Dad wouldn't be nearly as happy if he knew what else I've been earning this whole time.

Bronson Harford took a moment to tighten his tie again before he jerked the back door open and steeled himself to mingle with their honored guests and foundation benefactors with a mask of hospitality and enjoyment. The night was almost over, he told himself grimly.

CHAPTER TWENTY-ONE

Johnny and Lisa decided to stay at the Ritz-Carlton in San Francisco that night after the gala and the next morning, treated themselves to breakfast via room service.

After she'd finished a stack of pancakes, two orders of bacon, and two glasses of orange juice, Lisa leaned against the pile of real, fluffy, and supportive—and clean—pillows and nursed her third cup of coffee. "Wow. There is nothing like almost an entire week in the worst motel on the planet to make you seriously appreciate room service and real food."

"I could take or leave the food, darlin'." Johnny refilled his cup from the massive French press sent with their meal. "I ain't gotta leave the damn room for a coffee. That's all I care about right now."

"Well, it's enough." She smirked, sipped more delicious, hot, fresh coffee that hadn't come from a broken coffeemaker or a jar of instant coffee-flavored powder, and retrieved her tablet from the bedside table. "Why don't you get that list? We'll do a little more digging before we return to Yuba City."

"The list of Bronson's buddies?"

She looked at him and tilted her head. "That's the only list of anything we have right now, right?"

"Course it is." Johnny dug through the pockets of his off-white dress slacks from the night before and found the crumpled piece of paper with three names written in Jasper Harford's neat, precise handwriting. "Very upstandin' citizens, he said. I think all these young shifters look fantastic on paper but maybe not so much off it."

"We're still not a hundred percent sure Bronson and Carp are the same guy."

"Uh-huh." He handed her the list and sat in the plush armchair beside the king-sized bed. "Like we weren't sure Bronson with long hair in the photo his old man kept in the hall and Bronson with short hair takin' over the family business in a public way were the same guy either."

"Well, if Bronson is Carp and we met him for the first time at Kaiser's farm… Honestly, I don't think I could blame the kid for wanting to break free of the mold, you know?"

"The do-gooder with all your family's money and sendin' a hundred-somethin' kids to college mold? How so?"

She raised an eyebrow at him and settled the tablet in her lap for a moment. "You saw how much pressure he was under last night. Jasper practically came undone introducing his son as the next face of the Harford Foundation, plus all those people in the same room. All that money and everyone wanting to talk to Harford the younger and congratulate him and offer their loyalty and respect and whatever else. And the whole time, he's expected to simply put on a good face and pretend that three months is long enough to mourn Addison's death and move on."

"It ain't like the kid was forced into it." Johnny frowned. "You heard Jasper, darlin'. He tried to get his kid to reconsider and hold things off a little longer. Bronson could've taken the offer but he chose to arrange one hell of a gala instead."

"Just because an offer's extended doesn't mean it's the right one to take."

"What is that supposed to mean?"

Lisa shrugged and picked her tablet up again to start looking up whatever she could find on Bronson's friends. "I'm merely saying that in Bronson's case, there's more riding on his ability to keep moving forward like nothing happened. Or, at least, he's more likely to feel that way."

"Sure. With great money comes great responsibility and all that."

She snorted. "That's not quite how the saying goes."

"Well, the kid ain't a superhero, is he? Take his daddy's money away and what does he have left?"

"Hmm. His dad, for one, and his uncle. As far as we know, that's the only family Bronson has left."

"Sure. One of 'em's straight-laced and as proper as can be, and the other's nothin' but a disappointment."

"And he has his friends. Corey Vandermeer, Adam Hoff, and Jeffrey Glennis."

"Four good ol' boys tryin' to be young natural-born shifters in a world that still ain't open to seein' their worth despite the reveal of magic." Johnny frowned across the room at the blank TV on the dresser and shifted his position in the armchair. "I bet Bronson's little stint at Kaiser's farm is his safe, secret little way of rebellin'."

"Seriously?" Lisa rolled her eyes. "Whatever gave you that impression? Assuming, of course, our gut instincts were right last night and Bronson and Carp are the same guy."

"Assumin' so. Yeah. Hopefully, we're about to find out real soon."

It only took Lisa half an hour to compile a more detailed list of Bronson Harford's three friends in a nutshell. All of them were upstanding California citizens exactly like their upstanding California-citizen parents—born into old money on the Gold Coast and graduates of Stanford like Bronson. The difference, however, was that they were much easier to find in a search through recent local media.

Corey Vandermeer lived closest to the hotel in Polk Gulch, so the Johnny Walker Investigations partners decided to pay him a visit first before they moved down the list to the other two.

At 10:00 am, Johnny pulled the rental SUV to a quick stop in the parking lot of Corey's apartment building. He turned the engine off, lowered his black sunglasses down the bridge of his nose, and gazed through the windshield at the incredibly tall building that towered in front of them. "It's a nice place for a twenty-somethin'-year-old shifter kid livin' on his own."

"That's what big family money does, right?" Lisa opened the passenger door and nodded for him to join her. "It must be nice to live in San Francisco and not have to work a day in your life if you don't feel like it."

"I'll take livin' in the swamp and not workin' any day of the week over this, darlin'."

"Oh, I know." They exited the vehicle, shut the doors, and headed to the building's front entrance. "But I'm very sure you didn't get anything handed to you on a silver platter."

"Neither of us did, darlin'. Don't make us any better or worse than these kids tryin' to find their way." When he opened the front door for her, she stopped and smiled curiously at him. "What?"

"You constantly surprise me."

"How's that?"

"When I expect some judgmental Johnny-ism, you pull out a nugget of wisdom that takes most people a lifetime to grasp even half an understanding of."

"Well, I ain't most folks." They stepped inside and moved to the elevator. "And you and I ain't exactly spring chickens."

She laughed and punched the call button. "Speak for yourself."

Corey's apartment was on the seventh floor and even the

hallway that led to the different doors—which were all spaced far enough apart to betray the size of each apartment behind them—was richly decorated with clean, fresh carpeting, intricate wall sconces, bright but delicate lighting, and long, well-polished end tables covered in potted plants and brochures for *Enjoying San Francisco the Way It Was Meant to Be Enjoyed.*

"Huh." Johnny took one of these from the basket and studied the contents briefly. "It looks more like somethin' you'd find in a hotel lobby, not apartments."

"I think some of these are time shares or at the very least, vacation apartments in the heart of the city."

"Why folks would come here from anywhere and pay too much to sit in a city on the edge of the ocean that ain't even warm in the summer is beyond me."

"Well, it's a good thing all the tourists haven't discovered how amazing the Everglades are yet."

He dropped the brochure into the basket before he turned and pointed at her with a warning glare. "Don't even go there."

They stopped in front of Corey's door and Lisa cleared her throat before she knocked briskly three times.

The bounty hunter grunted. "I think we oughtta break you of the habit, darlin'."

"What?"

"That knock. You still sound like a cop at the front door."

"Sorry, did you want me to drum out 'Shave and a Haircut' instead?"

"Huh?"

Two deadbolt locks turned and clicked one after the other before the door opened to reveal a young, handsome, grinning shifter in sweatpants and a polo t-shirt. When he saw Johnny and Lisa standing there, though, his smile faded. "Oh. Hi. Can I help you?"

"Corey Vandermeer?"

"Yeah. That's me."

"Johnny Walker Investigations." Lisa retrieved the flip-down badge that used to hold her federal ID and now held a photocopy of her Driver's License above an official-looking business logo Johnny had never seen. She flashed it quickly in front of the shifter's eyes before she pocketed it again. "Can we have a moment of your time?"

"Oh. Um…" The kid frowned and tilted his head as he studied the bounty hunter warily. "Yeah. Sure. Come on in."

"Thank you." Lisa stepped quickly through the doorway but Johnny stood in the hall for a moment longer with a scowl.

She's still knockin' like a cop and still flashin' a badge like a fed, even when it doesn't mean a thing. At least she can still fool a kid into thinkin' we're legit enough for a sit-down.

When he stepped inside and the door closed behind him, he gazed around with a low whistle. "It's some place you got here."

"Hey, thanks." Corey grinned and nodded as he studied his apartment. "I only moved in last month. My last place in North Beach had more square footage and a waterfront view but I couldn't stand the noise."

Johnny snorted. "Of the water?"

The shifter chuckled uncertainly and scratched his head. "It's the seals, honestly. I guess most people living in the city get used to them eventually like any of the other background noise. But they kept me awake all night, barking away. And there's nothing you can do about it."

"Uh-huh." The dwarf scrutinized him with a neutral expression. "Shifter hearin' and all that, right?"

Corey looked startled for a moment and his smile faded a little. "Yeah… Sorry, who did you say you work with again?"

"We work with each other." Johnny strode across the pristinely polished wooden floor toward the leather couches arranged in a square in the middle of the high-ceilinged living room. "Do you mind if we take a seat?"

"No. Of course. Please." The young man gestured toward the

couches, then smiled uneasily at Lisa before he led the way. "Can I ask what this is about?"

"We're a private investigative firm looking into the recent deaths of an unfortunately large number of shifters," she replied.

"Oh. Wow. Hey, can I get you guys anything to drink? Perrier? Flat water? It's bottled."

"No, thank you."

Corey sat stiffly on the couch opposite the investigative team and leaned forward over his thighs. "Which shifters are you talking about?"

"It's a long list, son." He shrugged and rubbed his mustache quickly. "But they're all what the shifter community's callin' transformed. Have you heard of this?"

"Yeah." The young man heaved a sigh and shook his head. "I never understood what the big deal is in the first place."

"And you know about the increase in faction skirmishes?" Lisa added. "Specifically the last three months?"

"The last three?" The young shifter's eyes widened before he closed them with a nod. "You mean since…"

"Since Addison Taylor was an unfortunate casualty in one of 'em." Johnny nodded. "We think there's a connection and are tryin' to find out what it is."

"Well, I hope you do." Corey rubbed his hands along the thighs of his sweatpants and shook his head. "This craziness has to stop somehow."

Lisa shifted forward to sit at the edge of the couch across from him. "If we can get the right information, we hope to help put a stop to it too. We heard you were there with Bronson Harford the night Addison was killed."

"Oh, man…" He scratched the back of his head, sighed, and looked at his visitors with a pained grimace. "Yeah. I was there. Me, Bronson, and two of our other friends."

"Adam Hoff and Jeffrey Glennis."

"Yeah. It was… It was supposed to be a happy night, you

know? Bronson was gonna propose. She had no idea what was coming and we were there to help him. Then, those assholes with guns arrived."

"A giant shifter with a huge beak callin' himself Veron?" he asked.

The kid looked entirely surprised to hear that nugget of information. "Yeah. How did you—"

"And a witch with red hair who looked like you could snap your fingers and break her in two?"

Corey looked warily from one to the other but didn't say anything.

Lisa drew a deep breath. "You know about the skirmishes, Corey. You were there for one of them and happened to make it out alive again with your friends—which, as I'm sure you know, doesn't happen frequently."

"We almost didn't."

"Fortunately, you all were very lucky—unlike Addison, I'm sorry to say."

"Me too." He frowned at the glass coffee table between them, then looked up quickly again. "You know we all gave our statements to the police that night, right?"

"We sure do." The bounty hunter folded his arms. "But I assume the police didn't say a thing about the shifter behind the attack, huh?"

"What?"

"A guy who calls himself Kaiser. The transformed who end up on the wrong side of his attack hound and shifter-huntin' witch don't get to see his face but what we wanna know from you is if you—"

"Wait a minute. Hold on." Corey straightened on the couch. His eyes widened again and he shook a finger at them. "I knew I'd seen you guys before. You were at The Resort."

"The what?"

"Yeah, that's right." Another wide smile broke through his

previously pained frown. "At the farm up north. You guys were there talking to Kaiser."

"Huh. Answer the question, then."

"Wait." Lisa briefly pressed the back of her hand against Johnny's arm and leaned forward. "I remember you too. You and two other young shifters stood outside one of the warehouses."

"Me, Jeff, and Adam, yeah." Corey laughed. "Small world, huh?"

"Not as small as you might think," the dwarf muttered as he frowned while he considered this information.

We've been blind to all these shifter kids livin' double lives as pot farmers instead of the trust-fund babies the rest of the world thinks they are.

"So you and your buddies work for Kaiser."

"What? No. Not really." Corey shook his head. "We only stopped by that day to check the place out. I'm very sure we left right after you did."

"Check the place out for what?" Lisa asked.

"You know." The young shifter shrugged. "The same reason you were there, probably."

"Y'all're fixin' to pitch in for fifty—" He grunted when his partner elbowed him in the side and cleared his throat. "Fixin' to get into the enterprise?"

"I'm not all that into it. Jeff, maybe. Adam couldn't care less, honestly. But Bronson's been thinking about...broadening his horizons, I guess."

"Bronson took y'all to a weed farm in the middle of nowhere run by Kaiser." Johnny tilted his head and studied the young shifter carefully. "The same Kaiser who unleashed his gang on the transformed on the docks and caught Addison Taylor in the process."

"Yeah, it's... Look, I know it's weird. But from what I've heard, Kaiser doesn't run around handing out death sentences, okay?" Corey sighed. "That Veron guy? He's a little insane."

"Try a lot."

"I know. Believe me, I know." The kid raked his hand through his hair, sighed, and leaned back against the couch cushions. "I've met Kaiser too. So have you guys. He's not some lunatic on a bender, right? He does very well at The Resort and always has a job for anyone who wants one. And he doesn't care who you are or where you're from as long as you work hard and follow the rules."

"So you do work for him."

"No. He gave us a rundown and made the offer."

"And you didn't take it?"

"No. Not yet, anyway. Honestly, we were only there for Bronson. You know, for moral support."

"And y'all ain't got some kinda moral compass pointin' you away from growin', buyin', and sellin' marijuana?"

Lisa turned her head a fraction of an inch to look at him but he ignored her.

I ain't talkin' about us and we ain't fixin' to do a thing with what we paid for.

Corey shrugged. "Not really. I'm not interested."

"But if you were, you have enough money and clout on your own to go in on somethin' big exactly like Bronson."

"I don't think he'll do anything, to be honest. He's looking for a distraction, you know? Come on. He watched his girlfriend get shot and killed moments before he was gonna propose to her. We were all there. We all—" The young man swallowed thickly and shook his head. "We all saw it. No one's found the assholes who shot her and what else are any of us supposed to do, huh? If he wants a distraction, the least we can do is back him up and be there for him."

Lisa let herself smile softly and that was enough to keep Corey's gaze fixed on hers. "You guys have been friends for a long time, haven't you?"

"Yeah. Since high school—the four of us. And then with Addison, it was the five of us until…"

"Uh-huh." Johnny glanced at his partner, then leaned sideways against the couch's armrest and pointed at the young man. "That day y'all were at the farm last week—the day we all saw each other without knowin' it—Jasper Harford said y'all were in the hills at one of y'all's getaway mansion."

"Oh. Yeah. Adam's dad has a place."

"And y'all thought lyin' to Bronson's old man was the best way to show moral support?"

"We didn't lie to him. We merely didn't tell him the entire plan." Corey's gaze flicked from one to the other and he leaned forward quickly. "No, honestly. We went to the mountain house for a week and didn't even spend a whole day at The Resort. You guys simply happened to be there at the same time we were."

"And when did you decide to come back to San Francisco?" Lisa asked.

"Um…this last Monday. We came down Monday night."

"Okay, then." With a nod, she turned to her partner and shrugged. "I think that's everything we need, right?"

"Sure." Johnny slapped his thighs and pushed to his feet. "You've been a real help, Corey. Thanks for your time."

"Sure. Of course. Yeah, let me know if there's anything else I can do."

"We'll be in touch if we need to be." Lisa smiled and stood as well. "We can show ourselves out."

"Hey, wait." Corey lurched after them, and when they turned, he stood with a sheepish smile and his hands stuffed deep into the pockets of his sweatpants. "You're not, uh…you're not gonna tell Jasper about this, right?"

"Is there somethin' we oughtta tell him?"

"No, but he'd lose his shit if he found out his son was within a mile of a weed farm. Especially since Bronson's about to take over from him. That's why we didn't say anything about The Resort before we left."

Johnny scrutinized the young man carefully before he cleared his throat. "We're private investigators, son, not babysitters. As long as y'all have nothin' to hide, what you do with your time and money ain't none of our business."

"Okay." Corey sighed with relief. "Cool. Thanks."

"Thank you." Lisa smiled at him as Johnny opened the front door. "Have a nice day."

"Yeah, you too."

The two investigators remained silent until they stepped into the elevator and the doors closed in front of them. Lisa puffed her cheeks out and exhaled slowly. "It sounds like he's more afraid of what Jasper would do to Bronson than anything else."

"That's a real pal for ya, sure." The dwarf folded his arms and stared at the seam between the elevator doors. "Do you think he was bein' straight with us?"

"I didn't sense anything that would imply otherwise."

"Naw, me neither." He narrowed his eyes. "What does that say about us when a damn kid puts the pieces together before we do?"

"It says we have a reputation, Johnny." She shrugged. "And that we're not exactly the subtlest when it comes to blending in."

"The kid's sharp."

"Yep."

"If he ain't hidin' somethin', we have ourselves another dead end."

Lisa smiled slyly at him and tilted her head. "Not if his friends tell us a different story."

"Uh-huh." He pulled his cell phone out and typed rapidly.

"What are you doing?"

"Lettin' Charlie know his babysittin' duty has been extended by another twelve hours at least. We have a few more stops to make."

"Since when does he have a phone?"

"He doesn't. I paid the desk staff to take messages for him."

"Is that safe?" She frowned in concern but he grinned cheerfully. "It is if I don't put anything specific to the case in it."

When he finished typing the text, he took a moment to read through it.

Back late. Stay in the motel. Hounds need more food.

With a smirk, he sent the message and didn't even have to try to wipe his cousin, his coonhounds, and the two transformed witnesses under their protection out of his mind.

It looks like we finally have some work to do.

Adam Hoff and Jeffrey Glennis both lived within half an hour of Corey. The partners visited them in turn and each time, they were welcomed with perfect politeness and a willingness to answer whatever questions they had. Adam and Jeffrey recognized them too from their first visit to Kaiser's farm and neither of them tried to hide it.

More importantly, all three of Bronson Harford's friends gave the same story—they'd gone to Adam's dad's estate in the mountains for a week-long getaway, some R&R with the hopes of lifting Bronson's spirits, and had a brief tour around Kaiser's farm and the grow warehouses before they packed up and returned home to San Francisco on Monday evening.

The bounty hunter slipped into the driver's seat of their rental and grunted at the steering wheel. "Well, that puts a dampener on our leads."

"Yeah…" Lisa slid her aviator sunglasses onto her face and strapped her seatbelt on slowly. "I honestly didn't expect that to go as smoothly as it did."

"You and me both, darlin'." He started the engine and pulled away from the row of overly large and most likely overly expensive condos Jeffrey Glennis currently called home. "What I can't understand is why Bronson wanted to make friends with Kaiser in the first place."

"Right?" She leaned forward to turn the air conditioning up. "Those kids aren't stupid. Bronson certainly isn't. If everyone in the shifter world knows he's responsible for the ultimatums and for killing the transformed shifters if they don't take his offer, Bronson and his friends are playing with fire. But why?"

"It might be he's goin' off the deep end after the girl he was fixin' to marry was snatched away from him. You know, livin' on the wild side."

Lisa scoffed. "Like aligning with the guy responsible for her death by making him a new business partner? I don't think so."

"I still stand by my double-agent theory."

"Johnny, Bronson Harford is not a double agent. He's a twenty-six-year-old shifter in mourning who's about to take over his family's long-standing tradition of handling more money than you or I will probably ever see in our lifetimes."

"You and I will live a helluva long time, darlin'. Assumin' the end comes from natural causes, of course."

"Okay, let's move on from our mortality and get back to the point." She swiped strands of loose hair away from her face and stared blankly through the windshield as they headed out of San Francisco toward the I-80. "If Bronson does have some kind of ulterior motive beyond rebelling against his Harford responsibilities and trying to distract himself from his grief, what would that be?"

"Tryin' to put the pieces of the puzzle together himself, most likely. It might be he's fixin' to investigate on his own, yeah? Maybe he wants to understand why and how a gang of Kaiser's transformed-murderin' flunkies could screw up as badly as they did, crash a private engagement party, and shoot a young girl who ain't on either side of the fence and was only caught in the wrong place at the wrong time."

"You think he's trying to infiltrate Kaiser's organization and… what? Destroy it from the inside out?"

"Sure. Or maybe he's realizin' he ain't as much like his old man as everyone thinks he is." Johnny glanced at her, then shrugged. "It might be he thinks if bein' a lover instead of a fighter when it comes to the transformed shifters got his heart broken and his world turned upside down, the other side might have a little more to offer."

"Okay, we'll walk down that hypothetical road for a second." Lisa folded her arms. "Bronson Harford's done everything right in his life. He did well in school, graduated from Stanford at the top of his class, and kept his hands and his reputation clean in the high-society circles he was born and bred into. Currently, he's following in his dad's footsteps exactly like Jasper did. He meets Addison Taylor, daughter of a transformed shifter mother and one seriously ill human father. He doesn't see the world in black and white like he was raised. He sees love and decides to propose but the love of his life is shot and killed right in front of him, and—"

"All his plans go down the toilet."

"Yes, Johnny. That's a given." She laughed but it was immediately dampened by another confused frown. "But doing business with the guy everyone knows has indiscriminately killed transformed shifters? Kaiser's taking lives merely because those who want to live the rest of their days as normally as possible refuse to fully identify themselves with the shifter world and the magical world. That's it. He's the only one who has brought violence into this."

"Okay, so it might be Bronson thinks violence is the way out since peace, love, and understandin' didn't get the job done."

"Well, that would make sense if he started a gang of angry shifters to take a stand against Kaiser but not if he's aligning himself with the guy."

"He could simply want a little fresh perspective. Or he's bein' reckless on purpose and aims to drop the surprise on his old man in the near future, simply to get a rise. Just 'cause he can."

"There are so many other ways for a young magical like Bronson to 'get a rise' out of his parents."

"Uh-huh. We merely gotta find the one reason Bronson has for choosin' to do it this way."

She laughed despite her inner confusion. "Oh. Is that all?"

CHAPTER TWENTY-TWO

About a month earlier, Bronson Harford had finally relented and come downstairs to the breakfast room in the mornings to eat breakfast with his father. It had taken him at least two months after Addison's death to feel like he could handle either Jasper's constant light-hearted chatter that meant absolutely nothing or his comfortable, satisfied silence that seemed to mean even less.

He'd eventually conceded to join him for luncheons as well, most of them set out on the back veranda to showcase both the beauty of their estate and the unfailing skill of Armand's cooking, no matter what the meal.

But once he'd returned from the trip into the mountains with his friends, he'd fallen into his old habits again. Now, he took his meals in his private apartment on the top floor of the Harford estate and he'd come out only for the charity gala two nights before.

Only to keep up appearances. That's always the most important thing, isn't it?

Jasper hadn't once come to see him since the last straggling guests had finally left the ballroom on Thursday night, and the young shifter couldn't have been more grateful for his father's apparent disinterest. He stared out the bay window that served as the nook for the small bistro table he used for every meal now. Almost absently, he took another mouthful of his delicate breakfast crepe, swallowed it without tasting any of the complex flavors, and dropped his fork onto the plate.

This is taking way too long. The rest of the world is out there, still turning while everyone moves through their boring lives, and I can't even—

The sharp buzz of his cell phone vibrating against the china plate on the table whipped his attention away from his foul mood, but only for a moment.

I swear if he thinks a phone call from his study is gonna make me feel bad about any of this, he's officially lost his mind.

It wasn't his father's private number, however. Nor was it any of the staff either or his friends.

The number wasn't saved in his phone, but he recognized it all the same and answered quickly.

"Hello?"

"Bronson?" The woman's voice was short and clipped.

"Yes."

"Are you alone?"

He stared out the window at the sweeping expanse of the estate grounds and sighed. "I am."

"Good. And do you know who this is?"

Of course he knew. Did she think he'd simply forget everything after a week without contact?

"Why are you calling?"

The woman hummed in a low tone and the echo of metal tapping against metal came through the line. "We still have what you want, Bronson, and we're keeping it nice and safe. You waited patiently enough, I guess. So if you want to come take a look, now would be your chance."

His gut clenched and he fought to control his anger before it would surely have driven him to crush the cell phone in his hand. "Is this coming from you directly?"

"Nothing comes from me directly. You know that. Now, do you need a refresher course on the directions or can you get here without someone holding your hand?"

A low growl escaped him. "I know where it is."

"Good. I'll leave a light on for you." The call ended with a sharp click.

Bronson sat in silence while rage and anxiety churned madly inside him.

I can't expect someone like that to not seriously enjoy this. She'd better not forget who she's talking to.

He shoved away from the bistro table and stormed around his apartments to collect his keys, wallet, shoes, and a light jacket. Without a backward glance, he left his private home inside his home and headed quickly to the staff access elevator.

What I want. Keeping it nice and safe. He snorted as the elevator descended to the first floor. *She says it like she's the one responsible for this whole thing.*

That thought made him pause. Whatever happened after this —whether or not he could control himself when he came face to face with the one thing he'd wanted since that night on the docks —Bronson had no idea who was truly responsible for any of it. He'd grasped at straws for months but no more.

None of the staff bothered him as he rushed through the back exit and hurried to the detached garage filled with all six of the Harford family's luxury vehicles. Only one of them ever had much use as Jasper Harford hadn't left the estate for longer than an hour in at least the last three years.

I'm nothing like him. Not the way he wants me to be. He didn't fight for what he wanted and look at him now.

It was dangerous to get behind the wheel of any car with this much rage boiling through him. He knew that but he'd been offered an invitation he couldn't refuse. Even the thought of refusing was impossible—unthinkable. He'd denied himself this satisfaction for longer than he should have and this was his chance.

Plus, if he didn't take the invitation to go out there now, who knew how long the offer would stand?

Not long if he knew anything about the man who made it in the first place—through, of course, the dark witch with the seriously bad attitude, not to mention her shitty taste in clothing.

An hour and a half later, Bronson pulled his Bentley to a quick stop at the designated location almost five miles off the main road. A thick cloud of dust had billowed up behind the rear fender but he'd ignored every pebble ding and rocky scrape on the car's undercarriage so he could get there as quickly as possible.

The location was almost in the middle of nowhere. At least, that was how it appeared. But he'd been there once before and knew exactly what to look for.

He hiked up the rolling hill in front of him, his gaze fixed steadily ahead while his arms pumped at his sides. Once he crested the rise, the relief he thought he'd feel at the sight of the old, crooked, sun-beaten shed didn't materialize. Instead, more rage seemed to have surged in to take its place.

The young shifter clenched his hands into fists and hurried down the hill toward the shed. When he was halfway there, a rickety side door creaked open and the tiny witch dressed in black that contrasted dramatically with her crimson hair stepped out.

She held the door open and scrutinized him without any expression whatsoever. "It took you long enough."

"I'm right on time."

"Hmm. Of course you are." She nodded toward the dark interior of the shed and he gritted his teeth as he brushed past her. The door creaked shut again and it seemed they'd stand forever in the hot space with only the bright California sunlight that streamed through the gaps in the wooden planks to alleviate the sudden darkness.

In silence, the witch pulled a huge, heavy-looking lever built into a metal box opposite the door. A low, hollow thunk was followed by the jingle of lengthening chain before the low-powered lift descended with agonizing slowness beneath the miles of unfarmed, unused, practically forgotten land around them.

Bronson glared at her.

She can't seriously think she's running the show here. Of course she doesn't. She knows exactly who she works for and what her job is. That's all. It doesn't mean I have to like it, though.

The lift shuddered to a stop at the bottom of the shaft with another thunk and a series of grating clicks. The whole time, his silent companion stared at his face. Even when she gestured down the narrow passage in front of them, she didn't look away.

"I thought you wanted this," she muttered.

He did.

I'll get two for the price of one if she doesn't quit mocking me.

The shifter stepped out of the lift and stormed down the passage. Up ahead, the soft glow from the lighting installed in the room beyond filtered toward him. It wasn't enough to brighten all the crevices, but it was enough to cast a struggling shadow against the back wall of the room.

Someone was in there—someone he had itched to get his hands on for the last three months.

Finally, he could do something.

His rage flared anew when he stepped into the low-ceilinged room with concrete walls and nothing but an air-vent grate set in one to prove there was any access at all to the outside world. In the center of the room, another shifter sat on a dented metal folding chair. His wrists were tied behind the back of the chair and the same rope coiled around his arms and torso to hold him in place. His ankles were bound too, but the rope around them was tied tightly to two metal rings bolted into the floor.

This bastard wouldn't go anywhere.

Bronson couldn't help but snarl when he recognized him. He appeared to be around his age or maybe a few years older at most. Even with the dirt that streaked his face, his eyes wide with terror, and the stench of being chained there for the last week without the luxury of a working toilet, he was undoubtedly the shifter he had been looking for.

One of them, anyway.

"You—" The prisoner's eyes widened even further and he struggled against the tight ropes with a growl of alarm. "What do you want?"

"I want her back." Bronson stalked closer to the chair in the center of the boxlike room. "I want her alive. Is that something you can do for me?"

"Are you kidding?"

"What's your name?"

"My... What?" The terrified shifter gaped at him before his gaze flicked toward the mouth of the passage when the crimson-haired witch joined the party. "Listen. I didn't kill your girl, man. I swear."

"You mean you didn't pull the trigger?" His lip curled in another furious snarl. "Because the way I see it, the idiot who fired that gun isn't the guy I'm looking for."

"I don't know what you want."

"What's your name?"

"What's she doing here?" The prisoner jerked against his restraints again. "I'll tell you whatever you wanna know, man, but get her outta here."

The smack of something heavy and solid against flesh came from behind Bronson. He turned to where the witch stood with a monkey wrench produced seemingly out of thin air and dropped it repeatedly into her opposite palm.

"Maybe he needs a little encouragement," she muttered.

"Aw, Jesus." The shifter tied to the chair groaned and slumped against the back of it. "Come on. You already have me tied up. What do you need something like that for, huh?"

The witch stared at him. "Because it's fun."

"Not for you." The young Harford growled his annoyance.

She took a deep breath through her nose but didn't look away from the terrified man in the center of the room, even when she tilted the monkey wrench toward Bronson and offered it to him.

He took it, swallowed, and hefted the weight of the tool in his hand. "Get out."

"Can't a girl stick around for a good time?"

Bronson turned toward her, took one step until they were merely inches apart, and glared at her.

I could break her in half if I wanted to—unless she moved faster and got off a good shot first.

"Wait outside."

"No can do, pretty boy." She met his gaze head-on and the corner of her mouth twitched. "The only magical who gets to party alone with that washed-up dog in the chair is me. And yeah, that comes directly from the top too."

Bronson glanced at the entrance to the passage and resisted the overwhelming urge to shift and rip her throat out. "Then go and wait at the lift."

"Have fun." Her eyebrow quirked almost imperceptibly before she turned and stalked down the passage into the darkness. The hem of her black trench coat swirled around her ankles and her heavy, booted footfalls echoed behind her.

Only when her footsteps stopped did he turn to face the transformed shifter who'd been at the docks that night.

Him and the other pieces of shit who took her from me.

"H-hey, man." The prisoner's eyelids fluttered and he forced himself to swallow. He couldn't tear his gaze away from the wrench in his visitor's hand. "Seriously. I didn't do anything. I swear. I had no idea—"

"What's your name?" Bronson lunged toward the chair and swung back with the wrench.

"Hux, man! Hux!" the transformed shrieked. "My name is Hux! Fuck, please—please don't hit me with that. I didn't— I'm a regular guy, okay?"

The wrench was heavy in his hand. He glanced at it, still unsure whether he would use it on the defenseless guy strapped to the chair.

As much as I hate that witch, she sure knows how to tie a shifter so he can't get free.

Slowly, Bronson lowered himself into a crouch in front of the chair and glared at the other shifter, not even slightly concerned that the prisoner might lash out. Hux was terrified, that much was clear, and clueless. Even if he'd wanted to fight back, there was no way for him to do that now.

"Where are your friends?"

"Who?"

"You know who."

"H-hey, man. I have a lot of friends, okay? You're gonna have to—" Hux shrieked when the wrench swung toward his leg. Instead of striking flesh and probably splitting bone, the tool clanged against the metal leg of the folding chair. Despite the ropes that held him in place, the transformed shifter struggled again and tried to lean as far away from the shuddering leg of the chair as possible.

It wasn't much.

"Jesus Christ—"

"The other two who got off scot-free that night." Bronson growled impatiently. "One has a goatee and wears that stupid hat. The other one's skinnier than you and probably as much of a coward."

"I...I don't know."

Bronson lifted the wrench again and tilted it from one side to the other in front of Hux's wildly glistening eyes.

If I let him think it's coming long enough, he'll break without me having to use it.

"I'm serious, man. I swear." The terrified shifter licked his lips nervously. He panted now and still tried to shy away from his interrogator and the wrench. "Look, I was wasted at the bar the other night. We were all there, but your fucking war-witch knocked me out and I woke up here. That's all I know. They could be anywhere!"

Bronson swallowed the acidic precursor to the bile that threatened to rise in his throat and stood again slowly. "She's not mine."

"Y-yeah, okay. Whatever. Kaiser's witch or—I don't know. Hey, if you wanna get the guy responsible for killing your girl, man, talk to him. Kaiser. He ordered the—"

"You're the one I want!" he roared and spittle sprayed from his mouth as he leapt toward the other shifter and wrapped his hand around his throat. "You're the one who took her. The three of you! You took her and you wouldn't let her go until it was too late. Now, she's dead!"

"I—" Nothing more than a strangled croak followed from the prisoner's gaping mouth. Even though he struggled to breathe and his mouth opened and closed, he held his gaze. A flash of silver burst behind Hux's eyes but in the next moment, he'd completely ceased to struggle.

With a furious snarl, Bronson pushed him away from him by the throat. The chair rocked and would have fallen if the prisoner's ankles and feet hadn't been secured so conveniently to the metal rings in the floor. The front legs settled onto the concrete with a clang and he coughed and drew in raw, gasped breaths between fits of coughing.

Harford hurled the wrench at the wall and a few chips of concrete broke away to clatter on the floor with the heavy tool he was no longer willing to use at all. "If one of the others had been taken instead of you, where would you go?"

"No…" Hux shook his head and his chin rested against his chest as the rest of what little fight he had left drained out of him. "I have no idea, man. We couldn't even decide what to do when it was all three of us. Tying me to a chair doesn't change that."

"It seems not."

"Man…" The prisoner groaned again. "We already knew someone was coming after us. And now they know someone got to me first. I have no idea where they went and you can beat me all you want. I can't tell you something I don't know."

"I'll find them." He clenched his fists and stalked across the square concrete box and back without pause. "If I keep you here long enough, someone will eventually come sniffing around, trying to catch your scent."

Hux sucked in a sharp breath and his throat clicked audibly when he swallowed again. "How long have I been down here, man? Four days? Five?"

Six. It's hard to count the days when you're strapped to a chair underground, huh?

Bronson continued to pace.

"However long it's been, man, my friends aren't coming to get me. No one's coming near that witch Kaiser has on a leash." Hux coughed again and rocked his head back so he could get a better look at his interrogator. "But it won't matter anyway."

"And why's that?" Bronson snarled.

"Because Kaiser isn't the only asshole trying to carve through us transformed, is he? There's a new guy in town, right? Tyro." He hawked and spat on the floor.

The coppery scent of saliva-thinned blood filled Harford's nostrils, but he ignored it.

"He's targeted all the transformed shifters and doesn't even stop to give them a choice like your friend Kaiser. The asshole murders them in cold blood simply because we weren't born into this like the rest of you." The prisoner seemed to have regained his nerve and despite his panting, his voice grew louder. "So you can threaten me all you want. Turn the whole world upside down for two more transformed who you think killed your girl. You'll be lucky if you get any of us before he does."

"Tyro?" Bronson stopped pacing, his shoulders hunched, and turned his head to study the shifter intently.

"Yeah." Another round of hacking coughs wracked him. "That's all he wants. Every last transformed lying dead in the gutter. We already know it's coming and we already know no one gives a shit. You can't—"

The guy shut up and shrank against the back of the chair when Bronson whirled and stormed toward him. He thrust a finger in his face, leaned closer until their noses were inches apart, and muttered, "I'm not done with you."

Before he could no longer hold back the urge to rip this guy apart—like he knew he would if he played this game any longer—Harford spun away, stalked out of the room, and headed down the dark corridor toward the lift.

Tyro. All this bullshit about Tyro.

His fingernails bit painfully into his palms as he clenched his fists.

You know what? Maybe he will kill all the transformed, including the one down here. Then Jasper Harford's perfect son won't have to get his hands dirty.

He stormed into the lift and stood for a moment, breathing heavily and glaring at the floor. The witch leaned casually against the wall and paid more attention to the dirt she was digging out from under her fingernails with the tip of a switchblade than the angry, entitled, rich-boy shifter who fumed barely five feet away from her.

"Get me out of here," he demanded hoarsely.

She took another moment to finish her grooming, closed the blade before she shoved it into the pocket of her trench coat, and uncrossed her ankles before she pushed away from the wall. The lift trembled beneath her tiny frame as her combat boots thunked on the short ramp. She cranked the lever and the automatic winch grated and squealed as they ascended slowly.

Bronson stared directly ahead at nothing, although he could feel her gaze on him. He sensed that she tried to learn something from his face.

Whatever the hell she's looking for, she won't find it.

When the winch shuddered to a stop at the top of the shaft inside the rickety shed, he muttered through clenched teeth, "Do you have something to say?"

She stepped past him off the lift and headed to the shed door.

"I didn't think so." The second he stepped off the lift to follow her out, she whirled to face him and folded her arms. "What?"

"You're not gonna give Kaiser any reason to regret this little arrangement, are you?"

"Are you serious?"

She raised an eyebrow and cocked her head.

"No. I'm not going to give him a reason." He snarled with suppressed rage. "I know exactly what I agreed to."

"And you're a shifter of your word. Is that it?"

"I'm done here."

Rolling her eyes, the witch finally stepped back against the shed door and shoved it open. She turned and gave him enough room to brush past her into the suddenly blinding sunlight that flooded the valley.

He stormed up the small rise to where his Bentley waited at the bottom of the short slope on the other side.

How was this a good idea? If I can't get that asshole to talk and I'm too chickenshit to hit him with a damn wrench, why did I even come?

"Don't do anything stupid," the witch called after him. For the first time since he'd met her, he thought he heard a smile in her voice.

He didn't turn to check, mostly because he didn't want

Kaiser's witch to see him fall apart as the realization of what he'd done—and had almost done—set in. More than that, he couldn't let her see how much his hands were trembling now.

No, nothing stupid. Merely secret after secret, buried exactly like Mom said they had to be—forever.

Bronson reached his car and fumbled with the handle before he finally managed to jerk the door open.

With another furious growl, he threw himself behind the wheel, turned the engine on with a quick jerk, and froze. His heart pounded wildly in his chest and another warning surge of bile stung the back of his throat.

I have to keep the secrets. I'm the only one who can.

He forced himself to strap his seatbelt on, then looked at the top of the hill. There was no sign of Kaiser's dark witch, nor of anyone or anything out here.

After several deep breaths, he shifted into reverse and stepped on the gas to turn the Bentley in another spray of pebbles, dirt, and a massive cloud of kicked-up dust.

No one can find out. If they knew what I am and what Mom was, I'd be shit out of luck and there's no way to come back from that.

CHAPTER TWENTY-THREE

"You seriously didn't get anything?" Seated on the edge of the bed in the crappy motel room off 99, Galfrey gaped at the investigators and gestured wildly in frustration. "You spent two days in San Francisco and now what? We're back to square one?"

"Oh, man." Jake grasped his hair with both hands and groaned. "We're done. They're gonna find us and there's no way Hux isn't dead by now—"

"Dude, shut up!"

"All right." Johnny raised his hands to stop them. "We still have—"

"Shut up?" Jake leapt to his feet, whirled toward his friend, and ignored the bounty hunter completely. "Why? We've already spent a week holed up in here shutting up. A week without getting out of this shitty—" He snatched the remote from the mattress and hurled it at the wall with a shout of frustration. It bounced and the backing popped off and the loose panel and batteries rolled across the floor to disappear beneath the bed.

"Whoa, whoa, whoa. Hey!" Charlie turned toward him in disbelief and gestured at the broken remote. "If you gotta break something, man, break something we don't use all day, huh?"

"We're dead!" the transformed shifter shrieked. "Do you get that? We're all—"

"Everyone shut up and sit down!" Lisa yelled.

All four men turned to look at her with wide eyes.

In the other room through the open adjoining doorway, Luther uttered a low whine. "Uh-oh."

"Yeah, you'd better listen to her, two-legs," Rex added and the tip of his snout and one eye poked out from behind the door-frame for a quick peek into the other room. "You do not wanna make the lady angry."

"You won't like her when she's angry," Luther added.

Lisa put her hands on her hips, pressed her lips firmly together, and studied each of the transformed shifters before she nodded curtly toward the beds. "I said sit."

"Yeah, even we know that one," the smaller hound whispered.

Johnny snapped his fingers and pointed at the adjoining doorway. "That's enough out of y'all."

Rex's head disappeared immediately.

Charlie and Jake both lowered themselves slowly onto the edge of the bed closest to the exterior door. Galfrey dragged his hands down both cheeks and huffed a sigh. "We're screwed."

Lisa cleared her throat. "What part of shut up did you not understand?"

The bounty hunter snorted and tried to cover it by clearing his throat when his partner glanced scathingly at him.

Damn. Her kid is all grown up and out workin' on the other side of the ocean and she's still got the mama death-glare. Why is she fixin' it on me?

"Now. Here's the deal." She raised her chin and scanned the faces that returned her stare. "Johnny and I are still working on finding Hux. So far, we don't have any strong leads but that's never stopped us before. What we did find is cause for a little confusion at the very least, so we'll have to dig deeper into that until we find what we're looking for."

"What confusion?" Galfrey asked hoarsely.

"Bronson Harford and all three of his friends who were there with him at the docks the night Addison was killed have personal business with Kaiser."

"What?" Jake's eyes bulged and his mouth fell open. "Are you kidding me?"

Johnny snapped his fingers and pointed at the shifter. "Hey. Does she look like she's kiddin'?"

"You don't have to do that," she muttered.

"Well, he's askin' stupid questions."

Charlie sniggered. "There's no such thing as a stupid question —right, 'coz?"

"Wrong."

"Okay, I'm the only one who gets to talk right now," Lisa interjected. She raised her voice but nowhere close to its previous shouting volume. "So far, three of their stories all match. The fourth is from Bronson, which we don't have yet, but we'll speak to him too very soon. There's already a connection there but it's flimsy. You two and Hux were the transformed shifters who got away the night Bronson's girlfriend was killed in a faction skirmish. We knew that already. I think the hunch you had about these skirmishes getting worse after Addison's death— maybe even specifically because of them—is right on the money. Especially now that we know Bronson Harford and his friends were at Kaiser's farm."

"You think they know where Hux is?" Jake asked feebly.

"They might." The bounty hunter folded his arms. "All they told us was they were at that farm so Bronson could do a little business with the king of shifter-weed."

"That doesn't make sense." Galfrey shook his head. "Why would Bronson do business with the guy whose crew killed his girlfriend?"

The partners exchanged a knowing glance before she cleared her throat. "Like I said, there's cause for a little confusion."

"I'd call that big confusion," Charlie muttered.

"Either way, when we find out what Bronson wants from a deal with Kaiser, it should be cut and dried from there."

"Cut and dried?" Galfrey sighed. "That doesn't sound like it's gonna happen."

"What about his friends, though?" Jake glanced from Lisa to Johnny. "They'd know where Hux is, right?"

"As far as we know, they're merely a couple of Bronson's friends backin' up a buddy who has fallen on hard times." Johnny cleared his throat. "Emotionally speakin'."

"And what about our buddy falling on hard times? If he's still alive, we have to find him—"

"We will." The dwarf nodded and glanced at each of the transformed shifters, including his cousin, before he turned smartly on his heel and headed through the interleading doorway. "As soon as we find out who the hell else knows where he is."

"Oh, come on!" Jake started to stand but one warning look from Lisa made him settle on the edge of the bed again. "You should be interrogating those guys. They have to know something."

"We're working on it." She folded her arms, then called over her shoulder, "Johnny?"

"Yeah."

"Have you called to make that appointment to talk to Bronson yet?"

"It's still on my long list of to-dos, darlin'."

"Maybe hold off on that for a little longer."

The bounty hunter's face reappeared in the open doorway and he frowned at her before it morphed into a full-blown scowl. "Why? We already paid a visit to Bronson's three amigos and asked all the questions we could think of."

"True." She turned to face him. "And I believe they don't know anything. But maybe he's not in the habit of sharing his darkest secrets with his three best friends. He could be saving that for family."

"Hell, we already talked to his old man too."

"I'm not talking about Jasper Harford. I'm talking about Langley." With a sudden frown, she spun toward the transformed shifters and pointed at them. "Do any of you know anything about Bronson's mom?"

Galfrey shrugged. "Only that she died a while ago."

"Yeah, I know that. What was her maiden name?"

The shifters looked at each other and shook their heads. "How should we know?"

"Well, you knew Bronson, didn't you? Or knew of him."

"Why does that matter?"

"Because we're lookin' for Bronson's uncle. His mama's brother." Johnny squinted and stepped fully through the doorway again. "Jasper had no idea where his brother-in-law has been for years."

"I know. But we have a family connection—a first name." Lisa shrugged. "A last name would make finding him a hell of a lot easier, don't you think?"

Charlie snapped his fingers. "Appletini!"

"Dammit, Charlie. You ain't gettin' out for a damn drink. Who the hell drinks one of those anyhow?"

"No, no. Appleton. Apple…Appleman. Yeah!" The mohawked dwarf pointed at his cousin. "That's it. That's his mom's name. Helice Appleman."

Lisa grinned. "Are you sure?"

"Oh, yeah."

Johnny raised an eyebrow. "And how the hell do you know that?"

"Hey." Charlie raised both hands in surrender. "I'm not hiding anything I swear. Listen, I remember her name 'cause there was this huge charity auction twenty, maybe twenty-one years ago."

"Auctionin' away a Ms. Appleman?"

"What? No. It was a…a private thing, right? Put on by the Harfords—Mr. and Mrs. The kid was, like, barely out of diapers."

"I have a hard time believin' you were invited to a private anythin' by those shifters."

"Not a personal invitation. It was one of those underground things." Charlie whistled and ended it with a laugh. "Man. It's amazing what comes back to you when you spend enough time off the—I mean…" He cleared his throat. "You know."

"Uh-huh."

"I'm just saying, okay? The Harfords opened their doors to a horde of shifters—anyone who could make it and especially those of us who'd recently been…you know. Blasted in the face with dark magic that turned the whole world upside down for shifters."

"And you."

"Obviously."

Johnny scrutinized his cousin a little warily before he returned to the adjoining room. "Y'all stay put. You know the drill."

"Wait, what are you guys doing?" Galfrey asked.

"Lookin' up a Langley Appleman." The second the two partners stepped into the other room, he slammed the door shut behind them and locked it. "I can't believe I'm entertainin' this."

"It's not a horrible idea, Johnny." She snatched her tablet up and brought it with her to the bed. "The one guy who's not a part of all this—at least not on the surface, anyway."

"Not a part?" Johnny gestured toward the adjoining wall. "The moron's sittin' in the other room."

"I can hear you," Charlie called in a sing-song tone.

The hounds sniggered. Rex gave himself a back scratch on the stained carpeting and Luther nibbled at his forepaw.

"Wait." Lisa looked at her partner and lowered her voice. "You're talking about Charlie?"

"Uh-huh." He squinted at her. "Who are you talkin' about?"

"Langley. Appleman. At least I hope that's his last name."

"Right. Then we were talkin' about the same thing."

"No, you said you can't believe you're entertaining this."

The dwarf snorted. "I meant takin' my damn cousin at his word about a last name for a guy we ain't heard nothin' else about since we started."

"You don't think he can remember a name?"

"Appletini?"

She tried to quell her laughter and returned her attention to the tablet and the multiple searches she was ready to run on one Langley Appleman. "But you don't think it's the wrong idea to go talk to Langley."

"'Course not, darlin'. I think it's a perfect idea—the logical next step and all. And if we don't find somethin' out from Bronson's uncle, I—" With a glance at the door, he leaned toward her and whispered, "I don't know how close we're ever gonna be to findin' Hux and gettin' some closure to this whole mess."

"That's never stopped us before either, has it?"

"No. And we ain't gonna let it start now."

For the rest of the day, Lisa sat hunched over her tablet on the bed while she pored over social media, news articles, and whatever state and local case files she could still get her hands on. She even went through all the articles about the Harford family, hoping to find something about the late Mrs. Harford's brother Langley. Finally, she signed onto the FBI database to run a quick search for his name as a last resort.

With their last stock of non-perishables almost depleted, Johnny took the hounds out for a dinner run. By the time he returned, the motel room was filled with three hungry, grouchy transformed shifters ready to eat almost anything and another motel room with a haggard, exasperated Lisa Breyer who was one small step from pulling her hair out.

"Whoa. Did you find some bad news?"

"No, that's the thing." She growled and swiped the screen

angrily. "I haven't found anything. The only thing with Langley Appleman's name on it is a birth certificate and graduation records from both high school and college. That's it. There is nothing else."

"For real?" Johnny unwrapped two giant Slim-Jims and tossed them absently to the hounds as he joined his partner on the bed.

"Yes!" The animals scrambled across the carpet to lunge after the snacks. "Johnny, is it Christmas already?"

"You should get us more of these for Christmas, that's for sure."

"Wait. Do we ever get anything for Christmas?"

He grunted and peered over Lisa's shoulder at her disappointing findings. "The guy's married, ain't he?"

"Or he used to be. But I don't have his wife or ex-wife's last name, so it's not like I can look up marriage records."

"How the hell does the brother-in-law of Jasper Harford not have a damn thing on him?"

"Exactly." With a heavy sigh, she placed the tablet on the bed and glanced at the hounds who had swallowed the last of the Slim-Jim's and now peered into the plastic bag of leftover groceries. "Do you have any more—"

"Yep." He traded her the last Slim-Jim for the tablet and she stripped the packaging off and attacked it with almost as much enthusiasm as the hounds.

"Did you search for the wife yet?"

"I told you, I don't know her name."

"Not Langley's wife. Jasper's."

Lisa stopped chewing and looked at him with wide eyes. "Oh."

"That's all right. It's kinda hard to imagine how a wife and mama might have anythin' to do with all this when she's been gone…what? Fifteen years? It's worth a shot, though."

She swallowed and leaned toward the tablet. "Yeah. Langley's her brother, right?"

"Well, he sure as hell ain't Jasper's."

After a few more frustrating searches and more detailed instructions from his partner, the dwarf finally stopped scrolling and stared at the only headline they'd seen that might have been remotely helpful. "Hey. Look at this. *From Appleman to Harford, Her Biggest Joy Is Still Giving Back.*"

"It looks like an article on Helice."

"Uh-huh." He clicked on the link, which opened to an online article dated twenty-seven years earlier.

"Wow. This was before Bronson was even born."

"He wasn't even a bun in the oven at that point."

"Let me see that." Lisa took the tablet, settled it on her lap, and scrolled through.

"Darlin', if you're gonna take it from me, at least read it out loud so I ain't gotta sit here and—"

"Fine. 'The founding of any organization, outreach program, or charity non-profit opening its doors for the benefit of the community's youth is a cause for celebration in and of itself. For Helice Harford, it's a dream come true. Last summer, after a six-month engagement to California's Jasper Harford—heir to the Harford legacy in Sausalito and grandson of Reginald Harford, founder of the Harford Foundation—Helice couldn't have imagined how much her life would change. But marrying the man of her dreams was only the beginning. Merely one year later, the Harford Foundation broke ground this past Tuesday on its newest development project outside San Francisco, The Appleman House.'"

"Jesus." Johnny shook his head. "What is it with these folks and namin' all their crap after themselves?"

"Says the owner of Johnny Walker Investigations." Lisa shushed him before he had the chance to make another retort and continued to read. "'We had the incredible opportunity to speak to the Harfords after the ground-breaking ceremony, and Helice shared some surprising and yet heartfelt memories from her past with us. 'I count myself as one of the lucky ones. Most of the other kids put into foster homes never find where they belong. They simply aged out and had to make a life out on their own but I didn't. I found my family—my real family. Without them, none of this would be possible.'"

"Say what now?" The bounty hunter leaned closer to study the article on the screen, scrunched his eyes up, and shook his head. "Did that say Helice Jasper was adopted?"

"That's what it looks like."

"Huh."

Lisa scanned the article and nibbled on the inside of her bottom lip. "Yeah. Wow. Six years in and out of foster homes until Mr. and Mrs. Appleman took her in, fell in love with her, and adopted her as their own."

"What about Langley?"

"Right here. Langley Appleman. Seven years old when his parents took Helice in. They were best friends and did everything together. Right. So Helice opened The Appleman House for foster kids—'intended as a safe space for children still looking for their loving families to gather, find support and friendship, and get involved in their communities. Once the initial construction on The Appleman House's main facility is completed, the Harfords plan to build additions and open upward of a hundred beds to California orphans unsuited, for any number of reasons, for entry into the foster system.' Wow."

"A damn orphanage in California?" Johnny snorted. "They should have put all the LA hoodlums in there instead of buildin' them a damn school in the Everglades."

"Stop it. Those are totally different circumstances."

"Not really." He scratched his chin and glanced around the motel room. "So lemme get this straight. Helice Appleman was adopted and Langley ain't her brother by blood."

"He's still her brother."

"I said by blood. Meanin' he and Bronson ain't related at all either."

"Yes, Johnny. That's how family lineage works."

"Do you think Harford Junior knows anythin' about this? With his mama dead and gone thirteen years?"

"I have no idea. Oh, look. Here's a picture. 'Right: Jasper and Helice Harford. Center: Collin Haverlin.'"

"That's Jasper's partner-not-partner. The MC at the gala, right?"

"Yep. Twenty years younger. 'Left: Langley Appleman.' Now, we have a face to go with the—"

Johnny squinted and turned to look at her. "You forget the rest of the sayin', darlin'."

Lisa's eyes were wide and she leaned toward the tablet in her lap before she scrolled through the rest of the article and up again.

"Lisa?"

"You're not gonna believe this."

"Well, I can't believe a damn thing if you ain't fixin' to show and tell."

"Right there. Langley Appleman."

"You look like you seen a—" The bounty hunter frowned and leaned closer to get a better look before he reeled away from the tablet with a scowl. "What the fuck?"

"Yeah. Forget trying to find a listing under Langley Appleman. We don't even need to go to his house."

"Goddammit." He shook his head vigorously and sneered at the photo in the article. "That motherfucker's been runnin' us around like a couple of newly hatched chickens."

"What?"

"You know what I mean."

Lisa placed the tablet between them, turned to look at her partner, and shook her head slowly. "There was no way we could have possibly worked this out. No way."

"Sure. 'Cause he doesn't ever show his face anywhere but one place. No wonder he sends his goons out to do all his dirty work for him. If anyone put two and two together and found out Bronson's uncle Langley is the goddamn Kaiser killin' transformed shifters across the country…"

"Yeah, that would most certainly be the straw that broke Jasper Harford's back, wouldn't it?"

"Damn straight, darlin'." He stood from the bed and paced the small motel room.

The hounds looked at him, licked their muzzles, and turned their heads from side to side to follow their master's footsteps. "Johnny?"

"Are you okay?"

"I'm thinkin'."

"You don't usually move so much when you think, though."

Luther lowered his head but continued to stare at the dwarf. "Yeah, most of the time, you kinda stand in one place with that look on your face."

"What look?"

"You know. The look."

Rex chuckled nervously. "The one no one else would understand. But we do, Johnny. When you get that look on your face like there's nothing going on in that giant two-legs head of yours—"

"I said I'm thinkin'. Hush up." He snapped his fingers and the hounds returned slowly to their lazy snoozing on the stained carpet. The dwarf pointed at Lisa. "Do you think you can get someone on the line to find us an address?"

"What, for Langley?"

"Yeah."

"Probably. But…well, we can't simply go to the guy's house, Johnny. He knows who we are and we know who he is—or who he's not, technically speaking."

"It doesn't matter." The bounty hunter stopped pacing and turned to face her as he folded his arms. "Wherever he is, we're goin' right up to his front door to have us a little chat—with no games this time, and no readin' between the lines. I ain't fixin' to get the runaround any more than we already have, and this whole damn family has way too many dirty secrets under all their piles of money."

"Yeah." With a sharp intake of breath, Lisa pulled her cell phone out. "And those secrets are getting shifters killed all over the place, aren't they?"

"Someone oughtta air the dirty laundry. That shit's stinkin' like a chum bucket on a hot summer day. If the Harford boys and good ol' Langley ain't gonna do it themselves, it looks like we have some heavy liftin' to do."

"Assuming we can even find him."

"Make the call, darlin'. We'll find him."

CHAPTER TWENTY-FOUR

Fortunately, Lisa's contacts with the FBI were still willing to run a search for Langley Appleman's last known address, which happened to be only two and a half hours away in the town of Truckee. By the time they had gathered all the information they could possibly find, the sun had already gone down and the snores from the three transformed shifters asleep in the adjoining room rose loud and clear through the thin wall between them.

"We ain't goin' up there tonight." Johnny had kicked his boots off and climbed into the bed with the lumpy and completely unsupportive pillows. "I'll be damned if we go knockin' on the bastard's door in the middle of the night when neither of us can see a thing."

Lisa sighed wearily and slid under the covers. "Tomorrow, then."

The next morning, neither of them particularly looked forward to the drive or what they realized they might have to do when they reached Langley's house in the mountains.

"He said he was out of town for a few days, didn't he?"

"Yep." Johnny glanced at the GPS route on her phone in the

center console's cupholder and grunted. "If that ain't another one of his lies too."

"Okay, so if it isn't and he's gone, we…what? Break into his house and snoop around on our own."

"That's the plan."

"Johnny."

He turned onto a narrow dirt road leading up a steep incline and looked at her in exasperation. "This ain't me feelin' especially curious, darlin'. Bronson knows damn well who his uncle is and what he's been doin' as Kaiser this whole time. Langley's been playin' us, keepin' us close and makin' us think we're gettin' somewhere with a dumbass deposit on goddamn marijuana that ain't even been cut yet and all his bullshit about not mixin' his personal life with business."

"We can't break into someone's house because you feel like you've been played."

"I have been played, dammit." The bounty hunter slammed his palm on the steering wheel, then growled and shook his head. "Both of us. We've been tryin' to do this the straight-and-narrow way and look what we got for it."

Lisa shrugged. "To be fair, Kaiser's been a known name in the shifter world for a while now."

"All the more reason for us to do whatever the hell it takes to bring the bastard down. The longer we wait and tiptoe around the whole situation, the more transformed shifters we're gonna find dead, dyin', or runnin' from one of 'em."

"And what do we do if Langley's home, huh?" She looked out the window and studied the thick growth of pine trees that they raced past on the narrow road. "We need an actual plan, Johnny."

"We have one. Either we're breakin' into an empty house to dig up the dirt he's hidin' way too well, or we're sittin' down for another heart-to-heart with the asshole behind this whole mess."

They made the rest of the drive in silence and she didn't argue any further against the plan one way or the other.

When they finally reached Langley's driveway, Johnny slowed the SUV to a crawl and scowled at the massive home that came into view. "'Course he's got a damn mansion up in the hills. Everyone does around here."

"Compared to his nephew's house, I'd say this is humble-looking."

"It's only another coverup."

There were no other cars on the long driveway or parked beside the house. Johnny went straight to the closed garage door first and cupped a hand over his eyes to peer through the tiny windows into the interior. "Nothin'."

"Seriously?" Lisa moved to the front door at the top of a short flight of wooden stairs. "Maybe he drove out of town."

"It looks like it." The dwarf scrutinized the front door before he raised his hand to knock twice on the wood that had been painted a deep navy-blue.

"Seriously? You feel like knocking anyway because?"

"'Cause I got no idea what kinda funny business this asshole's tryin' to pull at any given time of—"

The front door opened and they both turned quickly away from each other. Langley Appleman stood in the doorway in jeans and a t-shirt. The shifter glanced at each of them, then looked past them at the SUV parked in his driveway and the lack of anyone else on his property. "Hello."

"That's all you have?" Johnny sneered at him. "Hello?"

"I assume you came here thinking I'd sing like a bird, is that it? Or maybe there's something else you'd like to get off your chest."

"Yeah. A hell of a lot, Langley." The bounty hunter pointed inside. "We're gonna talk."

"If you say so." The shifter stepped aside and removed his reading glasses before he looped one of the earpieces over the collar of his shirt.

Johnny strode into the house, which boasted a sweeping array of light-colored wood. The entire entryway and living room beyond was filled with natural lighting from the huge windows that comprised the back wall at the far end.

Lisa stared at Langley and frowned before she stepped past him as well. She looked over her shoulder at him as he shut the door but the shifter didn't seem concerned about finding unexpected guests at his front door—even those who'd previously known him as Kaiser.

"Are you thirsty?"

"Quit screwin' around." The bounty hunter pointed at him. "You said you were out of town."

"And yet you came all this way to my home anyway. I hope I haven't disappointed you."

"Naw, we're glad you're here. 'Cause now we have a chance to lay all this out on the table."

"If you want." Langley gestured toward the living room. "I'd rather not talk about it in the hallway, though. Please come in."

Lisa and Johnny exchanged a confused glance but they followed the man and stepped down the two stairs into the living room.

"I have to give you two credit for working this out all on your own," their host called over his shoulder before he turned and sat in an overly cushioned armchair. "Have a seat. You did work this out on your own, right? I don't have to go through my employee list and have a talk with each of them one by one?"

"So you can shut 'em up for good and leave 'em to rot like all the others?" Johnny stopped beside the arrangement of couches and armchairs but didn't sit. Lisa didn't either.

"I haven't touched a hair on a single head, Johnny. I think you know that." Langley crossed one leg over the other and spread his arms. "You can understand why I don't mix business with my personal life."

"Uh-huh. The same reason why your nephew wouldn't tell us

a damn thing about Langley or Kaiser when we had a little chat with him at the gala on Thursday."

The shifter raised his eyebrows as he stared at Johnny for a moment before his gaze flicked briefly toward Lisa.

Now we got him. The guy had no idea we were snoopin' at his nephew's comin'-up party.

Langley took the whole confrontation in stride and fixed them both with a calm albeit thin-lipped smile. "Bronson understands the importance of discretion. So do the two of you."

"Even when he's completely aware of who you are and what you're up to when you're not…" Lisa swept her gaze around the expansive living room. "Lounging around at home?"

"Yes. Even then. Of course, that might have something to do with the fact that he's also involved in my other work." Langley's expression remained unchanged. "I'm giving him a chance to make something of himself in this world—something that isn't tacked onto his father's legacy and everything that comes with being a Harford. I don't see anything wrong with that. Do you?"

"There ain't enough hours in the day to go through that whole list." The bounty hunter inclined his head and studied him with a jaundiced eye. "Do you know what I think?"

"No, but I assume you're about to tell me."

"I think you're feelin' more than a little left outta that Harford legacy, ain'tcha?"

Langley chuckled. "I have no idea what you're talking about."

"Well, it ain't a family thing. At least not the real kind."

The man's smile faltered and his eyes narrowed slightly, and Lisa glanced at her partner

There it is. We found the sore spot.

"You ain't got claim to Bronson the way you want. Not by blood and not by marriage anymore with his mama gone. It's only him and his old man now." Johnny dusted the armrest of the closest couch, sniffed, and sat there instead of on the cushions. He leaned forward toward their apathetic host. "So what happened, huh? You were kicked outta the Harford picture so you thought you'd pump Bronson's head so full of shit he can't tell up from down anymore? Are you tryin' to get back at his old man for marryin' your adopted sister and leavin' you out in the cold this whole time?"

Lisa kept her gaze firmly fixed on the shifter and watched the muscles in his jaw clench repeatedly.

Careful, Johnny. This guy's already on edge as it is.

"That's what you think I'm doing?" Langley responded with a wry laugh. "Do you think I don't have my nephew's best interests at heart?"

"Naw, I don't. The only interests you're followin' are your own, ain't they?"

The shifter leaned back against the couch cushions and drew a deep breath and his already tight smile twitched. "You know, most people have no idea that Helice was adopted. I assume you found the article about The Appleman House. Am I right?"

"When you clean out all records of yourself," Lisa said, "then yeah. That one stands out like a sore thumb."

"I'm sure. Well, if I wasn't already completely confident in your investigative abilities, I'd be convinced of them now. Without a doubt. But let me make this perfectly clear. Helice was and always had been my sister. We were incredibly close and almost inseparable. I can't remember anything before she came into our lives and Bronson might as well be my flesh and blood. I've certainly treated him that way. It's no less than he deserves."

"So how do you explain to your flesh and blood why you're killin' all these transformed shifters, huh?" Johnny's sneering smile made his mustache bristle. "What do you tell him to justify puttin' all those lives on the line? How do you brush killin' his fiancée under the rug?"

"I don't kill anyone." Langley leaned forward abruptly, slid forward onto the edge of the couch cushion, and folded his hands in his lap. "I offer them a choice. If they don't like either of the options, it's out of my hands at that point."

"Bullshit."

"Johnny…" Lisa warned.

"Naw, I'm sick of listenin' to this asshole go on and on about how he ain't responsible for a damn thing." He stood and stepped toward the shifter, faster than either of them expected. The man rose from his seat as well and stopped mere inches from him. He slid his hands slowly into the pockets of his jeans and sneered at the bounty hunter without looking away.

"Yes, Johnny. Go on and lecture me about responsibility."

"The kind you reckon belongs to you for helpin' Bronson with his life choices, huh? Tell me this. If you hate the transformed so much you gotta gun 'em down where they stand if they ain't willin' to join you, why make an offer at all? Why not simply target 'em wherever you can find 'em and wipe 'em off the face of the earth without hidin' behind this bullshit superiority, huh?"

"That would be completely beside the point."

"Not really. Tyro's been doin' it for months and he has shifters all over the place more scared at the mention of his name than—"

"That has nothing to do with it!" Langley snapped. "And nothing to do with me."

"Oh, yeah? 'Cause from where I'm standin', it looks an awful lot like you and Tyro have the same game plan here, only his has more balls behind it."

"You—" The shifter wagged a warning finger in Johnny's face, then growled and spun away from him to pace across the room. "How anyone could draw parallels between Kaiser's work and the indiscriminate mess Tyro's made of things is completely beyond me."

"You mean your work," Lisa clarified.

"I have absolutely nothing to do with what that shifter's

meted out to the transformed—without a conscience and without offering them a choice!"

"It's not a choice when your only other option is death, Langley." Lisa fixed him with a hard look.

"But at least it's a choice." The man stopped, spun to glare at her, and drew a deep breath as he ran a hand through his hair. "On the other hand, maybe it's a good thing this Tyro wildcard came into the picture when he did. Eventually, it might serve as a good lesson for the transformed who would rather pretend they have agency over their own lives and what they've become than accept my offers."

"What exactly have they become?" She glanced around the living room in disbelief. "Do you hear yourself right now? You send your teams out to murder these magicals if they don't join you in…what? Building yourself an army?"

"No." Langley pointed at her. "No, that's not what this is about."

"Well, you're doin' a piss-poor job of explainin' a damn thing."

"You don't understand." The man laughed bitterly. "You have no idea what it's like to be a shifter in this world. Thirty-odd years after the reveal of magic, we still don't have the respect we deserve."

"Killing your own kind seems like an incredibly backward way of trying to gain the rest of the magical world's respect," she said carefully.

"No, I protect my own kind." Langley nodded vigorously and stalked up and down behind the couch like a madman.

Like a rabid wolf, is what. He's completely lost his mind and he can't even see it.

"It's impossible to live halfway like those transformed have lived since they were…created," the shifter continued. "They have one foot in their old life and the other in the magical world. Can you imagine the damage that could be done if transformed shifters tried to make their own way? They have no working knowledge of magic and no understanding of its history—of our history. They think they can simply sweep what they are under the rug and it's no one's business but their own."

"It is no one's business," Johnny muttered.

"It's my business! All of us—every shifter on this planet who's been suppressed under the weight of every Oriceran race since we first got here."

The bounty hunter took another long look around him at the tastefully and expensively decorated interior of Langley Appleman's home. "It doesn't look to me like you been sufferin' that much under anyone's thumb. Most folks would be thrilled to have what you have."

"Ha. Tell me something, Johnny. If someone were to follow you home into the Florida Everglades and start burning down the homes of your friends and neighbors there, would you sit back on your private island, content to let it all happen because most folks would be thrilled to have what you have?"

"It ain't a private island. It's the damn swamp."

Lisa stepped toward her partner and put a hand on his shoulder. "We understand that things aren't as easy for shifters as they have been for the rest of us."

Langley scoffed. "You don't understand. You think you have an idea because you have a few shifter friends and took in an orphan to raise like you would a dwarf. Isn't that right?"

"We ain't talkin' about my issues, asshole." Johnny pointed at him. "And your analogy ain't exactly foolproof."

"What?"

"Someone burnin' the homes of my friends and neighbors. Is that how you wanna compare the situations? Fine. But I tell you what. If a thing like that happened where I'm from, I wouldn't be blamin' my friends and neighbors for their houses and their lives getting' attacked. And I sure as shit wouldn't send someone else out to kill 'em for me if they decided they didn't wanna come live in my little corner of the swamp 'cause it's safer."

The shifter snarled through a mad-looking grin. "This is about protecting what the best shifters among us have been working for generations to achieve. I'm trying to build a better world for my kind. And if those who haven't endured this struggle for their entire lives can't see the risks of heading off on their own to do whatever they damn well please with the abilities they were given, they're the only ones to blame for their blindness."

"The Dark Families didn't ask before they gave those abilities to anyone," Lisa said, her voice still even but with an undertone of cold fury running through it. "No one gave them a choice."

"Exactly. Which is why I am giving it to them now."

The bounty hunter shook his head. "Is that what you've been tellin' your nephew? That this is for a better world and you ain't the kinda monster everyone thinks you are 'cause your hands are clean and you ain't forcin' this life onto the transformed who didn't want it in the first place?"

Langley's smile twitched again. "I'm trying to give my nephew the kind of education he deserves—the kind he will never receive from his narrow-minded father. Helice should have taught her son these things before she died but he was too young. I'm the only one who can open his eyes to what's at stake here."

"Why's that, huh?"

The man straightened, rolled his shoulders, and regained complete control of himself again as quickly as he'd lost it. "That, Johnny, is personal family business."

"Oh, sure. It's about to get real personal, all right." The dwarf stalked forward but Lisa caught his arm to hold him back. She didn't have to try hard. The strength of her grip and her fingers digging into his arm gave him all the warning he needed before he realized why.

Langley glanced at his watch and drew a deep breath.

At the same time, she glanced at the ceiling and nodded subtly toward the top of the staircase. Her partner followed her gaze and his hasty scan located two different security cameras mounted inconspicuously in separate corners of the living room. Despite this attempt to keep them obscured, the tiny red dots of light proved that they were being recorded at the very least, if not watched from somewhere else and by someone else.

The shit's been tryin' to get a rise out of us all along.

"Now." Langley cleared his throat. "As entertaining as this little visit has been, I have a conference call I need to be on in four minutes so I have to ask you to leave now."

"Uh-huh." Johnny sniffed. "We'll get outta your way then."

"Yes, thank you." The shifter glanced from one to the other and gestured toward the door. "I trust you'll keep these things to yourself, yes? I realize how tempting it might be to let a few things slip but don't forget the sixty-two and a half thousand dollars of your money at my property in North San Juan. We wouldn't want that to slip out with the rest of it."

"'Course not."

Lisa moved to the door and waited until her back was turned to roll her eyes.

"We'll discuss how to move forward at another date," the shifter added. "When we've all had the chance to cool off. I think that's best."

"Sure you do."

She opened the door and stepped out into the bright morning sunlight and the fresh mountain air.

"Oh, and do remember to call me by the appropriate name depending on the circumstances." He grasped the door to hold it open as Johnny approached the front stoop. "Langley Appleman has never stepped foot on the farm. That's very important."

The dwarf spun to glare at the man's shrewdly calculating gaze. "There's one other little piece of information I'd like to get cleared up first."

Langley pressed his lips together in irritation. "As long as it doesn't take you more than two minutes."

"How did you feel about Bronson and Addison?"

"What?"

He shrugged. "You know, her bein' a transformed shifter and all. Not a hundred percent, mind. Her mama was the one changed by the Dark Families, but she's still transformed. Did that rub you the wrong way?"

The man's upper lip curled into a twitching sneer. "I didn't have her killed if that's what you're insinuating."

"Maybe Bronson thinks you did, though. Have you ever considered that in your little crusade?"

"No. Bronson knows exactly who's to blame for that death. Now get out."

Johnny raised both hands and stepped off the step of the doorway and onto the stoop before the front door shut swiftly in his face with a thud. "He has some nerve."

"Come on, Johnny." Lisa turned to walk up the driveway toward the rental after she cast a sweeping glance over the outside of Langley's home. "Let's get in the car."

He snorted and hurried after her. "Conference call my ass."

Through the narrow vertical window beside the front door, Langley watched the dwarf and his Light Elf partner enter their SUV. He took his phone from his pocket, dialed the number he knew by heart, and pressed the phone to his ear.

"Well, that was fast," Agnes said on the other end of the line.

"Did you hear all that?"

"Every last word."

"Good. Do you still have a bead on the transformed dwarf?"

"The biker?" She snorted. "Sure."

"I'm starting to believe your assumption that his ties to my guests are stronger than I gave them credit for." He turned away from the window and walked slowly down his foyer toward the living room again. His footsteps clicked hollowly on the wooden floor. "I want you to find the shifter dwarf, Agnes—however you have to—and get rid of him."

"Do you want me to leave a calling card?"

"It doesn't matter. We can pin it on Tyro for all I care. But Johnny Walker needs to stop asking questions."

"I'll get it done." She hung up before he did, but he was already lowering the phone from his ear to slip it into his pocket.

A smile twitched at the corner of his mouth.

CHAPTER TWENTY-FIVE

"Charlie." Johnny adjusted his hold on his phone in one hand and jerked the steering wheel sharply to the right with the other for a tight turn onto the side road leading to the highway. Lisa gasped and braced herself against the passenger door before she scowled at him in disapproval. "Listen to me."

"Yeah, I told you, 'coz. Everything's fine here, all things considered, right?" Charlie snapped his fingers and shouted, "Hey! Just because I'm on the phone doesn't mean you can change the channel. Turn it back. So what's going on, Johnny? Did you finally find the uncle or what?"

"We found a whole lot and you gotta do exactly as I say—"

"Hey, do you think you could buy more grub on the way back? A guy can only eat so many cans of beans before he loses his—"

"Dammit, Charlie. Shut your trap and listen to me!"

"Whoa, hey. Okay. You don't have to be so uptight all the time. I'm right here."

"Johnny," Lisa muttered.

"Hold on."

"Johnny. Johnny, slow down. There's a—" She shouted in frustration when the SUV hit a massive pothole in the road and the wheels left the road for a moment.

The bounty hunter hissed and almost threw his phone at the windshield but opted to toss it into her lap instead. "You talk to him. I'll drive."

"Oh, sure, because I didn't suggest that in the first place."

"What was that?"

She picked his cell up and brought it to her ear with a grimace. "Quiet, I'm on the phone."

He rolled his eyes.

"Charlie. Yeah. Listen. Get everything packed, okay? No, you cannot leave the motel but be ready to. We'll be back as soon as we can but there's a chance we're either being followed or will be shortly. Yes, everyone, including Galfrey and Jake. No, I don't— No. Charlie, that's not—" She gritted teeth, closed her eyes, and sighed heavily. "Sure, Charlie. Like the motel's on fire. Make sure everyone's ready to go when we get there. Yeah, maybe."

She slapped Johnny's flip phone shut quickly and slid it into the cupholder.

"What did he say?"

"A whole lotta nothin', Johnny." She turned to look at him with wide eyes. "Do you honestly think Langley's about to make a move?"

"After how hard he tried to get a rise out of us with his clever little confession? Damn right I do. If he ain't comin' after us himself, he's sendin' someone to do the job for him. That's probably more likely now that I say it out loud."

"So what's the plan, then? We get everyone out of the motel and…"

"Honestly, I dunno. I haven't thought that far ahead."

"It's called a plan for a reason."

"That's all the plan we got, darlin'. Listen, I ain't takin' two fugitive shifters with me from that motel to the airport. I ain't gonna put Felix at that kinda risk, for one."

She responded with a dry, disbelieving laugh. "You're worried about your jet pilot?"

"I'm worried about how far Langley's willin' to go to get what he wants outta this. And yeah. Felix is a good pilot."

"Well then, do you know anyone around here with a safe house? Something off the grid where we can hide Galfrey and Jake? Probably Charlie too, honestly. He'd only get in the way."

"I'm workin' on it."

"You are?" Lisa studied him as he tightened his hand on the steering wheel. "While you're driving."

"It's called multi-taskin' and I can't do it while you're lookin' at me like that."

She clutched the armrest on the passenger door and stared directly ahead while her foot bounced anxiously on the floor in front of her seat.

When they reached the motel and hurried to their room to pack their things, the confused trio of transformed shifters wouldn't take "shut up and let me pack" for an answer.

"What do you mean someone's coming?" Galfrey asked. "You didn't tell them where we are, did you?"

"I ain't said a damn word about you one way or the other." Johnny crammed his extra clothes into his duffel bag and tossed the pillow on the bed aside to check that it hadn't hidden anything.

"But you think someone's coming," Jake muttered and swallowed. "Like, for us."

"We don't know anything right now." Lisa pushed him aside so she could hurry into the bathroom. "But it's better to be on the safe side right now."

"Safe where?"

"I dunno. We'll work it out when we get there." Johnny whistled shrilly. "Boys."

"We're here, Johnny," Luther called from the other room.

Rex grunted. "Yep. Looking for…anything extra…left under—ha! Got it!"

"Dude, how'd you get your mouth so far under the bed?"

"Skills, Luther. I got skills. You don't."

"We're gittin' on, boys." Johnny zipped his duffel bag and slung it over his shoulder. "And the rest of y'all better make sure you have everythin' you need. We ain't turnin' back if you left somethin' behind."

Jake shrugged and watched the commotion with wide eyes. "We don't have anything."

"Even better."

"Okay, I think that's it." Lisa barreled out of the bathroom, tossed her few toiletries into her carry-on suitcase, then zipped it and hauled it off the bed. "Let's go."

"Rex. Luther. We're—"

Rex barked. "Johnny. Someone's here."

Luther sniffed the bottom of the door to what had previously been the shifters' room. "Uh-oh. Uh…Johnny? You smell that?"

"Do I smell— Boy, there are only two of us in this room who can't smell everythin' you can and I'm one of 'em. Now I said—"

"Wait." Charlie grasped his cousin's shoulder and inclined his head. "Hold on."

"What?"

"Shh…" Galfrey raised a finger, stepped slowly toward the door of Johnny's room, and pressed his ear against it.

It wasn't necessary. They all heard the idling engine and the car door open and shut before a quick snort and a woman muttering, "Nice bike, asshole."

"Shit." The shifter dwarf looked at his cousin with wide eyes. "That's her. That's the fucking witch, Johnny."

"Oh, man. Oh, man." Jake spun in tight circles. "We're screwed. We are so—"

"You," the bounty hunter snapped. "Shut up." He nodded at Lisa and moved his hand to his utility belt, which he'd taken from the back of the SUV when they'd arrived and had since strapped on for precisely this reason.

"Whoa." Charlie looked at the belt and smirked. "What the hell are those?"

"Mine. Y'all stay right here until I give the word, then make like a goddamn dark witch lit a fire under your ass, understand?"

"Johnny, there are too many moving parts here," Lisa muttered. "We can't cover all of them."

"Do y'all know how to fight?"

His cousin snorted. "Do you know me?"

"Not you."

The other two shifters exchanged a nervous glance before Galfrey shrugged. "Well, we didn't die the last time she tried to kill us."

"Okay, do that again and you'll be fine." Johnny stopped in front of the door and pressed his ear against it to listen. One hand rested on an explosive disk at his belt.

"We don't hear anything, Johnny," Luther whispered.

"Yeah. Like she…disappeared." Rex sniffed the bottom of the other door. "But left her stink behind."

Lisa snapped her fingers. "Get over here."

The hounds snuck quickly through the adjoining doorway and sat on either side of her.

Johnny slid the chained lock gingerly out of its slot and lowered it slowly.

The second that his hand settled on the doorknob, a deafening crash came from the front door of the adjacent room. Red light flashed, hissed, and sparked and shards of wood sprayed across the shifters' empty room into the back wall and the bathroom door.

Johnny jerked the other door open and pulled a disk from his belt. "Out!"

Galfrey and Adam barreled onto the walkway and ran to the

stairs, followed closely by Charlie and the hounds. Lisa backed out and summoned a fireball in each hand.

A low chuckle came from the adjoining room. "Oh, I was so right. You know, I heard dwarves were ridiculously loyal. Even to the point of stupidi—"

The bounty hunter tossed the exploding disk into the room as Agnes' crimson hair appeared in the adjoining doorway. The two partners turned and sprinted down the walkway toward the stairs.

The hounds bayed wildly and skittered across the asphalt of the parking lot as Galfrey fumbled to open the back door of the SUV.

"Johnny! You want help? We can help!"

"Get in the car, shifters." Rex snapped at Jake's heels as the terrified man dove headfirst into the back seat.

"Y'all get in," Johnny shouted and yanked another disk from his belt.

Charlie stood beside his bike, his keys dangling from one hand as he stared at Johnny and Lisa running down the staircase. "Tell me where, Johnny?"

"Same place we met when you got here," Johnny snapped. "Now get on the damn bike and—"

A thick bolt of crackling red-and-black light struck the staircase banister beside the bounty hunter's head. It destroyed it and made him and Lisa stagger down the stairs. He lobbed his other exploding disk up behind him, blinded by the flying sawdust and wood chips.

Agnes snarled and pressed herself against the wall before it detonated in mid-air. Chunks of the motel's exterior paneling were blown off and rained over the SUV.

"I got it, I got it." Charlie had reached the bottom of the staircase and grabbed Lisa's suitcase, which he now hauled toward the open rear door of the SUV as the hounds barked like crazy.

"Johnny," Agnes called. "This isn't about you. I merely want the idiot with the orange Harley no one else would be caught dead riding."

Charlie spun toward her as she stalked down the partially destroyed staircase and hissed through his teeth. "That's taking it way too far."

She launched another spear of red light at him and hissed fiercely.

The mohawked dwarf leapt away from the car and hurried to his bike.

"Johnny." Lisa tugged on his sleeve before she raced to the SUV. "Come on."

"And give her a chance to—"

Agnes' next blast struck the asphalt at his feet, and he spun toward her with another exploding disk in his hand.

"You can't keep running forever," the witch all but snarled. "And unfortunately, you don't exactly have what it takes to hold me off forever. I'll keep going until I finally finish the job."

"Yeah, you're a real goddamn Energizer bunny." He flung the next disk at her and with another snarl, she shoved her hands out toward the hurtling black device. It struck in a burst of red light that launched like a magical net, and she tossed it aside before it exploded in mid-air. Shards of ripped plastic launched around them.

"You." Agnes pointed at Charlie. "You're done."

"And you're batshit insane, lady." His lips peeled into a snarled grin and he crouched in a ready stance as his eyes flashed silver as they always did before a shift. "Bring it—"

The witch launched another red spear at him before he could take a step forward and his entire body grew rigid under the shock before he crumpled.

"Oh, shit!" Jake shouted.

"Hey!" Lisa yelled. Agnes spun toward her with wide eyes a half-second before the Light Elf targeted her back with a blinding, shimmering column of golden light. The witch snarled and hissed as the energy spell forced her against the outer wall of the motel. "Johnny!"

"Gimme a goddamn minute." The bounty hunter dropped to his knees in front of his cousin and shook him by the shoulders. Charlie groaned, then Johnny slapped him in the face and that seemed to do the trick. "Get the hell up."

"Jesus, all right. I'll—look out!" The shifter dwarf yanked him on top of him by the collar of his shirt and narrowly avoided knocking his Harley over in the process as crackling shards of red light exploded from Agnes' open palms. They gouged the asphalt of the parking lot and hurled thick hunks of rock in all directions.

"Christ, it's like she's gonna explode." Johnny struggled to his feet and snatched another disk from his belt. "Lisa! Get to the—"

One of the witch's wayward destruction sparks struck his partner in the thigh. She cried out and staggered back, her energy spell cut off as she clamped both hands around the open wound in her leg.

With a tiny smirk, their adversary pushed away from the wall and took two steps forward. "Whoops. You might wanna get that looked at before it spreads. I heard it gets bad. At least, that's what it sounded like from all the screaming."

"Did Langley send you after us?" Lisa demanded through gritted teeth as she limped backward toward the car. "Is that what this is?"

Agnes regarded her impassively. "Who?"

"You know damn well who." Johnny pointed at his cousin. "Get on the fucking bike."

Charlie wasted no time but scrambled onto the seat of his Harley and jammed his keys into the ignition. The engine roared to life but when the witch fired a red thread of magic at it, the tailpipe sputtered once before it emitted a startling crack.

"You're not going anywhere." Agnes pointed at him but before she could launch another attack, Johnny's SUV roared to life.

Galfrey and Jake screamed at the top of their lungs from inside the rental and the witch turned to see what all the noise was about. She had two seconds to see the terrified faces of the two transformed shifters who'd escaped her once—Galfrey in the passenger seat and Jake behind the wheel.

Before she could react, the front bumper of the SUV pounded into her and she catapulted into the wall again. Cracks splintered around her and a puff of dust followed, and she fell on the sidewalk in a heap.

"Oh, shit!" Jake shrieked. "Oh, fuck. I hit her. Did I kill her? I fucking killed her!"

Johnny looked at Charlie and pointed down the highway. "Forget the restaurant. Sacramento. And wait when you get there, got it? Quietly."

"Yep." His cousin kicked up the bike's stand and cranked the throttle. "But hurry."

The orange Harley accelerated out of the parking lot and down the highway at breakneck speed before the bounty hunter reached Lisa doubled over beside the back of the SUV.

"Get the hell in the back!" he shouted.

Both shifters opened their doors and scrambled out of the car to enter it again through the rear doors.

"Are you okay?" The bounty hunter helped his partner to limp toward the passenger seat.

She laughed bitterly. "I've been hurt worse."

"Yeah, and we're gettin' that looked at."

"Did I kill her?" Jake asked from the back. "Is she dead?"

"Who cares about her?" Luther howled.

"Yeah." Rex snarled as he leapt up and rested his paws on the back of the seat, then snapped at the air beside Jake's face. "You almost killed us."

"I almost… Sorry. I wasn't thinking. I only—"

"Shut up and sit down," Johnny shouted as he rounded the front of the SUV. He paused briefly to look at Kaiser's unconscious witch and snorted. "You ain't car-proof, that's for damn sure."

With the last disk still in his hand, his gaze settled on the idling Camry in the parking lot—the only other vehicle on a Tuesday morning parked in front of the worst motel he'd ever seen.

"Johnny." Lisa pulled the passenger door shut with a grimace and shouted at him through the open driver's door. "We need to get out of here."

"Yep." The dwarf pressed the red button on the top of his disk, grinned, and tossed it through the open window of the idling vehicle. That done, he turned and climbed casually behind the wheel.

The door shut and he yanked the gear shift into reverse. Lisa finished buckling her seatbelt and stared at him. "What did you do?"

"I'm merely havin' a little fun." He stepped on the gas and all his passengers—including the hounds—shrieked as the SUV spun madly in the parking lot.

Moments later, Agnes' car erupted in flames and shattered glass.

"Are you serious?" the half-Light Elf shouted.

He shifted into drive and they lurched forward through the entrance to the lot, fishtailed wildly for a second, and finally settled on the straight road heading south. "Why? Do you reckon it's too much?"

She spun in her seat to stare through the back windshield at the flames that flared from Agnes' destroyed car and the pieces of the motel's outer wall that continued to crumble into a messy pile on the asphalt. "You know what? I think the motel looks better this way."

"You guys are insane," Jake muttered.

"No, you're insane," Luther snapped. "You tried to drive us into a wall."

"Yeah, and you hit a witch instead," Rex muttered.

Johnny glanced at the wreckage of the motel in the rearview mirror and snorted. "We just saved y'all's asses is what we did. Insane or not."

Now we gotta decide how to get these guys somewhere not even a shifter-trackin' witch can find 'em. She ain't stayin' down for long and when she's up, there's no way in hell she won't come after Charlie with everythin' she's got.

He glanced at Lisa and she patted the back of his hand on the steering wheel. "He'll wait for us."

"If he doesn't, I'll kill him myself."

Agnes groaned and pushed off the sidewalk. For a second, she thought she'd gone blind until she recognized the problem as the thick smoke that billowed from her car.

"Shit." With a grimace, she slid her hand into the pocket of her trench coat and pulled her phone out.

What Kaiser doesn't know won't kill him. If I can't eliminate that stupid dwarf on a bike by myself, I'll call backup in. Either way, it gets done.

The thought made her smirk as she scrolled through the few contacts on her phone and made the call.

The line rang twice before it was answered. "What?"

"Hey. Miss me?"

"I don't have time for this, Agnes. What do you want?"

She brushed the rubble off her jacket as best she could and walked toward the exit of the parking lot where it fed onto the highway. "I hit what you could call a wall."

"Why should I care?"

"Because Kaiser wants a certain dwarf dead and my car was blown to pieces."

The silence on the other end of the line made her smile widen.

"Your failure to do your job is not my problem, witch."

"Oh, come on. This is a courtesy call, Tyro. I have put a tracker on a transformed dwarf's bright orange Harley. It so happens he was holed up in a motel with Johnny Walker. I know you know the name. Plus, guess who's with him?"

"I'm not in the mood for games."

Agnes sniffed and wiped a smear of blood from under her nose. "The bounty hunter has the rest of who you're looking for with him. Play this right and you'll have all four of them for the price of one. Do you want it?"

Tyro's thick swallow and sharp breath was all the answer she needed, but she let him come to it on his own time.

"Send me what I need."

"Yeah, I thought you'd be happy. You sit tight."

Get sneak peeks, exclusive giveaways, behind the scenes content, and more. PLUS you'll be notified of special **one day only fan pricing** on new releases.

Sign up today to get free stories.

Visit: https://marthacarr.com/read-free-stories/

AUTHOR NOTES - MARTHA CARR
JUNE 24, 2021

The world is reopening. It's kind of weird. We're in the In-between Days. Scatterings of masks still being worn, meeting in larger groups and finally seeing old friends and family.

The 'thing' we all just lived through has left a mark. We'll be dealing with it for some time to come. I see it in myself and in friends. I wonder why it's harder for me to relax than it used to be. Where did this new baseline of stress come from?

Then I remember and I actually take a deeper breath and… exhale. Of course. There's a reason that's not to be taken lightly. Whether we like it or not, the year 2020 left some pretty deep skid marks across our psyche.

When I remember, it makes it easier for me to stop searching for any other reasons and look for some solutions.

Like getting back to swimming at the Y. At the entrance I had to ask for directions back to the pool. I had completely forgotten. The memory was erased, replaced by a thousand new ones of figuring out how to deal with masks, quarantine, finding toilet paper, using curbside pickup, zoom.

The first time I got in the pool I picked the lane next to the wall – just in case. It had been well over a year and a few surgeries. I didn't want to be the talk of the Y when a lifeguard pulled me out.

As I started to swim down the lane, looking down at the familiar black stripe I keep laughing, blowing bubbles into the water. It was so normal. I only had eleven laps in me that day, but they felt delicious. Every one of them. I got out of the pool, bobbing along like I was still in the water, making a crooked path back to my flip-flops.

That's what I missed most of all. Very normal, small details to my routine that involved other people even if just in passing.

Next, I started a yoga class that ends with fifteen minutes of meditation and an actual gong. Feels like heaven and I look forward to it like a kid waking up on a Monday morning in August and no school. Just joy and anticipation.

On the second of July I'll be hosting my annual party at a local Vets center for the first time since 2019. It'll be nice to see familiar faces again. And then, on the 4th I'll be having people over to the new garden. A small crowd in fact. Even the Offspring has invited friends and some neighbors are coming. Totally normal stuff that in any other year wouldn't really rate so much hurrah. But it's 2021 and things are different and fortunately, a little the same. Party on people.

More adventures to follow.

Thank you for not only reading this story but these author notes as well.

One of the downsides of creativity is the addiction to the dopamine hits new ideas fire off. What do I mean by this? Think of it as the (supposed and highly suspicious) comments runners say they have with their "runner's high."

Personally, I think it is a group hallucination that there are benefits to running. But I am averse to pain, so "no pain, no gain" is actually a promise that if I don't try to gain, I won't be in pain.

I'm kind of paying for that lack of exercise when I step on the scale...

So, this morning, I'm having breakfast, and I remember an article I read a couple of mornings ago where the reporter was discussing crypto-currency mining.

According to the article, he was running a software program that used his powerful CPU to make a little spending cash each month. Install software, set up digital currency wallets, use the computer next to me that is powerful and under-utilized...

What could go wrong, right?

(Except the whole using electricity issue, but have no fear.)

Anyway, I probably spent at least twenty (20) minutes getting into the software, the companies, the different income styles (group pooling, solo, purchase units of computer power but no hardware) and finally realized…

Why the hell am I doing this?

Sure, my mind was going spastic at the idea.

Just think, the only issue with crypto-currency mining is the problems of electricity to run the hardware and cooling the damned things because they used up 1.21 gigawatts of electricity*.

So, in a nutshell, if I could solve those two minor issues, I could have unlimited crypto efforts.

Finally, my practical business mind stopped doing what it wasn't supposed to (read business stuff) and started paying attention to what my creative mind was working on (not stories), and I slapped the shit out of myself.

Business mind: *SLAP!* "What the *HELL* are you doing?"

Creative mind: "OW, you bastard! Why did you slap me?"

Business mind: "You aren't working on the publishing or writing business!"

Creative mind: "But the drugs! Wait, the fun of crypto-currency! Look, we could…"

Business mind: *SLAP!!*

Creative mind: "OW, DAMMIT!" *Rubs face.* "Stop that slapping shit!"

Business mind: "How much money is this going to take?"

Creative mind: "I don't know! It's going to be fun!! That's all that matters!"

Business mind: *SLAP SLAP!*

Creative mind: "FUCKER! Stop that slapping bullshit!"

Business mind: "Get your head outta your ass and I

will! You already have a very well-paying job. You get to create stuff for people to enjoy."

Creative mind: "But…but…It's not…"

Business mind: *Raises hand to slap...*

Creative mind: "Ok, ok. I feel your point. It's just a fun diversion from this stuff I call work. Plus, you know, *save the world.*"

Business mind: "Creatives… The bane of my existence."

Creative mind: "I heard that!"

Business mind: "Take your focus away from authors for ten minutes, I swear." *Heads back to read the latest Entrepreneur magazine...*

That was a moment in my existence. I hope your mind is not warped by it.

Ad Aeternitatem,

Michael Anderle

Solve a murder, save her mother, and stop the apocalypse?

What would you do when elves ask you to investigate a prince's murder and you didn't even know elves, or magic, was real?

Meet Leira Berens, Austin homicide detective who's good at what she does – track down the bad guys and lock them away.

Which is why the elves want her to solve this murder – fast. It's not just about tracking down the killer and bringing them to justice. It's about saving the world!

If you're looking for a heroine who prefers fighting to flirting, check out The Leira Chronicles today!

<u>AVAILABLE ON AMAZON AND IN KINDLE UNLIMITED!</u>

CONNECT WITH THE AUTHORS

Martha Carr Social
Website:
http://www.marthacarr.com
Facebook:
https://www.facebook.com/groups/MarthaCarrFans/

Michael Anderle

Website: http://lmbpn.com

Email List: http://lmbpn.com/email/

Social Media:

https://www.facebook.com/LMBPNPublishing

https://twitter.com/MichaelAnderle

https://www.instagram.com/lmbpn_publishing/

https://www.bookbub.com/authors/michael-anderle